PLAY OR PERISH

Arcane Auction Wars

Book 1

PAIGE ANDREWS

JOHN PERAGINE

SHERMAN & STONE

PLAY OR PERISH

Prologue

"Why do you ask what I wanna do with it if you ain't even gonna listen when I tell ya?" Gus snapped at the dark figure of Murray standing next to him. "I feel like we keep going around and around." He snorted even more obnoxiously than usual, almost like he was putting on a show. "You're making me dizzy, Murray."

"You're the one who keeps changing his mind," Murray argued.

"I changed it once. I've been resolute ever since."

"Whatever you say, Gus."

But Gus didn't like the way Murray was articulating himself. His partner had been acting weird for a while now, almost for the entire drive to the storage facility.

Gus stopped walking right before they turned into their row, both suddenly standing under a wash of cold light from an overhead bulb.

"We need to keep it close. I don't see why you have a problem with that." Gus looked down at Murray, using his extra two inches of height like a dare.

Murray looked behind him as if worried that someone

might be watching. "It wants us to play with it, man, so that's the last thing we should do right now."

Murray was really pissing him off.

And Murray felt the same about Gus.

That was so unlike either of them.

This situation with the Mansions of Madness board game was disconcerting. Gus wanted to hold the game close to his body even though he knew he needed to get it as far away from him as humanly possible.

Now, they were back at the core of the true argument that the two of them had been struggling with for days.

"I'll be the Keeper, and you can be the Investigator."

"To hell with you, Gus!" Murray started walking down the row. He stopped in front of unit #25 and turned back to his friend. "Sorry about that … I don't know what's gotten into me."

"You sure about that?" Gus spat.

Murray ignored the bait, kneeling down to unlock the rolling door with one hand before yanking it up with a flourish and shining his flashlight into their shared storage unit with the other.

Every inch of the room was covered in a maze of rusted steel and wooden shelves piled high with games. Neat rows of colorful boxes, their surfaces slick with dust. Some boxes were arranged in a grid, with each game meticulously placed to maximize the available space. An especially large pile consisted of odds, ends, and leftovers, the boxes cracked and faded, yet still too hard for either to throw away. Tangled ribbons of plastic game pieces, dusty dice, and the faint odor of a cardboard overdose were both nostalgic and enticing.

"All right, Gus…"

But Gus was still clutching the box to his chest.

"It's only going to get harder," Murray tried again. "You know I'm right."

"It's just a game!"

"You know that's not true."

Gus didn't have an answer for that, but he still refused to let the box go. He practically wanted to cry at the thought.

"You'll feel better once the door is locked," Murray said. "I promise."

Gus nodded, hesitant but resolute, as he entered the storage unit and gingerly set the Mansions of Madness (first edition!) box onto the nearest pile.

"See?" Murray rolled the door back down until it clanged against the concrete. "Don't you feel better?"

"Not yet." Gus didn't know how he felt, only that it was nothing like anything he'd ever experienced. He was furious at Murray and didn't understand why his rat bastard of a friend (who had always been so cool to him until about ten days ago) was being such a total dick about everything all of a sudden, practically begging Gus to give him a sock on the nose.

Murray locked the door, and a current of panic rippled through Gus's body.

He reached out and tried snatching the key from his buddy's hand.

But Murray had been expecting the move. He yanked the key away from Gus, hovering in a moment of indecision before he suddenly dropped it into his mouth and swallowed.

"What the hell did you do that for?" Gus yelled at him in disbelief.

Murray had gone nuts, refusing to answer him. He started walking away, putting distance between himself and

Gus, as well as the storage unit, until they reached their van.

Murray was sweating through his shirt, Gus saw, and acting more chaotic. He was fidgeting hard, almost frantic by the time he unlocked the van door.

Gus was breathing in heavy gusts as he climbed into the shotgun seat, his face flushed, and his brow furrowed with exertion. He was clearly uncomfortable in the heat, even though it suddenly felt like winter inside the van.

"What the hell?" Murray said as puffs of his breath became visible in the late summer air.

"Yeah, what the hell?" echoed Gus.

"We need to get out of here."

"Yeah, we need to get out of here."

"Knock that off, Gus." Murray started the engine.

Neither spoke, as if they were both too afraid to so much as mutter until they were safely on the other side of the security gate.

Not that they had anything to worry about.

Three blocks from the storage unit but still a half mile from the freeway, Murray asked Gus why his nose was bleeding.

Gus was about to protest that his nose wasn't bleeding, but then he felt it gushing out of his nose and turned the question back on Murray. "Why are your eyes bleeding?"

Murray looked into the rearview mirror, and sure enough, his eyes were leaking blood like a block of ice left in the sun for too long.

He was still staring in fascination at his bloody eyes when he blew through a red light.

A car horn screamed, and Murray swerved, nearly clipping a silver Infiniti.

"Shit." Murray wasn't exactly coming back to himself.

But he was definitely better than Gus, who was trying

to say something or maybe simply breathe, but it seemed like he had something lodged in his throat.

"Gus?"

Gus leaned forward in his seat, clutching his nose as blood drizzled between his fingers.

"GUS!"

Murray careened toward the freeway on-ramp.

Gus was pale, sweating, and trembling, struggling to breathe as pain radiated from his temples.

Whatever had just happened to Gus, the same thing seemed to be tearing through Murray. His foot fell onto the gas, and they blew onto the freeway, headed in the wrong direction, roaring toward an approaching F-150.

The driver tried to swerve, but it was already too late.

Murray plowed into the truck, and their van went tumbling off the road, rolling over and over, glass shattering, metal crunching.

Murray's neck snapped with a loud pop.

But Gus had one last moment of hanging upside down, imagining the Mansions of Madness box sitting safely where it belonged in the storage unit before his final exhale.

Chapter One

"No," I told Judith again. "I don't want a Sorrowful Mary or any other ridiculously named drink. Even flat on my ass, I would be bored shitless."

"Why are you resisting? A Sorrowful Mary might be just the thing to make you finally stop frowning."

"Fine. What's in it?" I asked.

"Vodka, tomato juice, Worcestershire sauce, Tabasco, lemon juice, and celery salt."

"I only like two of those things. One of them needs buffalo wings, and I keep telling you I'm not in the mood for the other one, no matter how many crazy-ass concoctions you want me to try. You promised me a fun time."

"This is a party, Shondra! It's like the most fun you can have."

"This," I gestured around at the stupid college party, "is not my idea of fun."

"It's not my fault if you're—"

"I'm not anything. Except bored, and I'm totally that."

I draped an arm around Judith, the one friend who still tried with me, and squeezed her. "I get that you brought me here to cheer me up, and I appreciate it in the same way I do when you randomly baked me that cake, even though I just started a diet."

"Everyone likes cake," Judith said. "I just can't stand seeing you so down. And sorry, I didn't know you were on a diet."

"I appreciate that you don't want to see me sad, but that's about *you*, honey." I smiled. "And this isn't about me being on a diet. I just don't feel like drinking tonight."

"Since when did you become a teetotaler?"

"Since when do you even know that word?" I asked.

"I know things." Then, because Judith was a little insecure, especially after she started drinking, she added, "This is a college party. I still go here. And *teetotaler* isn't that big a word."

I laughed. Judith was a sweetheart, and she really had been trying to be a good friend and cheer me up. I had been understandably down, but life did go on even after what happened to my father. I had avoided people, but tonight, thanks to Judith, I was surrounded by idiots. The last thing I felt like doing was joining them.

Although, watching their antics made me even happier with my decision to take a little break from college. Or maybe a long one, like for the rest of my life — a life that had suddenly changed overnight. I was already firm in my decision, but Mom's incessant voice in my head always got me to unnecessarily question myself.

I was months shy of graduation, so Mom did have a valid argument that I'd invested too much to quit the race this close to the finish line, but even without crossing it, I'd had enough of the college experience.

I had a wake-up call, and I needed to start living my life every day to the best of my ability, regardless of how many inches I was away from graduation. Dad would have called that a sunken cost, and he would have been right.

I felt trapped. Dying to get out of here.

"I'm bored," I said.

"So you keep saying." Judith sighed. "Go and find someone else to have fun with if you don't want to play with me."

"I would love to play with you. But does it have to be here?"

Judith didn't answer, so I hugged her and thanked her for putting up with me. I found a room with a PlayStation less than a minute later, but the stupid thing was frozen mid-update, so it was as useless as a dead controller. This place probably only had idiotic games like GTA, anyway. These guys were unlikely to have anything released in the past five years.

Maybe…

A chorus of giggles came rolling into the living room from the kitchen, then girls screaming, but in a tone and pitch indicating a good time being had by all. Probably alcohol-fueled — almost for *sure* alcohol-fueled — but still worth checking out.

I entered the kitchen just as the main bro in the room, Colin Stewart, was finishing what I guessed had to be some sort of scary story, based on the general reaction of his eager audience, about something called a Dybbuk Box, sitting like a prize on the countertop in front of him.

"You're making that word up because it sounds like *dick*," giggled one of the girls.

"Dib-buk," Colin stated the syllables distinctly. "It's a real thing, I swear, from Jewish folklore. A box or wine cabinet or whatever, haunted by evil spirits."

Colin turned to look at me, standing in the doorway. "Ah, Shondra, surely you've heard of a Dybbuk Box?"

"No." I shook my head. Why did everyone always assume I was the expert on all things weird and spooky?

"Check it out." Colin nodded to the item of curiosity resting on the counter with a grin, eager to tell his story again. "That box right there is haunted."

"Okay…" This was so much better than drinking. The box was a two-foot-tall wooden wine cabinet with double doors and a small drawer on the bottom. A small brass ring adorned each door, and a keyhole plaque was set on the side. The box was otherwise unremarkable except for some symbols or strange letters carved on the front.

"This Dybbuk Box was originally posted for sale on eBay by a dude named Ross, like twenty years ago. A student named Losif at Mizzou bought it and sold it to this other dude named Jason Haxton, who was the director of some museum. So that's how you know I'm not lying about this — Haxton actually wrote about his experiences with this Dybbuk Box in a book."

One of the girls batted her eyelashes at him metaphorically. "Tell her about the estate sale guy."

Colin gave her a wink. "So, Ross is the dude who put the Dybbuk Box on eBay. He initially thought he was buying a wine cabinet at an estate sale from this crazy old bitch from Poland—"

"Hey!" shouted several of the girls.

Colin looked abashed, apologizing with his eyes but not bothering to put that sorry in words before he continued. "The woman was a hundred and three when she died. Ross offered to return the cabinet to her great-grand-daughter, assuming it had sentimental value. But the woman wanted nothing to do with it. Everyone in her family was terrified of the thing. So, Ross took it to his refinishing shop basement. Then, one day, he gets a call from some frantic salesman—"

Colin cleared his throat as Judith appeared in the doorway, probably looking for me before he continued.

"That salesperson told Ross that someone had come into the shop swearing and smashing things. Ross returned to find his basement broken into and the whole place totally reeking of cat piss. The Dybbuk Box basically haunted him until he finally sold it to that Losif guy, but then Losif had to get rid of it after he and his roommates all got insomnia and started, like, barfing all over each other. Then it went to Haxton, who claimed that it reversed his aging … after a bunch of welts and hives and more barfing, most of which was bloody."

"Gross," said two of the girls.

"It's not like you were there," snapped a third.

Colin looked over at me and finished his story. "The Dybbuk Box went into a museum, and you had to, like, sign a waiver if you wanted to see it because the museum didn't want to be responsible for whatever happened to you, but my dad doesn't believe in that shit and dropped a *ridonkulous* number of bones for it as my birthday present, so if anyone wants to get their haunting on…"

He waved a hand grandly across the Dybbuk Box.

Of course, I wanted to call bullshit on his story. Colin had a showman's flair, kinda like my Uncle Kevin, who also loved all of this arcane stuff. I was fascinated and pestered him to tell me everything he knew. Still, I never got to learn as much as I wanted to because talking about things like haunted objects always agitated my mother.

My heart started beating faster, partly because I was suddenly feeling unsettled, but also because the lights were flickering, and in a way that I realized might only be for me because nobody else seemed to be noticing.

Is that you, Dad?

Not even Judith appeared to notice as she drifted

11

closer to Colin, enraptured by his tale, or maybe it was golden hair and sky-blue eyes. Or his swimmer's body and perfect teeth. Honestly, I never got what girls saw in Colin.

He was still talking, and the girls listened, oblivious to the flickering light show going on. They were equally unaware of the arguing in the other room or the voices growing louder and louder.

One of the voices was my mother, mercilessly dressing me down about my many inappropriate life choices, most recently about leaving college. But that was impossible — Mom wasn't here.

Did anyone see the picture on the wall glowing? Oh, boy…

I blinked and smiled, trying not to hyperventilate, certain that something was seriously wrong with me. But what could it be? I hadn't been drinking — could my supposedly nonalcoholic drink have been spiked?

Or was Colin's story causing my imagination to run wild?

Everyone smiled goofy grins, their eyes not leaving Colin as he continued weaving his fantastic tale.

Especially Judith's eyes. Her expression of blissful abandon never wavered when Colin suddenly pulled open one of the small doors, grabbed Judith's arm, and started shoving it into the Dybbuk Box—

I screamed, stepped forward without consciously deciding to, and punched Colin in his stupid, smug face.

My knuckles throbbed, and I stared down at the hand that had acted out on its own like it was attached to someone else. What the fuck? I had never done anything like that before and had no clue why I had responded with such unprovoked violence.

"You bitch!" Colin roared, doubling over as he covered

his nose, blood running over his top lip. "What the fuck was that for?"

My chest tightened in fear. I had no idea. Half the girls shouted at me in defense of Colin, while the other half moved in front of me to protect me, even though they didn't know why I'd done what I'd done. Because, solidarity.

Some girls began pushing. Red Solo cups full of stale beer flew everywhere.

Colin was righting himself and looking mad enough to murder me twice, and a few of his buddies came rushing into the kitchen to make me feel about five times more vulnerable than I already did.

They tried to get the unruly girls under control with little luck.

"You bitch!" Colin yelled at me again, this time lunging forward.

I stepped back, expecting him to jump me, but one of his buddies held him back. I must have really pissed him off because Colin thrashed hard against his friend. The girls stopped fighting and everyone stared, witness to whatever might happen next.

"I'll kill you!" Colin roared.

Judith looked terrified, unsure of what I might do next.

But she didn't need to worry because I did what any sane person would do after punching someone for no apparent reason. I doubled down. "I'll kill you twice!"

Judith rolled her eyes.

Then she grabbed my arm and yanked me out of the scene while Colin yelled curses after us. Fuck those guys.

We left the party and walked silently for a while, Judith letting out a few nervous giggles about Colin being a little "too intense." That had been some seriously traumatic shit back there. Still, Judith decided the best way to handle it was to pretend it hadn't happened. She started prattling on about the most inane college crap I couldn't find the energy to care about.

I still hadn't responded to her question — if I thought Professor Weiss liked her enough to recommend her. We were a half mile away from the party by that point, and I'd yet to utter a word. In that time, Judith had also made multiple comments about her shoes and outfit both being "not nearly cool enough for tonight," wondered once if she looked "hot enough right now," reminded herself not to break her Snapchat streak, and made a rather long series of remarks about life in general that I found about as interesting as knowing the details about her brushing her teeth.

Finally, I asked, "Do you think our friends are *really* our friends?"

Judith didn't answer my excellent question, which I'd been considering the entire night.

That was why I had no interest in the party. It wasn't about the drinking. It was about the company.

No. My friends weren't really my friends anymore.

And maybe they never were.

Because they never really saw or heard or understood me.

Judith kept prattling on as we walked.

I thought about the Dybbuk Box, imagining Uncle Kevin and how much the object would have fascinated him. Maybe I was more like him than I wanted to admit. Neither of us knew how to make real friends. And, like with my uncle, that scene didn't scare me nearly as much as it should have.

But then I remembered all those smiles in the kitchen and how they had stretched just a little too wide, and I shuddered.

Chapter Two

EVERYTHING KEPT GOING WRONG.

I was back at my mom's house, where I lived in the misery of her eternal disapproval. My two siblings were coming over for dinner, which would mean three times the usual amount of judgment if everyone hounded me individually. Still, there was always a (good) chance that everyone would gang up on me, increasing the judgmentalism exponentially.

I wanted to make a frittata with veggies so no one could make me feel guilty about meat, even though I was still using eggs, and that would raise my sister Rashida's ire a little. But my eggs got overcooked and rubbery, and I thought the veggies were too raw. They ended up burning when I tried again. However, both of those times added together were still better than my third stab at a frittata — which I usually had no problem making — because that final attempt started a fire. We ended up ordering a large Garden Vegetable from The Flying Saucer. The place had only delivered pizza fast once, but I was still banking on the memory. Of course, the pie was cold when it got there.

Rashida said, "This is really delicious, Shondra. I'm glad I came over for all of this cheese."

"Leave her alone." My brother Malik pretended to defend me. "You know how Shondra thinks. If a place is good one out of five times, you might as well try it a sixth."

I had no hope of Mom coming to my aid. Not only was I her least favorite child right now, but she already had her tablet out and was swiping to her latest news report, itching to see herself on-screen. Most people got to see themselves in selfies; Mom's job as a reporter on TV made a lot of her life like a selfie. She probably stared at herself for hours in the bathroom, with a playlist to bask in her own glow.

"Who wants to watch with me?" Mom positioned her tablet so everyone could see it.

I said, "I've seen it already."

"No, you haven't. And neither has your brother or sister."

Mom finished showing off what none of us really wanted to see, and then she started the part of our evening that I was dumb enough to think I might avoid if I had ordered cannolis from the Flying Saucer for dessert and watched her newest video with a smile.

"Can we have a conversation about your life choices?" Mom asked me. She wasn't even subtle.

I shrugged. "I don't know. Can we have an actual conversation instead of you listing all the ways that I suck for not wanting to work at Trader Joe's anymore?"

"I don't care where you work, Shondra. But I care that you have a job. You dropped out of college and worked there for, what, two months before quitting? What are you planning to do next?"

Rashida and Malik shoved cold pizza into their mouths, enjoying the show.

"You *do* care where I work, Mom. When I told you I got the job at Trader Joe's, you acted like I was putting in for the day shift at a strip club."

"I guess I was still reeling from the bomb that my daughter was dropping out of college."

"Taking a gap year."

"Just shy of graduation."

Malik and Rashida kept chewing and watching.

"We can't help when life happens to us, right, Mom?" I smirked at her, feeling like a jerk but needing to lash out in some way to make myself feel a little better. "Isn't that what you said?"

"We all miss your father, Shondra. But he's been gone for six months now. You can't just stop living your life. It's time to move forward, not just on."

"On is forward, Mom."

Rashida dropped her slice. "Mom's right. College is, like, essential."

"Is that what it's like?" I snapped at her.

Malik swallowed the last bit of his crust. "Seems like you're blowing it, Shon."

As usual, neither my stupid older sister nor dumber younger brother knew what they were talking about.

The mood was abysmal, and I wasn't sure if it could get any worse. Until Mom showed me a way.

"I'm just worried that you're going to turn out like … Kevin."

"*Like Kevin?*" Comparing me to my uncle, the dark sheep of the family, was *not* okay, no matter how much I loved him. It was an even sharper sting, knowing I'd made the same comparison just one night before. "Why don't you just call me a freak and a loser?"

Malik laughed. "I thought that's what she was doing."

Rashida slapped him on the arm.

"I thought you liked Uncle Kevin!" Mom protested.

"But you don't!" I shouted. "That's what makes it an insult!"

"I never—"

Mom was cut off by a tremendous *thump* coming from upstairs, followed by a terrible crashing sound.

I ran upstairs, and everyone followed.

Together, we looked into my room and surveyed the damage. My closet door was open, and an avalanche of my clothes and old yearbooks spilled out. On top of it was Uncle Kevin's trunk. It appeared the closet ceiling had given way, and the old trunk had fallen through from the attic, leaving a huge mess.

Dust and debris were settling in the air, stirred from the crash. The imposing trunk's surface was covered in cracks and dents from years of getting dragged through every damned adventure in Uncle Kevin's life.

Mom looked at me like it was all my fault.

"What?" I asked.

Malik started to laugh again, and Rashida started slapping him before he finished. That ended the evening for everyone. It was abrupt and unsettling but still better than getting emotionally egged for dropping out of college and relentlessly nagged to go back.

"I'll call a contractor in the morning," Mom said as the three of them backed out of my room, leaving me solitary amongst the shambles.

Had Uncle Kevin just saved me from another miserable night at home with the fam? If it was him, I wish he had been less messy about it.

After cleaning up the ceiling debris and making a new laundry pile, I was alone with Uncle Kevin's trunk, sifting through his mess, captivated and confused like always.

Kevin had been interested in just about everything, which was the thing that made him most odd, at least according to my mother. But such varied interests made it hard to find anything threading the objects, articles, and note cards from the trunk together. Other than my uncle's love of conspiracies.

The CIA killed John F. Kennedy.

The government is hiding evidence of extraterrestrial life.

The government is using psi-ops to keep the population in line.

Ghosts of our loved ones walk among us.

The moon landing was a farce and was filmed in a Hollywood studio.

The government controls the weather using high-powered lasers and other secret technology.

Uncle Kevin definitely didn't trust the government. But he also had journals full of notes about mysterious objects and fabled arcana.

A potion that could bring the dead back to life.

A sentient book that could answer any question.

A glove that could be used to control the elements.

A pair of opera glasses that will show you anything that's happening at that moment.

A spell that can create a doorway to another dimension.

All of it, unbelievable — and so was Uncle Kevin.

I'd seen them all before. Not that I remembered much. Maybe a percentage of what I wanted to. Kevin had disappeared when I was thirteen years old, over nine years ago. There was no evidence that he was dead, only that he seemed to vanish from existence. And since nobody ever wanted to talk about him unless they were talking shit, I didn't have anyone to answer my questions or help me to understand how I felt.

I didn't recall ever seeing anything in Kevin's trunk about a Dybbuk Box. But back then, I hadn't known what one was.

So, I started looking through his trunk for answers.

Two minutes later, I found a tattered magazine article in the trunk about a Dybbuk Box, along with a picture.

The article detailed a wine cabinet made by a Jewish scholar in the early 1900s, used to store the body of a dybbuk, a spirit said to possess people.

I looked closely at the picture. It might even be the same one Colin had been boasting about in the kitchen.

This felt like synchronicity, hearing that story at the stupid college party, then coming home and seeing that same story in Uncle Kevin's trunk.

I looked Colin up on Facebook and saw he was selling the Dybbuk Box. Did getting punched at his party make him want to get rid of it?

I clicked on a picture. It didn't make sense for my heart to start beating faster. In better light, the wood looked ordinary, with a worn and weathered exterior. But something (probably that time I just spent with the trunk) made me wonder (hope?) if the Dybbuk Box was imbued with some sort of dark and powerful magic. An evil spirit bound and determined to possess anyone who dared to unleash its malevolent energy into the world. That would be cool, right?

And in the background, everyone smiling those weird, unsettling smiles. I shuddered, clicking and clicking and clicking for more information, desperate to know where I could see the Dybbuk Box in person again.

Maybe I'd even buy it for myself. That way, I would be getting it out of the hands of apparent idiots.

But why? Did I have a self-destructive streak, and it wasn't enough to drop out of college, spitting distance from my degree?

I'm unsure if I thought it was a good or bad thing when I saw that the Dybbuk Box was being auctioned off the next day. But for sure, I was smiling.

Chapter Three

"THE DYBBUK BOX!" I YELLED, BUT THE GUY IN THE bowtie had no idea what I was talking about. Same thing had happened with the lady with hair the color of grape cough syrup and the grandma in stilettos. "It's wooden, with ornate markings and symbols, and…"

I stopped talking because people shifting on their feet and trying to get away from me while I was in the middle of a sentence made me uncomfortable.

"I'm sorry," said Mr. Bowtie. "But I'm afraid I've not seen the particular listing you're inquiring about. Have you considered asking someone who works here?"

"Well, thanks anyway." Good luck getting your lock of Marilyn Monroe's hair, or whatever it is you're bidding on, Orville Redenbacher.

I gave the guy a clumsy grin, then reviewed the listings again. Apparently, I was even more terrible and awkward around rich people than I had imagined myself to be. We had nothing in common. It's not like I could afford anything being auctioned, and all these monocle wearers could smell it on me. They were clearly not used to young,

Black, college dropout nerds in their midst. Maybe it was my worn jeans and Cat-o-mancy T-shirt that gave me away.

I looked through the listed lots again but came up just as empty.

Then I surveyed every item physically displayed, feeling like I was inviting too much attention with my nervously furtive movements. I was about to give up because, of course, this whole thing was stupid, and I was thinking seriously about leaving when I saw Colin standing off to the side, his face looking like a pummeled grape, with a pair of black olives for eyes squished into the top. His posture seemed defeated. He looked like an entirely different guy than the one I had seen just last night.

What could have possibly happened between the party and now? My fist clearly couldn't have done *that* much damage.

"Hey, Colin." But he didn't seem to know who I was. "It's Shondra. Judith's friend from the party last night. The one who, um, punched you?"

He nodded. Not the angry reaction I'd expected.

"Sorry about that, by the way. Something came over me." Still no real response. "Are you okay?"

He was rubbing his jaw. No, Colin didn't look okay at all.

"I will be soon." He obviously didn't want to discuss it but was doing me a courtesy just by standing there. "Once I get rid of that thing."

"What happened?" I asked, nodding at his face.

"My trophy case fell on me while I was sleeping last night."

"Ouch." I couldn't help making a face.

"It's fine." He shrugged. "Another couple of hours and

my legs stopped working for no reason. *Again*. At least they worked enough for me to get here."

"That happened before?"

"The last time, it lasted three days, and there was no explanation, so once was more than enough."

"I can imagine. Out of curiosity…" It was more than curiosity. "Why wasn't any of that in your story yesterday?"

He brushed off the question.

"I need to sell that thing." He sounded so sad and desperate, but then a spark of hope suddenly filled in the blanks. "Do you want to buy it?"

I kind of did.

But then he shook his head violently back and forth while grabbing a handful of hair from each side.

"NO. NO. NO." He shook it again. "I'm sorry, I didn't mean that. You don't want the thing. Trust me. Sometimes, my ears bleed for hours. I can't cook anything without a fire starting in the kitchen. I've fallen downstairs four times in the last three weeks. My tongue has stopped working twice, and I'm not sure how many times I've found myself driving without remembering getting in the car."

"Why were you boasting about owning it then?" He'd really been a total dick posturing about it. "If all this bad shit was happening…"

"Then there's also the tripping in a puddle of mud and dropping my cell phone into a toilet, but admittedly, those were probably just me." He looked straight then as if he were finally tuning back in. "I thought it was, you know, cool."

"It was cool up until you were almost crushed to death by a trophy case, you mean?"

Colin looked down in embarrassment.

"So … you're selling it?"

He sighed. "Before you decide to bid on it, I submit

Exhibit A." He waved a hand over his purple face. "If that fails to move you, then the Dybbuk Box is in the back room where people won't accidentally see it or open the thing or come anywhere near it."

"Can you show me?" Colin didn't mind selling the box so long as he didn't meet the new owner. But really, I was as good as anyone. "Please?"

I knew it was a bad idea, but I couldn't resist asking. I felt compelled, practically forced. But I'd never been good at stopping myself, so that was not necessarily any kind of ancient spirit curse.

He sighed again, seeming torn between wanting to protect me from my desire to purchase a death box and needing to unburden his curse upon someone else. He led me down one long hallway and around a corner to a closed door.

"That's as far as I go." Colin nodded at the door. "It's in there if it's still what you're looking for, though I really hope it isn't."

For a flash, his face said the opposite. But then he turned around and walked away faster after laying a few steps of distance between us.

I knocked lightly twice, unsure of whether I should just open the door, then turned the knob and swung it wide when nobody answered.

Two people were standing in front of the box, and each one of them individually made me feel like I was the grand marshal in a *basic* parade.

The man had a strong jawline and deep blue eyes, which I could see sparkling from the doorway. Tall and muscular, with a broad chest and powerful shoulders. More like Captain America than Thor, but I didn't hate it.

The woman was a stunner, her blonde hair framing

smooth skin, tan enough to have sand between her toes, cheekbones chiseled by angels, and a beautiful sneer.

I inched closer, trying to keep myself small while eavesdropping on what sounded like a healthy volley of sparring between the beautiful people.

"So, if I win, then dinner is off the table?" said the man.

"Dinner was never on the table, Darren."

"All this tension."

"There is zero tension. I will be leaving here with the Dybbuk Box, and you will be going home alone like always."

"I never go home alone," Darren said.

"In spirit, you always go home alone."

Burn. My money was on the blonde.

"I can pay for the box in cash."

"Congratulations." She shrugged. "I can pay more."

"We'll see."

"Looks like we will," the blonde agreed, nodding at the private auction just about to start.

My timing couldn't have been better.

Or worse, depending on what you believed.

Ken and Barbie in front of me only stirred my desire to see and hear and know more about the Dybbuk Box. Last night, I felt horrified at the thought of Judith touching it — or having her hand shoved in it. Now, I was imagining the brush of that wood against my fingers.

An auctioneer joined us, and the four of us alone made it feel like I was witnessing something special.

The bidding started at $100 but went up to five times that after only two rounds.

I told myself that I was willing to spend no more than one thousand dollars, even though Mom would murder me in my sleep if I even did that.

I caved and ended up making my first and only bid at $1200 after Darren added $300 to his opponent's prior bid.

They both turned to look at me. He scoffed, and she rolled her eyes.

"Who are you?" Blondie snapped. "Are you even registered to bid?"

"I, uhh…"

I was out of the game after that.

But Barbie and Ken kept going.

Back and forth, back and forth, until Blondie won the box.

Darren had a half smile as the auctioneer finished, but his eyes were narrowed, and he was chewing on his bottom lip, clearly upset at having lost the prize.

This seemed to be about more than the box. These two had history, and I felt as suddenly curious about that as I did about the piece of arcana that the woman had just won.

The Dybbuk Box was delivered to her hand, wrapped in paper, and nestled into her own bag. I felt even smaller as she passed me like I didn't exist.

I followed her out of the room, around a corner, and down one long hallway into the main auction area, where a livelier auctioneer was rattling lot numbers and opening bids.

I felt physically and emotionally distraught that the box was leaving and relieved that it was now farther away and less able to affect me.

The blonde looked back and saw me. She absolutely had to know I was trying to catch up, but I only walked faster.

I was almost running by the time she reached the door,

swinging it open right in time for me to slip out of the auction house behind her.

She reeled on me. "What the hell do you want?"

"I'm sorry." I felt so stupid. "I was just curious about … that." I nodded at her bag. "And I didn't know how else to—"

"This isn't a toy, and it's not some sort of college drinking game. Go home." Her eyes were icy blue but even colder as she gave me the order.

"I'm just—"

"*Go home.*" Firmer this time.

"Give the kid a break," said a voice from behind me. I turned around, already knowing to whom it belonged.

"You too, Darren."

"I'm glad you got it." He shrugged. "That just gives us a chance to get it back."

"Good luck with that."

"You can tell everyone at Darrow & Grimes that Nemicon—"

"Fuck off, Darren." The blonde turned around and walked away with the box, swinging in a bag on her arm.

Like an absolute boss.

Chapter Four

I'D SWORN OFF LOOKING AT MY PHONE WHILE WALKING many times, but I really meant it this time. My face still hurt from where it slammed against the hardwood after the rug slipped out from under my feet, sliding along the floor like someone had just rubbed butter on it, even though the rug had never moved like that before.

Then I bashed my knee on the banister while trying to right myself.

Now, I was being superstitious and trying to get out of feeling so clumsy, assigning all of the blame to the Dybbuk Box. I had only looked at the box, not even touched it. I tried to dismiss it as a made-up ghost story like one told around a campfire, but I still felt some sort of unexplainable connection to the Dybbuk Box. I felt cursed.

Just like Uncle Kevin, I couldn't turn my curiosity off, so after I iced my jaw and told Mom that it wasn't hurting nearly as bad as it was, I grabbed my laptop, climbed into bed, and started an online search with the three words that had been stirring around in my head like brew in a cauldron since hearing them outside the auction house: *Darrow, Grimes,* and *Nemicon.*

Nemicon was the more interesting name and thus earned my attention first. I hit a bullseye on the About page after clicking on the photo of Darren Dupree, the Paul Walker lookalike I'd seen at the auction house.

Darren was even sexier in pixels. His picture was below the boss, Mr. Rudolph Bramson, a man whose biography read like an entry on an adventurer's travelog. Dude should have been named Indy. He had visited public and private collections of artifacts from all across the world, spending years developing relationships to now deal in only the finest in high-end art and one-of-a-kind antiquities. Maybe by antiquities, what they really meant was *arcana.*

There was surely more to Rudolph, considering the depth of experience meeting such vagaries in his story. His company tagline, *The Past is Your Future,* was clever, but it said nothing about the founder.

I clicked around until I found a story about Darrow & Grimes without even searching for those keywords directly.

So, Barbie and Ken were connected for sure.

According to the article, Rudolph had a history with D&G, which seemed sort of like the crap version of Nemicon, from what I could tell. Not even an antique shop; it was a thrift store. The D&G website wasn't nearly as grandiose, and there was very little storytelling or pictures of what they sold, but it had the only thing I really needed it to have: an address that turned out to be just ten minutes and six traffic lights away.

A little bell dinged above the door as I entered the shop.

A woman looked over, smiling like she was starving and expecting a pizza. Her face was round and expressive, and her voice was full of vibrance. She had a smile like J-Lo and was about her age, too.

"Welcome to Darrow & Grimes!" she announced, standing in front of a large painting of a bunch of men in an old-timey saloon and surrounded by shelves of the junk the store signs referred to as *trinkets*. "Let me know if there's anything I can help you with. Just give me a holler. My name is Jackie. And yes, our fudge is as delicious as it looks!"

She nodded down to a meticulously arranged display on the counter. Hills of fudge on a glass cake stand, arranged in neat rows of varying colors, accented by sprinkles and candied nuts.

A pristine exhibit, especially compared to the rest of the bric-a-brac shop, cluttered with an assembly of antiques, relics, and trinkets. Despite its haphazard appearance, the place felt oddly charming, with a sense of order and decorum to the general chaos. Inventory seemed clearly labeled to make categorization and navigation easier, not that I could understand what differentiated the shelves.

The shop held a strange mix of old and new amid the old books, gilded vases, and ancient sculptures. There were slightly used Bratz dolls, old TVs, Disney paraphernalia, and a massive plastic marble run snaking around the shelves that was calling for me to drop a marble into it. There was a smell of mustiness, mingling with the warm and pleasant aroma of burning incense and sweet-smelling herbs, polished wood and leather, and natural dust and decay.

I wanted to touch everything but didn't dare to take my hands out of my pockets. The woman was staring at me, probably seeing right through me. She probably knew exactly why I was here.

"Can I help you with anything?" she finally asked.

"Just looking." I should probably say something about the fudge. I smiled and made my way over, then pointed at one of the piles. "Is that pistachio?"

"It is pistachio!" Jackie looked like she'd just won a prize. She beamed even wider through her pitch. "Chocolate, vanilla, and pistachios. Here, try some."

She was already cutting a tiny piece off of the brick.

"Thank you." I took it, wishing I had asked about the maple, the peanut butter and jelly, or the pumpkin spice. I don't even really like pistachio, but the green was just colorful enough to catch my eye first.

But it tasted incredible. Rich and sweet, a decadent nutty flavor balanced by the creamy fudge.

"Right?" Jackie must have made the fudge herself.

"Did you make it?" I prepared for my compliment.

"Nope." She shook her head. "It's from Costco. I used to make it. But that damn baby makes it near impossible to put in the time required."

"Oh." Did she mean *her* damn baby? Or was she also moonlighting as a babysitter.

"Were you looking for anything in particular?" Jackie laughed. "Besides free fudge?"

I figured that maybe I'd stop feeling stupid if I finally just spit it out. "I was at an auction earlier today…"

"An auction?" Her slow repetition sounded like an accusation. She was standing up straighter, and neither her mouth nor her eyes were smiling anymore.

I was already regretting this. "There was an item … I think someone from this place might have—"

"*This place* is—"

"I'm sorry, never mind!" I shook my head, trying to backpedal. "I was just curious … I can't stop thinking about the box and … I don't know…"

I had no idea why I was rambling. "Never mind. Sorry for wasting your time." I turned around and began to retreat.

But Jackie stopped me with a clear note of concern in her call. "Wait!"

I turned back around.

"What's your name?" she asked.

"Shondra," I said, as if that made a difference.

"Come here, Shondra."

I was standing in front of the counter two moments later.

"This will be weird, but I promise it won't hurt." Jackie ducked behind the counter, then circled back around, holding some sort of handheld device with a long, thin probe protruding from the front, dangling like a you-know-what.

She waved the probe up and down my body.

"Can I ask what you're doing?"

"I'm scanning your energy," Jackie explained, her movements precise, her expression confident and calm.

"For what?"

"Curse remnants."

"Oh." I nodded. "Of course, curse remnants."

No, not, *of course*. What was she talking about?

Jackie nodded, apparently finished, then tossed the device onto the counter with a clatter. The thing must be durable. "Come with me to the lab."

She had me at "come with me," but a lab was definitely something I wanted to see. Didn't most good adventures begin in a hidden lab?

Jackie held the door open, letting me step around the counter to the inner sanctum, and I entered the new space to see an older, imposing man (not quite Nick Fury, more Morgan Freeman) exuding an air of confident intelligence I could practically smell from the doorway.

He was at a long table, standing in front of a large steel cage.

"What's this?" he asked.

My fantasy of a secret lab run by a mad scientist was satisfyingly fulfilled. Mad scientist in a lab coat? Check. A Bunsen burner under a glass beaker? Check. Tables covered in unidentified devices with blinking lights, bundles of wires, and tempting red buttons to push? Check. Weird relics and menacing objects on shelves all around the room? Check, check.

I was home.

Jackie scurried over and explained in a whisper.

He slowly nodded. "I see."

He went to one of the other three tables that filled the lab and picked up what looked like a 1950s-era toaster with a battery pack on the side and a long translucent hose coming out of one end. He swung it like a lasso over my head while nodding the entire time.

I still had no idea what was happening. Was I being punked? No cameras in sight. This guy was for real.

He finished swinging his contraption, then put it away and picked up a bundle of sage from a plate not too far away, introduced himself as Clarence with an overdue smile, and finally explained himself while waving the now burning sage in a cloud all around me.

"You got a bad energy transference. Looks like it's from the Dybbuk Box."

I could barely breathe with all that reeking smoke, and my head was swimming.

"You'll be okay." Clarence nodded with a loose gesture that, when combined, clearly meant, *You should probably go now.*

But I couldn't leave without the answers I came for. Or ones to the new questions that popped into my head after walking inside.

"What is this place?" I asked. "What do you do here?"

"We are in the business of antiquities."

"I mean in *here*." I waved my hand around at the lab, then pointed at a table full of vintage dolls that seemed to be eyeing me in accusation.

Jackie and Clarence traded a look, but neither one of them answered me.

"I'll leave if someone can tell me about the Dybbuk Box. I just want—"

The door opened, and a newcomer entered the lab. A smaller man with fluffy hair and beady eyes, but also the first person to give me a smile since I'd swallowed the fudge. He had total Ant-Man energy.

He extended his hand. "I'm Brian Darrow."

"Oh." We shook. "It's nice to meet you."

"So, you met Ariel at the auction, I take it?"

The blonde? "It wasn't much of a meeting."

"Yeah." Brian gave me a knowing smile. "She can be like that. I'm impressed that you found us."

Neither Jackie nor Clarence seemed impressed in the least, trading another look that made me feel like shrinking into myself. Not that I blamed them. It wasn't like I'd deciphered a serial killer's elaborate code. I was decent at research, but there had been nothing to finding Darrow & Grimes.

"Where do you work…?"

"Shondra."

"Where do you work, Shondra?"

"I'm sort of between jobs right now." Aka, I'm literally doing nothing with my life.

"Well, we have an opening." Brian seriously smiled

more than Jackie had over that fudge. "How would you like to come in for an interview tomorrow?"

What was happening?

"I would love that!" I chirped — before I knew what job I was agreeing to interview for.

Chapter Five

I WAS SHOCKED THAT BRIAN ASKED ME FOR AN INTERVIEW but tried not to be put off that both Clarence and Jackie seemed even more surprised. Or annoyed, really. I went home, and there was mercifully no shit to be had — my bedroom was the same organized mess it usually was, but, luckily, there were no new trunks that had fallen through the ceiling, no strange voices or glowing paintings. Only peaceful dreams from the minute my head hit the pillow until I woke up. Maybe Clarence's smudging had worked.

I showed up ten minutes early to my interview, but the other person vying for the job must have been there at least eleven minutes ahead of the scheduled time because his eyes were locked, loaded, and looking down on me when I entered.

He was hotness-level ten: Chris Pratt (*Guardians of the Galaxy*, not *Parks and Rec*, obviously), smirkiness-level: Loki (TV show, not movies), and up-himself-level: Tony Stark all the way.

I still didn't even really know what I was interviewing for, but I did need a job (plus Mom would stop nagging me for a few moments), and if I couldn't stop thinking about this place and its many curiosities — like the supposedly haunted Dybbuk Box that brought me here — then I might as well get paid to nose around. I could be the lab assistant and scream, "It's alive!"

Not that I had a chance of landing the gig. The guy sitting across from me seemed to know exactly why he was there, while I didn't even know there would be more than one person applying for this mystery job.

"Did you read about the Abernathy Stone?" he asked me.

"I think so." I smiled because, of course, I hadn't read about it. Was this a test? Were there CliffsNotes?

"Looks like the ability to turn lead into gold isn't just a legend after all. At least not according to Professor—"

"Have you ever heard of the Dybbuk Box?"

"Of course, I've heard of the Dybbuk Box." He seemed offended but rebounded by proving his superiority and obvious right to this job by finishing his stupid little story about some professor of something or other who did a study on this thing called the Abernathy Stone that might or might not have at one time in ancient history actually turned lead into gold. Supposedly.

I didn't need to believe a word the guy was saying to know he'd be a shoo-in for sure. This guy thoroughly knew his shit, while I still didn't understand what this shit even was. He was confident and great-looking — though not nearly as handsome as Darren at Nemicon, because wowsers — but his general knowledge about the kinds of things sitting on the shelves in the shop and on tables in the lab made me feel out of place. Intimidated before he even introduced himself.

"I'm Kip." He smiled like this next part wasn't about to gut me. "Kip Grimes."

Grimes. Like the name on the fucking door. Great.

"I'm Shondra. Henry." A nervous laugh. "No relation to anyone here."

"Montague Grimes was my father."

"Do you really need to interview for this job, then?"

He laughed. "I guess you don't know Brian."

My odds of getting the gig were slightly better than *Freaks and Geeks* getting green-lit for another season.

"We met yesterday, but I have no idea why he asked me to interview."

Kip smiled. "Because he saw something special in you, I suppose."

He sounded sarcastic, obviously trying to unseat me. "I was just coming in to look for something. I don't know anything about any of this."

"You know more than—"

Kip didn't get to finish his thought before the door swung open, and Brian was smiling at us both. But, no surprise, he nodded to the eventual winner first.

Kip followed him into the lab, then the door closed behind them, and I was left all alone with my doubt. I had no idea what I was doing in the shop or what was keeping me glued to that seat, other than a million little mysteries whispering in my ear from all the bric-a-brac stacked on those shelves and the near certainty that if I did manage to stick around this place long enough, I would eventually get a glimpse of something on the other side of an invisible veil that most of the world could never experience. It was something I had waited for my whole life, and now here I was, sitting clueless and contemplating ghosting the interview.

I got up to leave three times, certain that I was making some sort of mistake. Or maybe I was the butt of a joke I didn't understand. There could be hidden cameras anywhere. Everywhere. They would be so easy to hide in numerous objects crowding the store. I pictured Kip and Brian laughing at me sitting there uncomfortably while Clarence joined them, or Jackie out front, peeking over at the loser sitting all alone, waiting to interview for a job she can never ever get, in between offering customers fudge.

But that made me mad, so I sat down again.

The door opened again, then Kip left the lab. He clearly had gotten the job, considering how wide he was smiling, but the jerk went ahead and insulted me anyway.

"Good luck," he said, though he couldn't have possibly meant it.

"Thanks." I smiled and nodded to prove that Kip wasn't getting my goat, then passed Brian as he held the door open for me.

The lab was empty except for the two of us.

Brian walked over to a desk, clear except for a computer and a landline. The hairs in my nose itched as we passed dolls, jewelry boxes, and an ornate mirror. I had a sense of unease, but it was muted by my excitement of just being here.

Brian sat on one side of the desk and gestured to the empty seat.

I sat, and he got right to it. "So, tell me about your fascination with the Dybbuk Box."

"What do you want to know about it?" I asked.

"How long have you been interested in it?"

"I just heard about it at a party a couple of days ago."

"Really?" Brian raised his eyebrows, appearing seriously surprised. "The story must have made quite an impact on you."

"It wasn't the story … it was the Dybbuk Box itself. This guy grabbed my friend Judith's hand and tried to put it inside, but then I—"

"Your friend — what's her name and address?" His tone was as urgent as his suddenly set jaw.

"Judith!" I blurted, more scared than I wanted to admit. "Judith Alderson … but you can't have her address!"

"Her bad luck could possibly be fatal if you don't give it to me."

Fatal?

"She lives at 4279 Briar."

Brian picked up the landline and punched a couple of digits. A beat later, he barked into the phone.

"I need you to send Ariel over to 4279 Briar. The girl's name is Judith. The odds of some lingering Dybbuk problems are highly likely … thanks, Jackie."

Then he hung up like there wasn't even anything super weird about that.

Brian's tone returned to normal, "So, you were resistant to the energy, even if the curse hit you a little."

"Sorry." I shook my head. "I don't know what that means."

"Why do you want to work here at Darrow & Grimes?"

"Why do *I* want to work here? *You're* the one who asked me if I wanted to interview yesterday, so…"

"I sure did. And now that you're here, I hope you can tell me what makes you right for the job."

I didn't even know what the job was, but I sure as hell wanted to be right for it.

"I didn't know about any of this a couple of days ago, other than what my Uncle Kevin used to talk about, but I'm fascinated by it all. Now that I know it's actually real … I … This spooky stuff is cool and all, but—"

"But?"

"But something happened. Something bad, and I hurt someone for no reason. I believe the Dybbuk Box made me do it, but I don't know how. You bought the Dybbuk Box, and something in my gut says that you did it to protect others from getting hurt. I want to be a part of that. I want to do what I can to make sure that other people don't get hurt."

"Like the way you helped your friend Judith?" Brian asked.

"Exactly."

And yet, I realized at that moment that I had never really thought about helping Judith or even wondered if she was okay. Both the question and the way that Brian asked it felt kind of strange, and that weirdness was only the start, with his questions getting weirder and weirder the longer he kept talking to me. I saw myself as a modern Lydia Deetz, for I, myself, am strange and unusual.

"If a human being's soul could be stripped from their body, leaving only the shell behind, what form would that soul take?"

"A wraith?" My long weekends of Dungeons & Dragons campaigns were paying off.

Brian smiled, seeming to like that. But then he frowned, so maybe he didn't. "Can you tell me the difference between ghost energy and spirit energy?"

"I'm … not sure."

"True or false: Ghosts have no individual identity, but spirits are complex."

"True?"

"Ghosts are an extension of the soul," Brian replied, and I didn't know if I got the answer right or not. "They bring back thoughts and emotions but no real personality. Spirit energy is different. Do you understand?"

No. "Of course."

"What would you do with an object that you knew for sure was haunted?"

I had no idea. So I said, "I'd bring it to Brian Darrow."

Another smile. "What if the item was dangerous?"

"Then I would *have* to turn it over to you."

He shook his head, still not what he was looking for. "Say it was a vase."

"I'd smash it?"

Now, he looked disappointed. "How would you handle someone who won't let go of a cursed object?"

"Does the object have sentimental value?"

Brian sighed, frowned, then seemed to reset himself. "You have no idea what I'm talking about, do you?"

"No," I confessed.

"What *do* you know about the arcane?"

"I like the movie *Poltergeist*, and I play RPG games."

Brain frowned again. A miss.

"I also do research." I rushed, trying to fill my gap in knowledge with confidence. "I learn a lot from internet searches."

Clearly, this wasn't impressive, so I tried again.

"And from Uncle Kevin, as I said. He talked about ghosts and curses and all sorts of crazy things. Everyone in my family thought he was nuts, but I believed him and thought he was fascinating. He disappeared years ago, but he left a trunk full of letters and objects and things."

"Well, that is interesting." Brian scratched at a non-existent beard. "Anything else?"

"No." I could feel my shoulders sag, so I tried to keep my face happy.

Another smile, but this one was different. "Thank you for your time."

"I'm sorry. I just—"

"You did your best." And this time, his smile was like a period at the end of our interview, or nails on my opportunity's coffin. "I'll walk you to the door."

Kip had yet to leave D&G, still basking in his father's legacy while yukking it up with Jackie out front. His interview had ended, but he'd hung around to rub his superiority in my face.

"How did you do?" he asked.

"I crushed it."

Kip smiled. "I'm sure you did."

So rude. I looked past him to the painting on the counter that I'd first noticed yesterday when Jackie was offering me fudge.

Now, Kip was looking at the painting, and I noticed that he looked just like one of the men in it.

"Did you pose for that?" I asked, gesturing to the canvas. "Or did you have to send in a photo to give yourself more time to stare into the mirror at home?"

Kip didn't reply, seeming suddenly flustered, his body sagging and cheeks flushed. He walked past me to Brian, gave him a hearty but abbreviated shake, then nodded to the room before leaving Darrow & Grimes without a word.

I watched him go, then turned back to Brian and Jackie. "Was it something I said?"

"Not exactly." Jackie pointed at the painting. "Kip's father was Montague Grimes, co-founder of Darrow & Grimes."

"I never would have guessed," I tried to joke.

"That's his father in *Saloon at the End of the World*." She nodded at the man, who looked a lot like an older version of Kip. Then, she explained what I had already figured out. "That's the name of the painting."

"Like in *The Witcher*?"

"I'm sorry?" Brian didn't get it.

"The painting's name, '*Saloon at the End of the World*.' It's like Tavern at the End of the World from *The Witcher*. It's a novel series. Andrzej Sapkowski."

His face was still blank.

"Maybe you've heard of the video game? Or surely you know that series on Netflix with Henry Cavill?" Most people had no idea that their favorite shows were basically *always* based on books. But Brian still didn't seem to recognize it. "Anyway, they use that name. Also, Star vs. the Forces of Evil has something like it. The Tavern at the End of the Multiverse."

"Oh." Brian frowned. "Not nearly as clever as I thought."

He might as well have been talking about me.

There was zero chance that I would be getting this job.

Chapter Six

I WAS HAVING A HARD TIME NOT STOPPING FOR A cheeseburger on my way home.

But even if I brushed my teeth before getting back to the house, Mom would still find a way to smell it on me. Her sixth sense was so good it was halfway to a seventh, and I didn't want to be nagged about why I was eating my feelings on top of everything else.

No, Mom, I won't be getting that job. Not a chance in hell. The interviewer practically laughed at me while ending things early after talking nonsense I could barely understand. He seemed to delight in my ignorance. He out-nerded me, except for that Witcher thing. Shame on you, Brian — you need to put it on your to-be-read list immediately.

The more I thought about it, the madder I got.

Almost angry enough to make myself a sundae. But there wasn't any ice cream in the freezer, and Mom came back from wherever she was a few minutes after I broke down, so I would have been caught vanilla-handed for sure.

"Have you eaten?" Mom asked.

"I was waiting for you."

"Then you should have been here earlier. I made quinoa."

"Quinoa? Since when do we eat quinoa?"

"Since Pilates Gourmet posted a recipe."

"Great. More Pilates Gourmet," I said, with a sarcastic smile, even though I actually liked all of the Pilates Gourmet recipes more than I would ever admit to Mom because she cared about that woman's Instagram way too much and acted like she didn't. The name Pilates Gourmet also felt insulting for so many reasons, even though I could never get her to understand why.

"Fine." She shrugged. "No bittersweet chocolate almond bark for you."

"Why does it have to be bitter?"

"I guess you didn't get the job?"

"Why do you assume my failure?"

"I'm not assuming your failure, Shon. I'm drawing conclusions based on your obviously mopey face."

"I'm not mopey." No way I could have gotten away with my self-delusion in front of a mirror.

"Maybe it's time to forget about trying to get a job and remember all the goals you were so close to just a few months ago."

"*Maybe.* I'm not sure that you've ever had any patience for any other perspective there, Mom."

"That's a little unfair."

"You're totally right. Thank you for finally admitting that."

"You're moping around the house. The whole point of going to college was to develop other interests."

"I have other interests."

"And you're using them to apply for a job at a thrift store?"

"It's not a thrift store."

"What kinds of things do they sell?"

"A ton of stuff. Including fudge."

"Have you thought about applying for something you're passionate about?"

"No, Mom. I only fill out applications for things that are for sure going to bore me. Please remind me to add this exchange to my resume."

"Why do you have to be smart with me?"

"It's something I'm passionate about, so I was trying to apply myself."

"Quinoa is in the fridge," said Mom.

Then she was out of there.

I dug through the fridge and grabbed a carton of what might have been cashew chicken, but it tasted like beef, and I couldn't remember what the lunch special had been last week when I ordered it.

What a dumbass. I totally should have gone with the burger.

I emptied the carton while taking a BuzzFeed quiz that nudged me into a little momentary self-reflection about whether or not I might be a clairvoyant since I was still smarting from my failed job interview and wondering if Brian's comment about being resistant to the curse meant I might be psychic.

Do you see things that others do not? Maybe.

Have you ever seen a ghost? Maybe.

Are you a night owl or an early bird? Depends.

Do you see the future? Not according to Mom.

I set the empty carton on my desk and nestled into bed with the laptop, looking up Nemicon because if Darrow & Grimes didn't want me, then maybe they would. The two companies clearly carried the same kind of supernatural inventory, given that they were both bidding on the Dybbuk Box.

"Nemicon, how may I help you?" asked a woman who sounded too fancy to actually mean it.

"Yes…" Her polished indifference had flustered me. "I was wondering if you were hiring?"

A long pause. "Hiring for what?"

"For people … to get the haunted objects."

"This is a gallery." Then, a clarification. "For fine art."

Then the woman hung up.

I was as done with the internet as the internet was with me, so I went to dig back into Uncle Kevin's treasures. I pulled a few of the more interesting pieces out of the trunk and put them on my bed. There were faded tags attached to each, yellow and smudged with time.

A pentagram necklace inscribed with the name *Zachary Jones* in Hebrew and English letters.

A pendant depicting a beaked woman in a gothic dress. Beneath the image read, *The Matriarch.*

A hand mirror with an illegible word scrawled in blood in the upper right corner.

A tarnished pewter crucifix with a bloody handprint smeared across its body.

A rabbit's foot from the Genesee River, according to its tag.

Plus, a stack of postcards that gave me the creeps: a black Mass being performed in a dark, dreary cathedral; a specter standing in the rain on a lonely country road; a haunted house with a message that read, *Wish you were here!*; and a child with glowing green eyes.

No words on the backs of them, though the postcards all did look like they came from the same maker, one that apparently didn't exist online, probably because the post-cards were even older than they looked.

I searched online for everything from the pentagram to the rabbit's foot as best I could, but Google kept delivering results that were barely adjacent to what I was hoping to find. Until I encountered a thread that led me down a series of rabbit holes and eventually into something called The Hold. According to the consensus among those who knew the object existed, The Hold was this world's most powerful piece of arcana.

It sure didn't look like much. Big and wooden, with metal hinges that looked like they had been stolen from an old drawbridge. Most of the articles I read agreed that The Hold was a spirit trap and worked by capturing a spirit in its sigil and effecting a sort of spiritual duplication of another being or a bit of energy. Not that I understood what that meant.

The Hold would give its owner the power to manipulate spirit energy, meaning they could wield other arcane objects.

What if I was onto something that Brian didn't know about? I was a beat behind Ariel when it came to the Dybbuk Box, but maybe I would come in first this time. This could be my way back in.

I had to call Brian.

But the phone rang in my hand before I could. Darrow & Grimes.

I couldn't believe he was actually calling to tell me that I didn't get the job. I wasn't sure if that was kind of him or humiliating for me.

"It's Brian. From Darrow & Grimes."

"Of course." Then, before he could get the word *unfortunately* out of his mouth: "I found something you might be interested in. You need to hear me out."

"Okay. What is it, Shondra?"

"The Hold. Have you heard of it?"

"Of course. Everyone in our line of work has heard of The Hold."

Our? "What do you know?"

"The same myths as everyone else, I imagine." A laugh.

"So it's not really true?"

"I didn't say that." It sounded like Brian might have been switching his phone from one ear to the other. "Myths are clues in our line of work."

"I found someone who might know where it is," I told him.

"Of course. I find one every time I go online." Brian laughed again, but he still sounded friendly. "I'm sure we'd already be onto it if it was legitimate. You'll find that true secrets are rarely found in message boards or chat rooms. But we do appreciate that kind of initiative around here."

Might as well get this over with.

"Why are you calling me?" I asked.

"To offer you a job, assuming you still want to work at Darrow & Grimes."

"But you ended the interview early? I thought…"

"Look, we both know that you don't know anything about the world we work in."

"Umm … I wouldn't say *anything*."

"But you have a lot of spunk, and everything else is trainable. So, Shondra, you've got the job."

Chapter Seven

"Shondra!" Jackie greeted me as I entered the shop.

She wasn't alone. Clarence, Brian, and Ariel were all with her.

But Jackie was the only one offering me fudge.

"No, thank you. It's a little early for me."

"Good to see you again," Clarence said. Judging by his expression, that was still a hypothesis. "We've got a lot to talk about."

Brian laughed. "That means that Clarence has a lot to say and that you have a lot of listening to do."

"The first thing to understand is that there is no magic in this world." The team all groaned, obviously having heard the lecture before. "Everything is energy. And what most people call 'haunted' really means that some form of energy is affecting an object. That could be ghost energy, which comes from former people."

"Dead people?" I asked. Clarence cleared his throat. Clearly, dead was not his preferred scientific term. "Are ghosts bad?"

"Only if the person was bad," Clarence continued. "It

could also be pure spirit energy — entities that were never human, or sometimes imprints of trauma. There's also—"

Brian held up a hand. "Shondra can learn as she goes. No need to give her the full list. What we do at Darrow & Grimes is find haunted objects, study them, and then destroy them."

"Why?"

"Because people get hurt." Ariel sounded bored. "Are we showing her around the lab or what?"

Brian nodded, then led the way. "Ariel prefers to skip the formalities."

She also seemed like a bitch, but the kind I wanted to be when I grew up.

"I heard that," Ariel said.

I was afraid to wonder if she could really read my mind.

"That big steel cage that was here last time…" I pointed to the empty table to distract my brain — and Ariel, if she was reading my mind. "Where did it go?"

"It had to be dismantled," Clarence answered with disdain.

"The cage was for a mirror we were trying to get, but it ended up going to Nemicon," Brian said in defeat.

"Fucking Nemicon," Ariel growled.

"Fucking Nemicon," echoed Jackie, though she seemed less than comfortable with cursing.

"Why do we hate Nemicon?" I asked.

"Because they think their white walls and big open spaces are fancy," answered Jackie.

"They are barbarians when it comes to the science," Clarence added, his bottom lip curling.

"Because they *sell* arcane objects to their rich, and generally power-hungry, clients," Brian said vehemently.

"Because they are dicks and weasels," Ariel grumbled.

"You mean Darren?" I asked.

"Fuck that guy," Ariel replied.

"Kip's not a dick or a weasel." Jackie turned to me. "We're so glad you're here, though!"

Oh. Got it. Kip landed a better offer from the fancy pants art gallery with white walls and big open spaces where the glossy snob laughed me off the phone. So, out of a two-person race, I came in second. Yippee-skippee, super happy to be here.

"If we have to show her around, then can we please show her around?" said Ariel. I wondered if she was going to hate me forever.

"I don't hate you," Ariel clarified.

I tried not to think about anything else.

Clarence got going on a long tirade about how gloves had to be worn at all times inside the lab and that all lab personnel were subject to impromptu screenings for psychic abilities. Then he started in on a few tired-sounding reminders not to touch anything on the Clarence Table — said directly to me but clearly meant for everyone in the room — and finally, another warning to never, ever, under any circumstances touch anything in the lab without wearing gloves.

I dutifully pulled on the offered gloves.

"What's this?" I asked, picking up a doll from one of the tables a few minutes later after Brian managed to momentarily redirect Clarence and what seemed like a beat before he was about to get going again. "It's pretty. Do you think—"

I screamed.

The doll was crawling up my arm and up to my neck, opening its mouth and biting me with what felt like razor-sharp teeth that couldn't possibly really be in its toothless plastic mouth.

Not that I could see while I was flailing around, still screaming, trying to make words instead of the broken yodeling rattling out of me as I tried to shake the doll away.

"Get this thing off of me!"

The doll dangled from my neck, giving me a hickey I could feel in the making.

Ariel rushed over, wielding a pair of tongs like a sword, then using them to pry the doll off of my body. It didn't go easy, the doll still sinking its impossibly tooth-filled maw onto me again, grabbing a handful of my hair that it couldn't *really* be gripping in those tiny plastic fingers.

Ariel finally yanked the doll off of me in her now twisted tongs, its plastic still clutched a small hank of my hair. I swear that thing was *smiling* at me. Clarence stood by the open incinerator as she dropped it into the fire.

Clarence closed the door, and I watched the doll beating its little plastic fists against the window as it slowly burned, flames flickering bright pink and then orange before the blackest of blacks turned to ash without sound under the incinerator's name in big block letters: Dale & West.

Clarence opened the Dale & West door again, and Ariel scooped up the ash. She dropped it into a container marked *Coffee* and told me a lie. "It was just a doll."

"More like a puppet," said Clarence.

"For a demon," clarified Jackie.

"Goddammit," Brian grumbled. "We could have used that with Monique."

"Used what with Monique?" I dared to ask.

"No way." Clarence shook his head. "That one was too dangerous."

Ariel rolled her eyes. "Obviously."

"Too dangerous for what?" I tried again.

"We have to save that woman from herself," Clarence said.

"Who is Monique again?"

Jackie took pity on my confusion. "Monique is a nice yet eccentric woman…"

"Crazy," Ariel clarified.

"…who collects dolls."

Clarence grimaced. "Energetically inappropriate dolls."

"She talks to them like they're her children," Ariel said.

Brian was indignant. "She pays excellent money to do so. Not to mention the information she gives us."

"It's sweet when you think about it. Monique—"

"Then don't think about it," Ariel interrupted Jackie.

"—fights to save dolls that other people think are haunted."

"Because they *are* haunted."

"They're lost souls, not bad souls."

Ariel shrugged and, for the first time, actually seemed to care about talking to me. "Most of the time, when souls are lost, they turn into total assholes."

"Got it." I nodded, feeling like I'd gotten a slap on my back from the cool kid.

More explanation from Jackie: "Monique has a deal with Darrow & Grimes. She helps us find some of the objects that collectors are talking about."

"She has ties with some darker collectors of objects who hate us because of our policy of destroying the arcane," Brian added.

"They don't *hate* us," said Jackie.

"In exchange, we give her any dolls that come through that we deem safe," Brian finished.

Clarence glanced at the incinerator.

"How about I give Shondra the tour, and you can all

applaud when I'm done?" Ariel nodded at me, then started the tour before anyone could argue otherwise.

The Dale & West incinerator received an unusually reverent introduction to get things going, and Ariel didn't seem reverent about anything. But Dale & West was apparently a big deal, having once been a historical landmark in the city. An entire building once used to burn trash and animal carcasses had been shrunken into an industrial-strength burn-o-matic that now torched everything from plain old furniture to poltergeist-ridden toys. It released the ghost energy from objects, attaching people to them and then moving on to wherever souls went. I thought I understood how the soul thing worked from Sunday school as a little girl, but now, I wasn't sure about anything.

"That's Gnomey." Ariel pointed to a creepy garden gnome that gave me shivers inside and out of my body. Its blue hat had a gaping hole, and it was missing an ear. But what made it truly terrifying were the huge eyes that seemed to stare right through me. "No matter where we put him at night, mushrooms grow up the wall around him." She pointed to the wall, where there weren't any fungi. "Clarence probably made his omelet already."

"I did not," Clarence retorted.

"Fall asleep in Gnomey's direct line of sight, and you'll wake up with a problem," Ariel warned me.

"I certainly don't want a problem."

It seemed like an appropriate thing to say, even though I wasn't really that worried about falling asleep in front of a garden gnome in a place where I would never be sleeping.

"I mean it," Ariel warned me again. "Clarence will tell you that Gnomey is nothing to worry about, but ask me how many things in that little asshole's line of sight got a hole in it. Or ask him about all of those cracks in the wall."

Clarence dismissed her. "It's not *really* dangerous."

"It *is* creepy," said Jackie.

"We do have to move Gnomey every night," Ariel continued. "But no matter where we put the thing, including inside a box, mushrooms still grow around it, and there are still holes in—"

"His energy signature is low!" Clarence huffed. "No one has anything to worry about!"

"*His?*" I repeated.

Jackie was right about Gnomey being creepy, but he was still better than the Earworm.

"If you listen to music played on this gramophone, it gets stuck in your head." Ariel pointed to the ancient-looking record player.

"So don't do it," Brian warned.

The gramophone was large and black with a horn-shaped speaker, crank handle, and large spinning disc covered in engraved swirling patterns, all housed in a dark wooden cabinet with ornate accents and hinges. It was pretty.

"The music literally can't get out of your head," Ariel explained. "It drives you more and more insane until a large worm eventually pokes its head out of your eye."

"Oh my!" I gasped.

"Exactly. But you can pull the worm out with tweezers, and the song will stop playing in your head."

"Three days." Brian shuddered. "It takes three days."

Ariel nodded at him. "Experience."

The ghost phone gave me chills for a different reason.

"The ghost phone connects to the other side. It can be used to talk to ghosts and spirits," Ariel said.

Of course, I wondered if I could maybe someday talk to my father about it.

Ariel once again seemed to read my mind. "You can't

control who you talk to on the ghost phone. It's Russian roulette whenever you pick up the receiver."

"Can we still say 'Russian roulette?'" Jackie asked.

Ariel touched the receiver, but Clarence put a hand over hers. "Not worth it."

"We don't use the ghost phone," Ariel said, looking disappointed. "But that doesn't mean we don't talk to ghosts."

After a long pause during which something unsettling flashed on her face, she added, "Beatrice says you remind her of Lisa Bonet with a little meat on her bones."

"Thank you?" I replied, looking around.

Beatrice must have kept talking because the entire room was focused on the same spot, just to the left of Ariel, but I couldn't see or hear her. It was unsettling, especially when they all laughed at nothing.

Jackie gave me the skinny. "Beatrice is a ghost. She died in '95 at the age of seventy."

"1895?"

"1995, so she knows all about *Friends*, but not that it went on for ten years or that everyone thinks that Ross kind of sucks now."

I nodded. "He does kind of suck. How did she die?"

"No idea." Jackie shrugged. "She came into D&G on some object years ago, but somehow she survived the Dale & West."

"And everyone else but me can see her?"

Brian said, "You won't see her until you earn her trust. You'll see her in time."

"Maybe." Clarence clearly still wasn't sold on me.

Beatrice seemed to have finished her mysterious monologue. Ariel turned to move on, rubbing at her jaw.

"Snuggles again?" Jackie looked concerned.

"Yeah." Ariel nodded but then walked away, clearly not wanting to talk about it.

"*Snuggles?*" I repeated in a whisper to Jackie, thinking that it might be an abusive boyfriend and that we should probably intervene.

But Jackie was obviously not worried and had already walked away.

"No one is talking about any of the science!" Clarence complained. "Haunted is just shorthand for science without the proper vocabulary around it."

Ariel nodded. "Except, I'd argue that your lab coat says plenty."

"Science has yet to catch up," Clarence argued. "Everything is energy."

"I think *haunted* is a perfectly wonderful word." Jackie seemed to be arguing with herself from across the room. "Underrated, really."

After another few items, Ariel seemed to be boring herself.

"So," she said, abruptly ending the tour while changing the subject. "Are we going to the estate sale or what?"

"Yes!" Brian and Jackie chorused.

"Estate sale?" I asked.

Chapter Eight

ARIEL INSISTED ON DRIVING, SO WE ALL PILED INTO HER car, and she drove us to the address Jackie had given her. The house was old but even creepier than the place should have been, considering its age. Even in full daylight, the exterior was shrouded by dark, twisting trees, its windows boarded up and covered in grime.

A cold wind blew through the overgrown garden in front of the house, and I felt unreasonably uneasy as we approached the door.

Watched, as if someone was waiting for me to misstep. Probably Ariel. Or a ghost.

Paint peeled from the decrepit exterior walls, and the air around the house seemed heavier for some reason, with an eerie sense of foreboding that either no one else felt or appeared to care about.

"This is the place?" I asked, trying to sound brave.

"Yep!" Jackie chirped as Ariel opened the door.

This house felt like a mistake just one step inside. The lights were all on, but the interior was dark and musty, with a layer of dust coating every surface. Had someone seriously been living here until recently?

Something beyond the neglect was making the hair on my neck stand at attention … something about the house itself.

"Welcome to the Mathis estate sale." Ariel waved a hand across the room. "Sorry about the smell."

"You didn't make it!" Jackie assured her.

"It's not that bad," Brian lied.

In truth, it reeked like the stagnant air had been trapped in this shuttered dungeon for years. The faint hint of mold, accompanied by a bitter tang, old and earthy, the aroma of time lost lingered in the air like a specter…

I looked around the cluttered living room. "Where are we supposed to go?"

I had imagined many items with neat labels dangling from them. Instead, random merchandise was haphazardly strewn about the dimly lit space. Tables and shelves were piled high with an eclectic mix of yellowed books, heirloom jewelry, tarnished silverware, and other knickknacks of every shape and size. Old furniture leaned precariously in the corners on top of torn upholstery and threadbare rugs.

I shuddered as a cold, damp breeze flowed through the open windows, carrying a mustiness that hugged everything in the house.

"Wherever you want!" Jackie said.

"What are we looking for?" I asked since no one had replied when I'd wondered out loud in the car.

"The Soul Mirror," Ariel answered.

"Instead of reflecting back the face of whoever is looking into it, the mirror shows someone who's going to die in the next seven days," explained Brian.

"Don't look in it. You don't want to know," Ariel said.

I wasn't sure if I agreed with Ariel about wanting to know, but I definitely didn't want to look into that spooky-sounding mirror.

"It doesn't really work," she added.

"It might work," Brian argued with Ariel.

She shrugged. "Hey, you're the boss."

"Is that it?" I pointed to a gorgeous antique mirror that time had abused, framed in tarnished silver, with intricate carvings along the edges, glass coated in enough dust to obscure the reflection.

"Nope." Ariel shook her head and then walked deeper into the living room.

Brian followed her like a puppy.

"Where are they going?" I asked Jackie.

"Ariel is going to find the guy and submit a bid for the Soul Mirror, and Brian is following her because he appreciates a good rejection."

"Looks like it already happened." I nodded at Brian as he trotted back.

"Does it say 'Soul Mirror' on the auction form?"

Jackie laughed. "Of course not."

"Shit," Brian muttered.

"What?" Jackie asked, but then she followed his gaze and said, "Oh."

I looked too, and my only reason for being offered this job — Kip Grimes — was walking next to a distinguished-looking gentleman. One who was much more impressive in the flesh than the small picture on his company's website.

"I'm shocked to see you out in the field, Rudolph," Brian said to the other man before looking around. "And isn't this place a little lowbrow for you? I thought you only sold art in your—"

"You're always so adorable when you start getting worked up." Rudolph cut him off with a laugh and then nodded at me. "I see you've brought your second pick on her first day."

"First pick, Rudolph!" Brian snapped. "The only reason you got that guy is because I didn't want him! No offense, Kip."

"None taken." Kip gave Brian a shrug.

They started going back and forth, faster and louder. Jackie seemed to appreciate the exchange as if this was a new episode of an old favorite show.

Kip sidled up to me as if the two of us had anything in common beyond him leaving me with his leftovers. "So, how do you like the job so far?"

"It's my first day."

"Right." Kip nodded, still smiling. "That's why I asked how you—"

"It's great. I like it a lot. Love it so much. Super glad to be working for Darrow & Grimes." I was letting him see my irritation a lot more than I wanted to, but I couldn't stand that he was mocking me, so I added, "Mr. Grimes."

He looked taken aback, but he quickly recovered, smiling as he said, "Well, if you ever want to talk about it or anything, I'm always here."

"What *are* you here to do, Kip?"

"I'm here to help."

"And what is it that you think I need your help with?"

"Nothing. Never mind." Kip turned away from me, his smile and easy manner both gone as if he never really even meant them in the first place. "Have a nice time at the auction."

Jackie cleared her throat as a newcomer approached the group.

"Rudolph!" exclaimed the man with a smile, ignoring everyone else.

"Grayson." Rudolph shook his hand and gestured to Kip. "This is Kip *Grimes*, the newest associate at Nemicon."

"Oh?" Grayson raised his eyebrows, surely at the mention of Kip's impressive last name. "Are you here for the Soul Mirror?"

Rudolph shook his head. "No need to deal with trifles like that."

Brian shifted on his feet.

"Have you heard about the Mansions of Madness game?" Grayson asked.

"It's here?" Kip exclaimed.

Rudolph shot Kip a look.

"No." Grayson laughed like the notion was ridiculous. "Of course not. But the game has been tracked to a storage unit, and—"

"Perhaps we should talk somewhere more private," Rudolph interrupted him.

"What?" Grayson shrugged. "Why? We can get it if—"

Rudolph took him by the arm and wasn't especially gentle by the look of it, then escorted him away while he was still loudly going on about some mysterious sounding board game that had apparently been tracked to a storage unit.

"What is Mansions of—"

"It's a board game." Jackie had already whipped out her phone and had a wiki open.

But Brian looked over her shoulder. "I've never heard of it. What does Rudolph want with some board game."

"It looks like Warhammer or HeroQuest. Do you know those games?" I interjected, following links on my own phone. Jackie and Brian looked impressed.

"I haven't played this one, but they all follow the same general rules. There are heroes and villains," I explained. "They come as small figures users can paint. Though, in this case, there's also an app." I didn't add that I'd gone through a phase of painting Warhammer figures or that I still had boxes of them in my hall closet.

Jackie scrolled and started to read. "Horrific monsters and spectral presences lurk in manors, crypts, schools, monasteries, and derelict buildings near Arkham, Mass-achusetts. Players can spin dark conspiracies or wait for hapless victims to devour or drive insane."

"Fun," I said.

Jackie continued. "It's up to a handful of brave investi-gators to explore these cursed places and uncover the truth about the living nightmares within."

Brian took out his own phone, following another tangent as Jackie gave us the rundown.

"Each game takes place within a story with a unique map and combination of plot threads that affect the monsters in that specific game. One player takes on the role of the keeper, controlling the monsters and other mali-cious powers in the story. Other players take on the roles of investigators, searching for answers while struggling to survive with their minds intact."

"Dude, I'd so buy this." I doubted either of them would, though.

"Ah, there is definitely a haunted copy. The rumor is the first owner could never get anyone to play with him, so now his spirit drives wedges between the owner and others," Brian interjected, scrolling through a Reddit-like board, but one I'd never seen before.

Rudolph and Grayson were supposedly out of earshot, but I was sure that I heard Grayson shout, "Hold—"

Kip was still lingering at the side of the room. No doubt to eavesdrop, or more likely, rubbing his new role at Nemicon in mine and Brian's faces.

Ariel came storming into the living room before I could

ask anything else about the arcane forum Brian was totally going to have to hook me up with. I noticed her slipping something into her bag that looked like a cellphone, except it had a pair of strange antennas sticking out of its sides.

"We didn't get the mirror," she complained.

"Why?" Brian asked.

"Because our number was too low! Exactly like I said it would be."

Brian looked toward the door Rudolph had disappeared through. "He always was a liar."

Kip smirked, and I wondered if I could trip him without being obvious.

Ariel gave Kip a dirty look. "Let's go."

Once outside the house, Ariel leaned closer to Brian and whispered just loud enough for me to hear while walking behind them. "*By the way, this entire place is haunted. Energy signatures — totally off the charts.*"

"Can a whole house really be haunted?"

Ariel turned back to me. "A house is an object, too."

"What kind of energy?" I asked.

"Poltergeist," she said.

Chapter Nine

"ARE WE LEAVING ANY TIME SOON?" JACKIE ASKED. "SOME of us have babies to get home to. He doesn't like it when his mamá is late, and Lucy has to get home to her kids."

For once, it wasn't Ariel rushing us along because even though we were all in the car with her behind the wheel, she and Brian were engaged in a vibrant exchange about their next best move.

"Apparently, the auction is happening soon," Brian said, telling us all what he'd learned while sitting shotgun and speaking directly to Ariel. "It could be bullshit or a distraction, but this game might also be there."

"Grayson is a discriminating collector — only wants the rarest, the most expensive, and highly volatile arcane objects. If he's interested, then I'm sure this Mansions game is the real deal."

"And dangerous!" added Jackie.

"We should talk with Monique."

Brian shook his head. "We can't. We don't have anything to give her. She'll want—"

"We can owe her," Ariel cut him off. "Monique always

knows something about something. Rudolph sure as hell isn't going to tell us, and we don't have the resources to track him to the auction."

"I could follow him … if you wanted me to," I said. Obviously, no one wanted me to, but they didn't even have the decency to respond.

"He'll probably just send a lackey on his behalf," Brian said.

"So, are we going to Monique's or what?" Ariel didn't wait for an answer. They just started the car and pulled away from the poltergeist-riddled estate.

"Wait, what are we going to do about the haunted house?" I asked.

"What would you like to do about it?" Ariel snapped.

"Well, uh…".

"Exactly." Ariel shoved the transmission into reverse and spun some gravel.

"Don't worry. We'll deal with it later," assured Jackie. "I guess I need to call Lucy *again* and tell her I'll be late. Mi Deo! Working at the shop was supposed to mean I'd be home more often, yet here I am again chasing ghosts. The overtime is killing me. Brian, we need to talk about a raise here! Baby needs a new pair of shoes — literally."

Brian shrugged as we drove too fast down the highway.

Monique's home was a small suburban bungalow situated dead center on a perfectly normal street that looked about as haunted as the average Bed Bath & Beyond. Two stories with white siding and a gently sloping roof. Tidy landscaping. Quaint, with bright shutters that looked freshly painted. The street was well-maintained, with trimmed grass and swept curbs. The air was clean and fresh, with a hint of lavender and basil rolling in from a nearby garden. Freshly baked bread was alive in the air, mingling with the aroma of roasting meat from a backyard grill. But, of course, things got weird inside.

"Oh my gawd!" Monique exclaimed as she opened the door. "I can't believe you're here!"

Brian had called on the way. But Monique seemed like the kind of woman who lived her life as a surprise. She had a round face, with bright, sparkling eyes and a wide smile. Her hair was a vibrant red, cut short in an exuberant pixie cut. She was dressed in every shade of pink. This was true for both Monique's attire and her decor.

The walls were painted in shades of blush, and the furniture was upholstered in frilly pink fabric. The windows were adorned with mauve curtains, and the floors were covered in plush sand-colored carpeting. Knickknacks and accessories came in many shades of pastel. Even the bookcase was pink, filled with mysteries. I scanned the titles but didn't recognize a single one. The books were organized by the color of the spine. I bet she'd have a huge following on BookTok.

"I'm so excited to meet you!" Monique squealed.

"Me?" I touched my chest because this didn't make sense.

"Of course, you!" Monique threw her arms around me, then pulled me over toward the peonies once she finished her embrace. "You're the newest member of the Darrow & Grimes team, from what I hear, and you guys make my good life even better! Cookies?"

Monique changed subjects like a person realizing that their freeway exit was just three hundred feet away. Her cookies must be delicious, especially the way everyone turned into bobbleheads and looked like they were about to salivate.

My first bite told me that the enthusiasm was the Darrow & Grimes gang kissing up to her, and the second bite confirmed it. Not a bad cookie, but also perfectly marginal in every way. Bland yet sweet, with a crumbly texture that fell apart in my mouth a few chews too early. So dry. Milk — where was the milk?

"This is amazing!" Brian exclaimed with a full mouth.

"Mmmm…" Jackie made a noise, probably so she wouldn't have to lie.

Ariel earned my admiration (again) by saying nothing and showing no artificial pleasure on her face as she dutifully chewed.

"This is great." I lied like a coward.

Ariel slowly shook her head at me.

I was halfway through my cookie when Monique shrieked with delight. "Hey, Shondra!" And then, with undiluted glee, when I looked over: "Do you want to see my doll collection?"

Monique could have made an absolute fortune showing her doll collection by charging a curiosity-based admission price, then followed it up with an even more expensive ticket to escape after a glimpse of what looked like hundreds of dolls staring back with little marble eyes.

Then I remembered they were haunted. I wanted to scream my lungs raw.

"They're so … pretty!" I said.

"Beautiful," exclaimed Brian with manufactured awe.

Ariel and Jackie held their tongues.

A bedroom full of scary-looking dolls, most of them vintage, posed all over the room and on the furniture.

The rest of Monique's house was warmly lit, but this dim room filled with dolls of every shape and size didn't have any windows. The eerie-looking dolls were positioned in a wide array of macabre poses, staring back at us with glittering glass eyes. The vintage dolls should have been dusty and worn from age, but their delicate features weren't pitted or faded. They looked brand new, or maybe Monique had just given them all a bath.

"My babies live here in the middle of the house because they keep getting out otherwise."

"Getting out?" I repeated.

"Of course!" She laughed. "They *love* to escape. They think it's funny. See how they rearranged themselves?"

Monique pointed at her dolls, even though I had no idea what they looked like the last time.

Monique laughed again. "You should have seen them last night."

I was glad that I hadn't.

"Today, my babies will be doing the scene where Father Karras first meets Regan before the exorcism."

Only then did I realize that many of the dolls' macabre poses had something in common. They were lined up as if watching a play, hands raised in what I realized was frozen applause and not the extended claws I'd taken them for.

This was the first thing I felt truly frightened of since my tenure at Darrow & Grimes ... all six hours of it.

My heart was a loping cheetah while looking at all those glassy marble eyes.

I had to turn away.

"They really get you, don't they?" Monique sounded wistful as she touched her heart. "Have you heard anything about Lulu?"

Another abrupt change in topic.

Though Brian seemed to have been expecting it. "Lulu is too—"

"I've heard she might be coming to the area. Have you heard anything, Brian?" Monique still sounded sweet, but there was also a stinger in the bee now.

Brian smiled to soften the blow. "Lulu is too dangerous, Monique. We can't give it to you."

"*Her*," Monique stressed.

"Her, of course." Brian smiled. "Either way, Lulu's last owner clawed her own eyes out."

"You can't blame that on Lulu."

Brian looked uncomfortable.

"Well…" It was the best Jackie could do.

"So. Mansions of Madness," Ariel said. "Have you heard anything?"

Monique shrugged. "I'm sure I've heard something."

"Like…" Ariel prompted.

Brian perked his ears now that Ariel had done his work for him.

"I'm not even really sure what I heard. It barely piqued my interest." She shrugged again. "Because … no dolls."

"Any details would be great," said Brian.

"It's at a storage auction." Monique sighed, a long exhale to let them know she was doing them all a favor. "I'll go get the details. You can stay here with the babies. See if anyone wants to play Iago from *Othello*. It doesn't matter who says yes. They're all so good at it!"

Then Monique was gone.

And it felt like the Darrow & Grimes group could finally exhale.

"She's so—"

"NO." Ariel cut Jackie off, looking around the room at all the dolls. "Not in front of *them*."

So we stewed in the weirdest silence of my life. It lasted a couple of minutes that felt like fifteen, with all further discussion orbiting safe topics, like me explaining several intersecting storylines of *Warehouse 13*, which the gang had surprisingly little interest in given how closely it resembled their actual jobs.

Monique returned, grinning with victory. "You guys are going to love this! The game was found in some storage unit, but before it got to the Tweedle-Dee and Tweedle-Dum that owned it last, the game belonged to Jared Leto." Then she gave us the reason for her buzzing excitement: "Jordan Freaking Catalano himself! So gorgeous."

Also, creepy AF in *Morbius* and *Requiem for a Dream*, but she probably didn't want to hear that right now.

"He's an incredible actor," Brian agreed.

Ariel nodded. "Hot."

"Jared Leto loves haunted things," said Jackie.

Monique redirected them. "Anyway, I think the game is just regular haunted, not a spirit or anything."

"What does that mean?" I asked.

"She's so cute!" Monique told the room. "It does make the user stronger — but everyone that owns it dies. Apparently, in ten days."

"But Jared Leto isn't dead ... is he?"

Monique didn't answer me.

"Why would anyone want to own something like that?" I tried.

Monique blinked twice to let me know that I'd asked an idiotic question. Her enthusiasm for me was definitely dwindling. I had to say something to keep her attention.

I looked around at the dolls, and though I managed not to shudder, I asked a question I couldn't help asking. "Have any of these dolls ever attacked you?"

"Heavens, no." Monique touched her chest again. "They would *never*."

I should have stopped there when I saw the way that the D&G gang was looking at me. It was as if something compelled me to dig my grave in short measure. "One attacked me this morning. It crawled up my arm and bit me right on the throat. Ariel had to throw it in the Dale & West incinerator."

"She *what*?"

"Well…" I stuttered. "It was—"

"You murdered a *doll?*" She jabbed her finger toward the hallway. "Get. Out."

"But I'm—"

"GET OUT!" Monique roared over me.

Ariel fumed on our way outside. Monique slammed the door, and I expected Ariel to start yelling at me. Instead, she turned her rage on Brian.

"What the hell is wrong with you? Bringing an amateur to our best source?" She shook her head in disgust and stomped off toward her car.

"I'm so sorry," I apologized to Brian.

"It's okay. You didn't know better. It wasn't your fault." Brian sounded less than convincing.

Same for Jackie. "It'll be fine, dear."

But my vow was the most ridiculous, considering.

"I promise I'll make it up to you guys."

Chapter Ten

I couldn't wait to get back to Darrow & Grimes the next morning.

Most people probably mess up on their first day of a new job. Right? Especially one that dealt with haunted objects. There was no playbook for this. And my actions yesterday might have been like a rite of passage. Although, it felt more like that time the priest from the Indiana Jones movie pulled the beating heart out of the guy's chest.

Ariel didn't speak to me for the rest of the day, but that probably didn't have anything to do with what happened at Monique's. Jackie didn't offer me any more fudge. Brian was still acting quietly injured by the time I went home, but he had to be over it by now. That was all in the past, and I was ready for a brand-new day as I entered D&G for my second day of work.

Jackie wasn't working the counter or seemingly anywhere in the front. I looked around and found her almost immediately, pacing a back aisle while gripping the phone, looking frustrated as she ended the call and caught my eyes.

"Oh. Hey." Even a plate full of fudge wouldn't have made Jackie seem happy to see me.

"You seem upset." I started listing the reasons I was to blame in my mind, though there wasn't really any reason to count when it was probably almost for sure because of what I did at Monique's.

"Some lady wanted to know if we had a suit of armor. I thought we had chain mail back here, but when I came to look, it wasn't where I thought it would be."

"Is it enchanted chain mail?"

"No." Jackie shook her head, clearly thinking I had asked a dumb question. "Just regular chain mail. I told her we might have a morning star from a lot coming in next week, but that only seemed to irritate her. She yelled at me and implied I was too stupid to know the difference between armor and weapons."

"People are very particular."

"Ha." Jackie snorted. "That might have been the easiest question this week."

"What other kinds of things do people ask for?"

"Everything. Literally."

"They can't *literally* ask for *everything*. So, what kind of—"

"An entire wardrobe made from old kitchen curtains; a Rubik's Cube that's already been solved; a box of old VHS tapes with literally *anything* on them; a used jigsaw puzzle that has all the pieces, a used coffin—"

"A *used* coffin?"

"—a rusty old pitchfork; a jar of mayonnaise that's been opened but never used—"

"*What?*"

"—a vial of blood belonging to Abraham Lincoln—"

"Now you're messing with me."

"—A taxidermized beaver; a fake can of peanuts with

a spring-loaded snake; Mexican jumping beans; a lava lamp; and a bear trap."

"The lava lamp seems normal."

"We always have lava lamps," Jackie declared. "We average one per storage unit haul."

"So the customers are annoying you?"

"No. I like our customers. Whenever someone isn't nice to me, I give them the benefit of the doubt and assume they're being haunted. I've seen how irritable that can make a person."

"But you seemed upset when you were getting off the phone."

"Oh. That." Jackie sighed. "I'm trying to find a new doll to appease Monique. She's still stomping her foot about what happened yesterday. No offense."

"None taken." I smiled, feeling like I was in trouble. "Anything I can do to help?"

I was obviously bothering her, but Jackie was way too nice to make it obvious. "I've got this, dear. Why don't you see if Clarence would like your help with anything? And if not, then you can man the front."

I laughed. "Don't you mean woman?"

Jackie didn't join me, walking off to hunt for a potentially haunted doll. At least I had permission to see Clarence. He would help me feel better.

"Do you think it's my job to make you feel better about shitting the bed at Monique's place yesterday?" Clarence said two minutes later. "Don't come to me expecting me to shovel some wise old man bullshit into a pile for you. I'm not your grandfather, and as much as I may sound and look like Morgan Freeman, I'm not him either."

Did everyone here read minds?

I was really screwing up, and all I wanted to do was make a good impression. Dad would have known what to say to me, but he was gone. I could no longer just pick up the phone and call him when I was having a bad day.

The ghost phone sat on the table, mocking me. Begging me to pick up the receiver.

"Don't even think about it," Clarence warned me without turning around to catch me looking.

"How did you know?" I asked him.

"Beatrice." He said her name almost wistfully. He seemed at ease having a ghost roaming around untethered.

Not me. I was creeped out, knowing there was a spirit there watching me, an entity I couldn't see or hear. It made me nervous.

"What will happen if I use the phone?"

Clarence turned to look at me, shaking his head. "You don't want to know."

I did want to know, and that was exactly why I'd asked, but I couldn't press the question because Ariel entered the lab with a black eye.

"Snuggles?" Clarence said.

"What do you think?" Ariel sighed and nodded at me. "Are you ready?"

"For what?"

"We're going to a storage war."

"Sounds fun!"

"It's not fun," Ariel said. "It's work."

"Great. When?"

"Now. I think it's a bad idea, considering yesterday, but Brian insists. I'll meet you at the car."

"I don't think she likes me," I said to Clarence after Ariel left.

"Then maybe you should be on your way to the car instead of standing here complaining," Clarence replied.

The storage auction was a thirty-minute drive, tense

because Ariel and Brian both still seemed pissed at me, and I wasn't sure why I was coming along for the ride.

Not that I was going to ask.

I hadn't been around them long, but I could feel tension — sexual tension between Brian and Ariel. Well, mostly Brian. He kept flirting with her but pretending like he wasn't. Ariel drove fast, as if eager to end the trip, cranking the radio to muffle Brian's voice when he started telling a story about some strange entity that disrupted electronics so they didn't work anymore.

"It's called an EMP," Ariel said as she turned the radio up louder. "Hello, It's Me" began blaring from the speakers.

"You like Todd Rundgren?" I asked from the back seat.

"No."

I was worried about Ariel's black eye and wanted to ask her about it, but we weren't friends. Yet. My concern would surely be met with rolled eyes or scorn. Almost surely both.

I tried to imagine Snuggles with his ironic gangster name. A cold-hearted criminal. Ruthless, with fierce and piercing eyes over a sneering grin, striking Ariel for daring to contradict him. Probably had a face tattoo.

"Knock that shit off," Ariel said out of nowhere. "I'm fine."

It was another three Todd Rundgren songs before she pulled into the parking lot and announced their arrival.

"It's a storage unit," I announced.

Ariel turned to Brian. "I can totally see why you hired her."

"Have you ever seen *Storage Wars*?" Brian asked me.

"Only a couple of times." Not even once.

"She's never seen it," Ariel said.

"Yes, I have." Did she know I was lying?

Ariel shook her head, obviously disappointed in me.

Even if I had never seen the show, I got the gist from the deluge of ads on TV for it: a storage unit was packed to a suffocating level of claustrophobia with someone's old shit. Contestants bid on crap, trying to claim the most valuable items, scrambling over piles of old clothes and furniture, while bidding wars erupted over rare antiques and collectibles.

Ariel left to register us.

There weren't as many people as I would have expected at a storage auction, although I had nothing to compare it to. People huddled in small groups of two and three, whispering, making notes in little notebooks, and squinting their eyes at one another. The tension was thick, but there was something else under all that. It was a similar feeling to the atmosphere at Colin's party just before all hell broke loose.

The air was electric, like accidentally touching a bare wire. It hummed and thrummed under the service. I felt the same uneasy energy at the house with the soul mirror, except there, it was all around — in the walls, doors, ceiling. The same was true of Monique's doll room and Clarence's lab of arcane horrors.

The uneasiness felt more focused, like I had felt around the Dybbuk Box, but darker. I didn't pay much attention to it before, dismissing it as new job jitters. The darkness crept into my head, and a pall fell over my mind. As we walked like a flock of turkeys on the Wednesday before Thanksgiving, the feeling became stronger, and my skin itched. There was something really bad here. Something evil — and it was waiting for me.

"Stay on the lookout," Brian said, pulling me out of my moment of unnatural despair.

"For what?"

"You'll know."

I didn't, but I wondered if Brian might have meant the super weird guy who came over and said hello to me. He wasn't rude or anything. In fact, the guy was overly polite. The dorky little tip of his hat was made dorkier by an embarrassing lack of a hat.

"Milady." So yes, the guy could get even dorkier. He smiled, looking almost normal. "Hey."

I smiled. "Hey."

It seemed like the right thing to do. The guy wore a black Magic The Gathering tee at least one size too small, as his belly button peeked out the bottom like a winking eye. His pale skin was an indicator of too many hours in a basement game room. His baby face hid his true age, which I guessed to be his thirties.

Please don't be a serial killer. Please don't be a serial killer.

After a long minute of painful silence that left me wondering where Brian had run off to and when he might be back, the dorky guy finally broke it.

"What's your favorite kind of ice cream?" the dork asked.

"Moose Tracks." But then I thought that might have said too much about me and amended my answer. "Vanilla."

"I like beet ice cream." He looked hopeful, then crestfallen. "It tastes a lot better than it sounds."

"Does your last name happen to be Schrute, by any chance?"

"No." He shook his head with a laugh. I'm pretty sure he didn't get the reference.

Brian finally came scurrying over to rescue me.

"Nemicon is here," he said, in almost a whisper, gesturing over to Kip and Darren since they were apparently besties now. They were both standing with arms crossed, definitely giving off some Winchester brother vibes. Too bad they were assholes.

"I don't think they can hear you," I told Brian.

"What's Nemicon?" asked the dork.

Brian turned to him, then me. "Who's he?"

"Justin." He held out his hand, but no one shook it.

"I should go say something." Brian looked over at the Nemicon reps. "Do you think I should say something?"

I had no idea, but him saying anything to anyone other than me would leave me alone with Justin Schrute, so—

"I'll be right back," Brian said.

"Who is that?" Justin asked.

Maybe being trapped in the conversation would be better than that terrible silence. "My boss."

"Does he suck? Is that why you're sad?"

Who said I was sad? "It's only my second day at work, but things haven't been going too well so far. I'm trying not to get fired, but that joker over there is going to make it hard for me."

I nodded at Kip.

Justin grinned at me. "He looks like a joker."

I smiled back, for real, this time.

"Hang in there," Justin said, then mercifully left.

We arrived at the source of energy, and it crawled over every nerve in my body now like I was directly plugged into a wall socket.

The auctioneer, a man in a dirty t-shirt and overalls, began describing the next lot on the tour of units. The auction would start in five minutes.

Of course, Kip was bidding on the same lot as we were, even though Nemicon supposedly "only sold art." And, of course, he came over to smirk at me as the auction got going.

"Really?" I snapped at him. "There's no other place you can stand?"

"Whoa!" He raised his hands, palm out, about thirty-seven times more dramatic than he needed to be. "What the hell is your problem?"

"You mean besides your giant teeth?"

That didn't even really make sense because his smile was beautiful.

"Now you're insulting my appearance?"

"Just leave me alone, Kip."

"I'd like to know what I did to—"

"SHUSH!" snapped someone from the crowd.

We were getting louder, but that was only because the auction was going on.

"You shush!" I volleyed back.

"Maybe you should drink less coffee," Kip said.

Then we were shouting at each other.

Brian and Darren both turned to see what was happening, but Darren tripped on his shoelace and slammed into Brian. Brian thought that Darren had pushed him on purpose and took a swing while recovering his balance.

Darren ducked but punched Brian in the nose as a reflex.

Brian doubled over, clutching his nose. It was happening again, just as it did at Collin's party. Did all curses end with getting punched in the nose?

"Sorry, man. I—"

"Sold! To the guy in the *All Your Base Are Belong to Us* t-shirt!"

"Dammit!" Kip cut him off. "We just lost the game to that guy."

He nodded at Justin.

And, of course, Beet Ice Cream Boy was grinning from ear to ear.

Chapter Eleven

I WAS THE WORST.

I had beaten the shit out of a proverbial piñata and spilled the candy everywhere. Because of me, Darrow & Grimes would get none of it, and Justin, the Imperial Weirdo, would be getting it all.

If I had been mature enough to ignore all the many ways that Kip had been annoying me, I wouldn't have ruined D&G's chances at winning the bid. Now, I needed to prove that I deserved my job by making things right. Besides, the curse had made me do it — it wasn't really my fault, right? I needed to figure out how these arcane objects worked so I didn't find myself constantly in the center of fisticuffs.

I slipped away from my new coworkers (and *hopefully* someday friends) to greet Justin at his recently opened unit.

During the auction, I'd been too far back to get a good look at the contents of the unit. Now, I blinked in wide-eyed surprise at the staggering display of games inside. Old shelves packed with board games. The unit was bursting with long rectangular boxes in every possible color. All of them were dusty except for the one on top.

I tried not to gasp but did a little anyway.

There it was, Mansions of Madness, the supposedly haunted game that my new friends (or probably just coworkers) lost out on because of me.

Justin stopped riffling through the stacks of games and smiled. "See anything you like?"

I pointed at the Mansions of Madness box. "That's the one!"

He grinned even wider and nodded at the game. "Have you ever played it?"

"Of course." No, I absolutely had not.

"Cool."

He seemed so happy, and I really wanted the game, so I kept going. "Do you like board games?"

"Of course." Justin laughed, looking around at all his many stacks.

"What do you like most about them?" I tried to make my voice sound sexy but not too sexy, so the effort was more like a stutter.

"I love that games teach strategic thinking. And to lose with grace. The pieces feel nice in my hands. I like the sound that dice make when they hit the board or rattle around in a cup."

Now, he was just listing things.

"Do you want to play a game with me?" I leaned in and whispered, again exercising my feminine wiles. "Winner's choice."

Justin backed up from me, seemingly uncomfortable.

I batted my eyelashes before glancing at Mansions of Madness. "I've always loved that game."

But now his expression didn't seem so nice. Justin's

entire body stiffened, and it seemed like he was looking through instead of at me.

He reached out and grabbed the game. It looked like a jolt of something shuddered through his body, and his limbs flailing and jerked by unseen forces for a horrifying second.

And then he was back to normal. Ish.

"How do you like the app?" Justin asked.

"I love it!" I'd never even seen it, so I really hoped the app didn't suck.

"What do you love about it?"

"Everything."

"Like…" Justin narrowed his eyes at me.

"The graphics are cool."

"They're alright. When did you start playing the game?"

"You mean the app or the real thing?" I looked at the board again, wondering if maybe I should just offer him a bunch of money. Invest in my future with D&G instead of whatever this was.

Justin stared at me, not answering.

"I played the app first, and I liked it so much that I bought the game."

"Edition one or two?"

I looked at the first edition in his hands. "First, just like that one. That's why I want it so much."

"The app didn't come out until 2016 with the second edition, so nice try."

"But I was playing—"

"I said *nice try*." Then he turned his back on me.

"My game was the second edition, I just—"

"I asked you to stop it."

You actually said *nice try*. "Please. Can—"

"You know the sad part?" Justin waved his hand, not

just at Mansions of Madness but at the entire storage unit full of games. "This was for you. A grand gesture. I bought the entire lot so that you could impress your boss."

"That's so nice! You—"

"But you are clearly a manipulative bitch, so—"

"Hey!"

His demeanor had definitely changed from dorky beet ice cream guy only a few moments earlier. Could a curse act that quickly? Clarence had made me swear to always wear gloves before touching any arcane object. Justin had the game tucked snuggly under his left arm and gripping it tightly with his other hand.

"I have decided to keep MoM, and all the rest of it, for myself."

Goddammit. "I'm sorry. Really. I didn't mean to—"

Wait, did he just say he's keeping his mom?

"You did so mean it!" He snapped at me. "You're only sorry because I called you out on your stupid eyelash batting. I know what you were trying to do, and you didn't have to do it — if you'd just asked me for the game, I would have gladly given it to you. Now MoM will be with me forever."

"You don't live in a hotel with your mom, do you?"

"Huh?"

"Never mind. Can I have the—"

"No!" Justin huffed like a toddler stomping his feet.

I smiled. "I'm sure we can work something out."

"Work something out?" Justin repeated with a scoff, laughing at me (almost maniacally) before finishing his nonsensical thought. "You can't win in a game of wits against DragonSkinner69."

Whoa. "I'm sure you're right."

I really wanted that game.

"I'll always see right through you," he said.

I nodded. "Like a poltergeist."

"You mean ghosts. Poltergeists are the restless spirits of people who have died young or in violent circumstances."

You can still see through them, dork. But I smiled. "Right again."

"Don't patronize me!" Justin was getting huffy again. Sweat beaded on his brow, and he was licking his lips. A lot.

I didn't know what to say, but I also didn't need to figure it out. Ariel was suddenly there, yanking me away from the unit. I considered yelling out a final offer, but Justin's back was already turned, and this situation was embarrassing enough already.

"That was embarrassing," Ariel confirmed on our way to the car.

And she was only talking about what had just happened between Justin and me, though I wasn't sure how much she heard or saw. My embarrassment was like a mogwai eating after midnight compared to the relative shame I was feeling when Kip saw me getting marched out to the parking lot.

He actually laughed at me, like I was a punchline for him to punch again later.

Kip climbed into the passenger side of Darren's car, a sleek, silver Audi with a chrome grille and tinted windows. Flashy enough for me to question the size of Darren's manhood in any color, but it was cherry red, so I figured Darren was probably hung like a pimple. Kip, too, for getting into it. Too bad for them.

Oh my God, I was so mad. And Ariel looked even more pissed than I felt.

"You win some, you lose some," Brian said like a loser, even though I was the one who had lost him this round. "Let's get out of here."

"Back to the shop?" I asked.

"I think we're done for the day," Brian said. "We can try again tomorrow."

We meaning *me*.

I swallowed my sigh and nodded with a smile, wondering what was worse, being sent home early or knowing that tonight was dinner with Rashida and Malik. To celebrate Rashida. Like always.

Chapter Twelve

"CONGRATULATIONS!" MOM EXCLAIMED TO RASHIDA FOR the ninety-seventh time since dinner started. "I'm so proud of you."

"Thanks, Mom!" Rashida replied, and I knew what was coming.

Mom dropped her fork into some remnants of mashed potatoes and turned her attention to me. "Rashida has only been working at Alliance for five years, and she's already the human resources coordinator, responsible for—"

"Onboarding new employees and ensuring that all company policies are followed," I finished. "I was here. Not just for the reading of the job description for her new job—"

"Promotion," Rashida chirped.

"—but for this celebration dinner, all of it. Nobody asked me about my new job."

"You keep telling me that you don't want to talk about your new job," Mom replied.

"That's because you'll insult me."

She scrunched her nose at me. "You don't know that."

"Tell us about your new job," said Malik.

"We buy things from places..." I paused, trying to figure out a better way to end my third stab at an explanation.

"From what Mom said, it sounds like you work at Goodwill," offered Rashida. "You know, a *thrift store?*"

I wasn't sure if she lowered her voice because Goodwill was a curse word or if my sister was trying not to insult what she saw as my ignorance.

But the misunderstanding wasn't entirely their fault. It was difficult to describe how cool the work at Darrow & Grimes actually was without talking about the ghost phone, the Dybbuk Box, or Monique.

"It's not a thrift store. It's a..." I searched hard for the word, and everyone started trying to help me.

Mom: "A swap meet?"

Malik: "A flea market?"

Rashida: "That twice-worn shop on Magnolia?"

Mom shook her head. "That place is called Rummage Around."

"We sell haunted objects!" I blurted. "I mean, we sell a bunch of stuff, not haunted stuff, but we *look* for haunted objects, and then we get rid of them. So they don't hurt people."

"Goodwill can't do that!" Malik declared.

"Darrow & Grimes has a shop, so that is one side of the place," I explained, whether they thought I was crazy or not. "But we also hunt for haunted objects."

"Like with guns?" asked Malik.

"Our toaster used to turn on in the middle of the night." Rashida nodded like a sage. "It was totally haunted."

"It's not like it was making toast," argued Malik.

Mom shook her head. "Objects can't be haunted."

Things were spiraling quickly. I expected nothing less, but once, just once, I'd love for my family to understand and support me. See me. I didn't, nor would I ever, fit nicely into the mold my mother expected me to fit into. Instead, I was the perpetual joke of the family. This job was important to me, and dammit, they needed to try to understand what the shop was and why this was such an exciting opportunity for me.

"Of course, objects can be haunted. Haven't you ever heard of a haunted house?" I asked, then answered my own question into the silence. "Amityville, the Winchester Mystery House, the Myrtles Plantation?"

They all looked at me with blank stares.

"The Queen Mary," I added another when the silence continued, then another when it came to me. "The White House!"

"It's fine that you work at a thrift store." Mom gave me a smile that made me burn with fury. I'd prefer a frown to pandering.

"What if I really was working at Goodwill?"

"I said that would be fine." Mom gave me another condescending smile.

"But it's *how* you said it," I argued.

Mom sighed. "Do you get an employee discount on stuff, or is everything so cheap that you don't need a discount?"

"I just told you guys that I work for a company that hunts haunted objects, and your only questions are about discounts?"

"What do you want me to say?" Mom shrugged dramatically. "You give me news like that, and I'm not supposed to start worrying about you?"

Why could my family never just believe in me?

"You don't have anything to worry about." The words came out strong, but it still felt like pouting.

Malik shifted uncomfortably in his seat.

Even Rashida was smart enough to not say anything stupid.

Mom said what everyone was thinking. "You're starting to sound a little too much like your Uncle Kevin."

Dead silence after that.

Until I said, "I don't see what's so wrong with that."

I seriously didn't.

But everyone else did, so the few remaining minutes of our supposed celebration meal passed in relative silence, with only the clinking of flatware against the plates.

I went to my room after dinner with a terrible aching. Marching up the stairs was like walking in the aftermath of a furious storm after the deluge of water had turned dark and slimy.

That's what it was like missing Dad — reaching out for someone I could never touch again, feeling a cold blade slithering between my ribs whenever I tried.

I needed a distraction, so I studied up on the Mansions of Madness game to dull the aching, returning to the message board and combing through countless threads in search of answers, skimming over several other mentions of The Hold because proving myself by getting the board game back felt so much more immediate.

I scrolled through page after page, losing myself to the search by delving deeper and deeper down the rabbit hole. I was clueless about what to believe because bullshit and fact were the bread and butter of the forums. I had to follow my gut, stitching threads until there was finally enough of a tapestry to stare at.

I followed the path to a chatroom, where three friends had been batting rumors back and forth all night. By the time I was done reading, I knew everything about Mansions of Madness, from the game's general history to the haunting of one Alexander Gorman, a prior owner of the Mansions of Madness that had most recently ended up in Justin's possession.

The game was set in the 1920s, when the fictional city of Arkham, Massachusetts, was plagued by strange occurrences, horrific monsters, and mysterious cults. Players assumed the role of investigators who must solve mysteries and stop evil forces from taking over the city.

Mansions is loosely based on the works of horror writer H. P. Lovecraft and includes elements of his stories *The Call of Cthulhu* and *The Dunwich Horror*. The game could be played with or without a mobile app (but only after the second edition), and when fully explained, it sounded like something I would totally play. If I had a friend to play it with. Since going to college, my regular D&D group had broken up and moved away. College had taken up most of my time and left little time to find another group of nerds to play with.

Alexander had been obsessed with the game for years. He wasn't this version's original owner. He found his copy in an old house that was getting torn down (I'm sure there was a story there, but Alexander's possession was as far back as I could get the story to go).

He would have been overjoyed at having found the full set if Alexander had someone to play with. The game was meant for at least two players, but he lived his life at a table for one. Sounded familiar to my own life. I was, at heart, an ambivert — an introvert most of the time, but I could turn up the extrovert when I needed to. It was exhausting, and that's why I hated going to parties like Collin's.

Alexander came up with a solution to his isolation. If

he couldn't play it with someone else, then he would bring the game into the real world.

The game became his life, and he memorized every monster, trap, and puzzle. If the mansion had been an actual building, he could have navigated it blindfolded. Easier than his own house, which he never left, not even when it caught fire and burned down around him.

Alexander kept a journal of his time with the game.

All ten days.

The fire claimed his entire family. Both the game and journal were discovered lying in a patch of grass about fifty yards from the house by a fireman on-scene and were unscathed by the fire.

The fireman died ten days later in his own inferno — a risk of his profession, for sure, but it seemed more than just coincidence. Ten days later, his daughter electrocuted herself, and ten days after that, his son suffocated in a plastic bag. And Mom hung herself from grief ten days after that — an entire family died in a month. This curse took no prisoners.

Mansions of Madness then went to a man named Harvey Law. He bought it at an estate sale and presumably enjoyed it for the next ten days of his life before he was hit by a bus while crossing the street and no longer had one.

Leticia, Harvey's daughter, lived for another two years, but only because that's how long it took her to locate the game on a shelf in the basement. She spent ten days rolling her eyes at the legend, having the gall to call the awful deaths before her time with the game "coincidence," until a brown recluse spider crawled into her open mouth while she was sleeping. Ick.

Murray, Leticia's brother, found it next when cleaning the house in preparation for its sale. He was looking forward to the money from the sale that would soon be his.

His gambling debts would be cleared, but alas, he had died in a terrible wreck just recently along with his housemate, Gus, not even a mile from the storage unit where Justin eventually had bought the game.

Monique was obviously wrong about Jared Leto. Even though he was clearly weird enough to have owned a haunted Mansions of Madness game, he had almost for sure never possessed this one.

But I had still almost certainly just condemned Justin to death.

Another thing that was all my fault.

Why were all of these bad things happening to me? Maybe Clarence hadn't cleared all the residual bad mojo from the Dybbuk Box. Curses be damned. I had a mission now.

Save Justin.

Chapter Thirteen

I FELL ASLEEP IN FRONT OF THE COMPUTER BUT WOKE UP the next morning with a clear purpose. I marched into Darrow & Grimes armed with my research, ready and eager to tell anyone and everyone all that I had learned about the game and to let them know that we needed to do something about this Justin guy from the storage auction who only had ten days to live thanks to me.

"You don't really believe that, do you?" asked Jackie.

Ariel rolled her eyes. "Of course she does."

"That kind of story is usually urban legend," Clarence explained. "Your friend will be fine."

"He's not my friend. And how do you know what's real and what's rumor? Didn't we go there to *get* the Mansions of Madness game from that unit? To protect people?"

Ariel nodded. "Yeah, but the energy readings were low. That's not always the most accurate predictor, but it's still nothing like that house we found yesterday. No question, it's a much bigger threat."

I disagreed because that game gave off some seriously

scary vibes, but how would I convince them? I didn't want them to think I was nuts on top of incompetence.

"The ten days adds up." I showed Brian the pages I had printed out, thinking that would be more impressive than screenshots on my phone.

"You've really done your research here," Brian replied with a sideways smile, "but we can't help everyone."

What the hell? Was I misunderstanding the purpose of hunting haunted objects? If Justin was in the line of fire, and we knew it, then wasn't it our duty to move him out of it?

"She doesn't get it," Ariel said, turning to Clarence. "Can you…"

Clarence didn't need her to finish the thought, starting in on a lesson about the different energies and how they work. "How can you tell the difference between ghost energy and spirit energy?" He spoke slowly now that I had joined him over at his personal table, strewn with potentially haunted objects that I'd not seen yesterday, not that Clarence would ever use the word *haunted*.

I said, "Maybe … ghost energy is cold like my mom and spirit energy is warm like my dad."

Clarence smiled. "Ghost energy doesn't usually kill."

"What about that doll that tried to kill me?"

"Spirit energy. Of course, ghost energy *can* kill in some instances," he amended.

Great.

Clarence smiled again. "With spirits, energies from a *living* human can get stuck to an object."

"How?"

"Through trauma."

"So, like poltergeists?"

He nodded. "Plus your dybbuks and whatnots.

Though, those are generally spirits that aren't former humans."

It sounded like I was living in a Dr. Seuss book.

"What about curses?"

"Curses." Clarence sighed, not like I had offended him so much as he might be about to offend me. "Curses are like an uber blending of energies. Generally, it's both."

"Does that mean they'll get lost on Atherton Road and then give *me* a one-star review?"

Clarence ignored me. "It means the caster of the curse leaves some of their soul behind as the curse takes hold."

"You do realize that this is confusing, right?"

"Left unchecked, a curse can grow in power and eventually possess a person." He shook his head. "Not good."

"I'm pretty sure the game must be a curse. It has a ten-day limit. What makes you think there's no danger there?"

"Brian signing my paycheck." Clarence nodded, encouraging me to continue. "Go on. Tell me what you know."

I told him all about the trail of deaths, with more detail than I had allowed myself the first time. But then I shared a bunch of other stuff that I had read about. Crazy stories about things that happened to people under the Mansions of Madness thrall.

According to the journal and what I could piece together from eyewitness accounts of each owner's behavior (I based the order of ownership and times of death), Alex had started watering the family cat whenever it was sleeping and eventually cooking elaborate meals for the feline using items from the pantry.

According to his fellow firemen, Frank had gotten into the weird habit of having long conversations (and escalating arguments) with trees. His children both started running around naked without warning, with Billy singing opera and Allison waving a sword and shield. Mom quit work (even though she needed the job more than ever after losing her husband) while dressed as a Knight of the Round Table.

Harvey started knitting sweaters (that doesn't sound weird, but according to the witnesses, you had to know Harvey). Leticia was the most dangerous, which is why her story was the only one that made the news. It wasn't her biting the head off of a live chicken in front of her neighbors, but what she had done to chase that chicken down.

Clarence nodded when I finished. "I've got good news and bad news."

"Give me the bad news." That was the flavor I was most used to.

"This does sound serious, and according to the origin story you just shared, we have ourselves a dead dude for sure. And that means spirit energy, maybe even a curse."

"Okay."

"But you don't have to panic." His telling me that I didn't have to panic definitely made me feel more panicky.

"Let me show you something," he added, gesturing for me to follow him.

"I already met Gnomey," I said when we were both standing in front of the creepy haunted garden gnome.

"Gnomey is definitely an evil spirit, but so far, he's staying contained."

I wasn't sure how that meant Justin was safe, but it gave Clarence a decent excuse to show me how Gnomey's dangerous eyes worked by having me stand next to the thing and holding a piece of bread in its line of sight long enough to smell it toasting.

Butter melted right into the nooks and crannies when I

tore it in half, and yes, the toast was delicious. But I still wasn't willing to try any of the mushrooms Clarence taught me to scrape off the wall.

"We'll all be killed by the spores if we don't scrape them off daily. I'm not sure what the effects of just breathing them every day might be doing to us."

The King of Understatement and Burying the Lede. Would people be offended if I came to work with a medical mask on?

I chewed on my Gnomey toast, monetarily distracted from Justin, and looked at all the strange objects, curious about what each of them did.

"What's that?" I asked, pointing at another strange ceramic, which was displayed high on a shelf above Clarence's desk. It looked like a donkey that had mated with a wheelbarrow and like something my grandmother would have owned. That was apparently the perfect design for a beast of burden that could carry a jug of mescal on its back and keep a trio of teacups dangling from its side.

"Don't go anywhere near that," Clarence warned.

"That's not an answer," I said.

"Sylvia's vessel is lined in lead, so we can't get an accurate reading of its energy, but that thing is rumored to contain the world's most horrific curse."

"Then why is it *here*?"

Clarence shrugged. "Could be nothing."

I didn't know what to say.

"We've been too scared to open it. The rumors are that unsealing it means instant death."

"Why not throw it into Dale & West?"

He shrugged. "Maybe fire releases the curse."

"Isn't there any way you can tell if the object is dangerous?"

"The energy readings are normal." Another shrug. "We might not be getting anything serious because of the lead, and maybe there's something impossibly deadly within."

"How do you sleep?"

"The lab cots are actually deceptively comfortable."

I saw where Clarence was going with this. Clever.

"How can you tell the difference between rumor and fact?"

"Everything's a rumor until you can prove it. Simply Occam's Razor. Don't believe anything you hear and only half of what you see. I live by the scientific method, not unvetted internet gossip," Clarence said. "That's the point I'm trying to make about your friend Justin."

"He's not my friend."

"Sylvia's vessel is a rumor, while Gnomey is not."

By this logic, even if Justin died in ten days, it might not prove anything. It could be coincidental and anecdotal at most. I was a huge supporter of science, but I also had experienced things in my life, and just in the past couple of days, that challenged what we knew of the universe.

"How about The Hold?"

Clarence shuddered. "Fact."

How could he be so sure of that? Had he seen it up close and in action?

"The Hope Diamond?"

"Rumor, as far as I know. But the painting of Montague Grimes is fact. Because we've interacted with it and tested it. Scientifically."

"The end of the world painting? Like from *The Witcher*?"

"Half of that sounds right." Clarence nodded.

"What's the rumor?"

"Fact," Clarence corrected me. "Montague Grimes has

been trapped in that painting for almost fifteen years. The rumor, what we feel we know but can't prove, is Rudolph Bramson, the jackass Philistine that owns Nemicon, placed him in the painting. We don't know how, and until we do, poor Montague remains trapped."

"What do you mean by trapped?"

"Montague is *in* the painting. Didn't they tell you?"

"It's not a painting *of* him. He's actually in it?" My insides went cold. No wonder Kip hadn't liked me ribbing him about it. "So, what does that mean? Can Montague see us?"

"I imagine. Poor bastard can probably see and hear everything. He's been inching around the tavern for years but has never left through the door in the back. If you keep an eye on it, you'll see that the door is never in the same spot from one day to the next. We're all dying to see what happens when he finally makes it to the door."

"How do you know for sure that Rudolph is responsible?" I asked.

"We've heard things, but we have no proof."

"That sounds like a rumor."

"Exactly. And just like you feeling very certain that your friend Justin is going to die in ten days, the internet search still amounts to rumor until we can get this game in for testing."

"Not my —"

Clarence turned his head to the empty space beside me and got caught up in a conversation with the open air, which must have been Beatrice, and it was suddenly like I didn't even exist.

I was steering clear of Gnomey and Sylvia's vessel. I shuddered, thinking about getting anywhere near it, but I was getting pulled over to the table of new items almost against my will.

"Stay away from everything unless I tell you otherwise," Clarence said when he was done with Beatrice.

"Why am I even back here?" I asked. "Is there something I can actually help you with?"

"I'm sure Jackie will be here momentarily, so you can help her out front. Until then, I'm supposed to teach you about safety protocols and remind you that—"

"I always need to wear my gloves?"

I wish Justin had known that rule.

"And that there is a scientific explanation for everything."

There was no way I was going to allow Clarence to minimize and dismiss my concerns about Mansions of Madness. A life, a human life, was on the line, not some sweet little lab rat. Okay, even a lab rat didn't deserve to die needlessly in the name of science. Two can play at this game, Clarence.

"Is Beatrice still here?"

"No, she's floated off to do some research of her own. She'll ask on her side about your game."

"You seem to like Beatrice," I said, hoping for a smile.

"Beatrice is fine." The ghost of a grin appeared on his lips.

"Of all the bric-a-brac shops in all the towns in the world, how did Beatrice come to haunt Darrow & Grimes?"

"Beatrice isn't haunting anything. We incinerated the flowerpot she came in on a few years ago, and she's been around ever since."

"What is she attached to now?"

"No idea." Clarence shook his head, hanging it low as if this lack of knowledge carried physical weight. "We've been ruling things out that Beatrice might have reattached to ever since."

"It's his lab coat. We're all sure of it." Jackie announced as she entered the room. I laughed, thinking it was a joke.

Clarence and Jackie didn't join me.

"So, is Beatrice real?"

"Of course she is," Clarence replied in an indignant tone.

"Can you prove it? Can you prove she was actually haunting a flowerpot? By your standard of the scientific method, she shouldn't exist at all, especially since the vessel you *think* she was attached to was incinerated."

"Is there a point here? I'm rather busy." Clarence was clearly upset, but I wasn't going to let up. This was too important.

"My point is that not everything can be wrapped up neatly with a bow. Sometimes, you have to go with your gut, even if it means believing the new girl and her crazy theories."

We were standing nose to nose, and I wasn't going to be the first to blink.

"Okay!" Jackie interrupted. "I've got everything lined up for the de-haunting."

"Good news," Clarence said with a nod, sounding like he didn't actually care. He walked away, gesticulating and venting vigorously to the empty space next to him.

"It'll be tomorrow night," said Jackie.

I took a deep breath to compose myself. What was wrong with me? I wasn't usually this confrontational, except with Mom. But virtual strangers? Never.

"What are we de-haunting?"

"The house." Jackie looked at me like I should already know this. "The estate sale? Surely you remember."

"Right." That place had been creepy AF. But de-haunting sounded awesome. "What can I do to help?"

"Go home." She smiled. "Rest up for tomorrow evening."

"Oh. Okay." My smile faltered.

But then Ariel stepped through the door and saved my day. "I have something she can do."

Chapter Fourteen

"It's actually called The Carnivale Arcane?"

Ariel turned to me, taking her eyes off of the road but keeping her hands on the steering wheel, still the most badass bitch I had ever laid eyes on.

"It used to be called The Festival of Shadows, but people didn't get it. So, they changed the name, and now the place is like if Costco was owned by Spirit Halloween. When it comes to town, it's only here for a short time." Ariel looked back at the road. "Fortunately for us, the first rush is over, and the place will be relatively empty. Unfortunately…"

I really hated the word, *unfortunately*.

"…it also means that we'll have a hard time finding what we want."

"And what do we want again?"

"A doll. For Monique. Because you fucked up, and now Brian is wetting himself."

So I was on the way to The Carnivale Arcane because I had become Ariel's problem to solve.

"You said 'when it comes to town.' Is it like a circus that travels from place to place?"

"More like a carnival." Ariel turned her head again, just long enough to let me know I should feel stupid, and then she looked back at the windshield and finished her thought. "The Carnivale Arcane is a traveling museum of curiosities."

She could have just said that when we got in the car. I wish that Ariel would stop making me feel small, and I *really*wished that I could quit thinking that she looked so smart and cool while doing it.

"We're here," Ariel announced ten minutes later as she pulled into the parking lot of a nondescript warehouse.

"It doesn't *look* weird." I was underwhelmed, imagining a sad little flea market selling trinkets and sandalwood incense inside.

"Oh, it will." Ariel got out of the car and started walking toward the entrance without waiting for me.

Holy Lucifer, she was right.

The Carnivale Arcane was an elaborate maze of oddly unsettling displays. Every surface was covered in stuffed animals, eerie mannequins, and bizarre artifacts, ranging from common household items that had been modified into strange shapes to actual human body parts preserved in jars, from ears to pretzel-like penises. It got weirder and weirder the deeper we went.

Surreally twisted exhibits. Strange creatures, freaks, and artifacts from unknown corners of the world. My underwhelmed turned to overwhelmed quickly.

I saw a wax hand that moved on its own, a chamber pot that played a lullaby when full, a cursed mirror that distorted the reflection of anyone who looked into it, a haunted suit of armor that supposedly screamed in the night, and another one that was apparently always wet (it definitely was when I touched it); a cursed vase that caused accidents when moved; and a glass eye that wept blood.

But we only saw one doll in the entire place. A porcelain figurine with pale skin, a wide smile, jet-black eyes, and long dark hair. The thing seemed to move on its own, its head turning sharply from side to side as if on permanent lookout, sending several strains of chill down my spine.

"The doll is not for sale," insisted the Carnivale's owner, Parker, for the second time after Ariel tried to badger him into it.

"Sir." She gave him a flirty smile that he didn't deserve.

Parker shook his head. "No dice. Dollie is one of my biggest draws. I'll tell you the same thing I told the last lady who came in here nagging me out of one when I only had two: What's a museum of curiosities without a haunted doll?"

Ariel walked away, obviously chewing on a thought.

"What do we do now?" I asked her.

"We're leaving here with Dollie."

"But he said—"

"That other lady was Monique."

"How do you know that?"

"Are you kidding me?" Ariel gave me another one of her "*Why are you so dumb?*" looks. "She'll know exactly how hard we had to work for Dollie, and she'll appreciate the hell out of it when we deliver it to her."

"So what now?"

"We kill some time." Ariel nodded to herself and then walked off into another wing of the museum as I followed.

A minute later, I was standing in front of something truly horrific. A long line snaked its way to a charred recliner with a sign above it that read *CRAY-Z-BOY* and issued a challenge:

Sit on this chair quietly for thirty seconds and win $10,000!

"Gross," said Ariel, looking disgusted.

I read the exhibit's backstory next out loud to myself because, Ariel, of course.

This chair was owned by Harriet Little, killed while sitting on it by her abusive husband, Merl. He set her on fire while she sat on it.

The chair was saved, but poor Harriet was not.

Apparently, Merl got what was coming to him, spontaneously combusting the next time he tried to sit on his former favorite chair, and the Cray-Z-Boy has been haunted ever since. Now, anyone who sat on the chair exploded in some way, according to the placard. Sometimes it was a verbal explosion, crazed laughter, or loud singing, occasionally vomiting, and in some of the worst of situations, the Cray-Z-boy forced its occupant to uncontrollably shit themselves. The cleaning bill for this chair must be insane.

People who finally reached the front of the line were allowed to sit on the Cray-Z-Boy to try and win the ten grand — hard enough with the recliner being haunted, but nearly impossible as the crowd shouted questions and the chair's occupant blurted answers that were so horrific and uncomfortable that they absolutely had to be true.

I couldn't believe some of the things I was hearing:

"I'm glad my husband is dead!"

"I posed for Playgirl in my 20s!"

"I don't want to be a mom anymore!"

"I'm not gay, but I still want to fuck my neighbor!"

"I slept with my best friend's wife seventeen times!"

"I did cheat on you!" confessed the latest stooge, blurting his admission to a pretty yet gut-punched brunette standing a few feet away from him.

She stomped off.

The guy hopped off of the chair and ran after her.

Someone else sat down.

I shook my head. "No ten thousand dollars for him."

"This isn't right." Ariel was walking away from me again. "I'm talking to Parker."

The owner laughed at Ariel. "You've gotta be kidding me. First, you want Dollie, and now you want me to get rid of my biggest earner — just because it makes you a little uncomfortable?"

"It doesn't make me uncomfortable," Ariel argued. "It's unethical. You need to stop people from sitting on that chair before someone gets seriously hurt!"

"They can get off any time they want to!" Parker laughed. "Stick around if you want. Sometimes, they get off *in the chair.*"

Ariel wasn't backing down. "How can you profit from something that's so obviously dangerous? Something that makes people feel terrible after they leave? How do you sleep at night knowing that you profit off of people's misery?"

"Stacks of cash make a mighty fine pillow, lady." Parker was no longer laughing, pushing back on Ariel, his hackles clearly raised. "Every single one of those people stands in a long line waiting to embarrass themselves. They see what happens and are either still willing to take the risk, or they see themselves as the exception."

"You manipulate the experience so that people are engaging in behavior that they wouldn't normally even think of."

"Don't tell me what I'm doing, lady. I sleep just fine. I hope you two had fun here at The Carnivale Arcana. Now get the fuck out."

Parker turned away from us, but Ariel didn't leave, instead marching back toward the Cray-Z-Boy.

"What are you doing?" I called after her.

"Fixing this!"

I had no idea what that meant. Was Ariel going to warn everyone away? Try to sit on the chair and win the ten thousand dollars to prove a point? Maybe destroy the haunted object?

I never got the chance to find out.

Because as Ariel approached the Cray-Z-Boy's occupant, a petite woman chattering at the speed of a plane crash confession, the woman turned toward Ariel and projectile vomited far more than anyone that size could possibly hold. Ariel was covered.

"Fucking hell," Ariel said.

Chapter Fifteen

THE DRIVE WAS PAINFULLY SILENT.

This latest disaster felt like yet one more thing that was all my fault, even though I had nothing to do with what happened.

Ariel had seen the nightmare firsthand; she should have known to stay out of the spew zone. Because she was so driven and stubborn, I was a little shocked we were leaving without the doll or shutting shit down. Maybe being covered in stranger vomit was her limit.

"Where are we going?" I finally asked. Ariel glanced in the rearview mirror, so I took that as a cue to mean doing something about the drying crust on her face. "Somewhere to clean up?"

"My place. It's not far from here."

Another seven minutes, to be exact. Then she turned onto a street, and I knew which house was hers before we stopped in front of it. A small bungalow, charming from the porch to eaves, with gleaming windows and a welcoming front door painted in a jubilant red. Lush greenery lined the front walk.

The interior made me feel like even more of a loser. The place was clean, with bright rooms, both from the ample light spilling into each one, but by the touches of simple decor and clean-lined furniture that filled her house with an air of sophistication and delicate grace.

This was the place of someone who exuded confidence, someone who knew who they were and what they wanted out of life. *Better Home and Gardens*, here's your next front cover.

I still wondered what the hell I was even doing here.

Ariel said, "Don't get lost. Or touch anything. But you can make yourself comfortable. I'll be ten minutes."

She went to shower, and I was tempted to start going through drawers because I felt more curious about Ariel than I did about anything else, except for the ghost phone, and that was only because I missed my father like a limb hacked from my body.

I couldn't snoop. Even if Ariel wasn't able to read my mind (I still had no idea if that was only my paranoia) or have secret cameras recording me — this whole thing with the Cray-Z-Boy could be a setup — it wasn't right to betray her trust. So I sat on the couch, planning to kill my ten minutes there.

But then I heard a yell, loud and sudden enough to shove me off of the sofa and race down the hall.

"Snuggles!" Ariel bellowed when I was halfway there. "What did you do!"

Panic drenched me in those last few steps to what I assumed was her bedroom door, where I was sure her angry shout had been coming from.

I had forgotten all about Snuggles, and now it sounded like I was about to confront the threat head-on. I grabbed a candlestick holder from the hall table, ready to do battle *Clue* style, but when I burst into Ariel's bedroom, I found her shaking an accusing finger at a weird-looking teddy bear, with blood seeping down all walls around it.

"What? Where is he? Is someone hurt?" I was panting. "I have a loaded piece of overpriced décor, and I'm not afraid to use it."

Ariel glared and shook her head. I lowered my weapon.

"This is Snuggles," Ariel explained, glancing down at the stuffed animal.

"I thought—"

"I know what you thought. But no, I don't have an abusive boyfriend or any boyfriend at all. I've had Snuggles since I was a kid. My Great Aunt Mildred might be inside of it."

"Are you … do you like it?"

I couldn't help grimacing at the worn, dirty-looking bear. Patches of fur were missing, and what was left was crusty with dark stains. Where one of his plastic eyes should have been, someone had sewn a yellow patch with bright red thread over the space. The thing was hideous, and I felt some of that icky energy emanating from it. So much so that I wanted to snatch it from her and chuck it into the garbage disposal.

"Snuggles can be kind of an asshole, but sometimes he's cool." She looked at the walls and shook her head. "Not cool today, though, Snuggles. Not cool."

Even though the stuffed animal's face didn't change or animate in any way, the bear still somehow managed to look ashamed.

"But yeah, we're buds," Ariel said. "Snuggles doesn't mean all the blood stuff. I wake up with scratches all the time, and my walls occasionally bleed, but he's always sorry."

"Too bad he can't help you clean it," I joked, but what I wanted to do was scream, "Get rid of it!"

"How about you help?" she said.

"I would love to help you!" And I actually meant that.

Soon, we were each holding a rag and sharing a large bottle of her homemade blood cleaner.

"I'm still thinking about what to call the stuff," Ariel said. "I had to do something because the commercial cleaners cost too much, and so I make mine with vinegar and baking soda and some other stuff."

"Other stuff like what?"

"Don't worry about it," Ariel said.

It was hard not to worry after she said that. Maybe I should be wearing gloves, but at least Ariel was finally being nice to me. So, I focused on the positive while we scrubbed her walls. I thought it was sweet that she wanted me to forgive Snuggles and clean his mess. Maybe her secret formula could remove whatever was matted to his fur. I know just the thing to fix him — gasoline and a match.

Every few minutes, she would make another excuse for him.

"Snuggles just has a temper sometimes."

"He's a little rough around the edges, but he always means well."

"All that fluff is really hiding a lot of hurt."

It was probably just my imagination, but Ariel almost seemed sad while dropping me back off at my car an hour or so later.

"Thanks for the help."

"It was a pleasure to clean blood off of your walls." I dared not ask her the obvious question: where all the blood came from because I wasn't sure I was ready for the answer.

Ariel surprised me with a laugh. "Take the morning off

tomorrow, then meet Brian and me at Home Depot. Six o'clock."

"Okay. Why?"

"We're going to get some duct tape and hammers."

"Sounds like a party."

Ariel laughed again. "Home Depot is always a party."

"Just Home Depot? Or any home improvement store?"

"Oh," Ariel said, stone sober. "It's got to be Home Depot. The Husky brand."

"I can't tell if you're kidding."

Ariel shook her head. "Clarence won't let me joke about Home Depot. Especially Husky."

"Let me guess. There's a bunch of science to explain it."

"Boring science," Ariel agreed. Then she remembered that we weren't really besties. "But it's a science that you should learn."

She rolled up her window and drove away.

I was all alone, wanting nothing more than to hear Clarence tell me all about the science behind Home Depot's Husky brand.

I tossed and turned all night, waiting for tomorrow.

Then I had to wait through the longest day, wanting to visit Darrow & Grimes, even if I wasn't on the clock and couldn't get paid. Curiosity burned inside me, and that was a fire I didn't want to put out.

Night finally came, and I met Ariel and Brian at Home Depot as planned. I picked out some hammers but got chastised by Brian for either not seeing or understanding the difference between the Husky and higher-end Husky Pro brands.

Brian was probably irritated because one of the employees had come over and barked at him for making so much noise. Brian insisted that the aisles were empty and that it seemed like the best place to try out the swing of the hammers by whacking them into the aluminum shelving units.

"Why do you need to hit the shelves?" asked the employee, Ray, according to his nameplate.

"Because we're going to de-haunt a house." As if that explained everything.

I looked from Brian to Ray, fascinated by whatever might happen next.

"Why do you need to make so much noise? It's hurting my ears," Ray asked him, seeming nonplussed about the mention of a haunted house and more interested in Brian's hammer testing process.

Brian whacked the shelf one last time and held his ear close to it. "My home workshop lacks the necessary acoustics to make sure they create the exact vibrations needed. This is very precise testing — you understand, right?"

Ray looked at the cart full of various sizes of Husky brand hammers, bags of water softener salt, and large rolls of duct tape. Yeah, we were giving off that serial killer vibe- hard. "Can I help you to the register with that?"

Brian complied, and then we all walked to the counter together. I smiled as if the transaction was just a normal Thursday night. Nothing to see here.

Brian could have definitely handled this errand alone, but I thought it was sweet that Brian had wanted Ariel to join him and even sweeter that he wanted me to tag along.

Even though it actually made us both kind of pathetic when I thought about it. So I stopped thinking about it.

Ray looked sad to see us go.

"That de-haunting ... can I come with you?"

Chapter Sixteen

Maybe we should have let Ray come with us.

This place had been creepy during the day. Still, the haunted house was so much creepier at night, looming in the darkness, cowering in shadows as if scared of the eerily glowing moonlight. Wisps of cold mist drifted across its creaking, gaping windows and weathered doors, blanketing the place with an even more foreboding appearance.

Echoing wind and rustling leaves filled the night, accompanied by a low, ominous growl of an unseen creature, either rumbling from the bowels of the house or born entirely from my imagination.

"Brian and I are going inside," Ariel said, leaving me to finish her thought. "You are going to make a ring of salt around the perimeter of the house."

"And duct tape," Brian reminded her. "Around the base."

"What does that do?" I asked.

"It contains the spirit energy inside," Brian explained. "We don't need this thing getting away."

Use #5,956 for duct tape.

"You think it's spirit energy and not a ghost?"

"Of course. You should know the difference by now."

Of course, I didn't. I understood that ghost energy was a person once, and spirit energy could be a spirit that was never human or residual energy from a traumatic event, but beyond that, I hadn't a clue how to tell them apart.

"I'm still trying to figure this out," I admitted.

"Are we going to stand out here all night? We don't look suspicious or anything," said Ariel.

"Is it okay for us to be here?" I asked. "I mean, I feel like we're trespassing or even breaking and entering."

"This is what we do," replied Ariel. "Sometimes we have to break the rules to get the job done. Are you sure you're up to this?"

I nodded. I didn't want to argue the finer points between rules and felonies and only hoped that bail money was part of the benefits package.

Being all by myself in the dark wasn't as scary as I'd expected, but it made me even lonelier than usual. I got right to work anyway, glad to finally be useful.

I felt certain that someone was watching me the entire time, but I made the circle anyway. Salt and tape, salt and tape, salt and tape, intermittently gripping my hammer until I no longer felt the need. Brian was right, the hammer did have a nice weight and grip to it, but I wondered how useful it was against a ghost.

It was peaceful inside the circle. Safe. Maybe I could finally—

A terrible banging and shrieking came rolling out of the house.

I froze and peered into the darkness.

Someone screamed, and I ran toward the porch with my hammer raised.

The house rattled on its foundation and stopped me

cold. I felt the dark energy seeping out from inside and wondered why I hadn't felt it as strongly the first time we were here.

I swallowed, frozen in place, perhaps willing yet still physically unable to take another step forward. In the attic window that had suddenly illuminated, I could see a shape in the window. It didn't look like Ariel or Brian, though. It was big and broad, and a sense of recognition jolted through me. Could it really be my dad?

But then, my body began to move of its own accord.

I ran toward the front door — how could I not after seeing my father?

I drew nearer as the banging and shrieking from inside grew louder, more desperate. But I didn't care about any of that. I was following a cloud of my father's aftershave. A whiff of spice and pine, musky and woodsy enough to make me sick with memory. I longed for the cure and kept walking.

I heard his voice but had no idea if it was only an echo inside me — my name over and over in his comforting tone, like a lullaby, more soothing than a warm blanket on a cold night.

My heart pounded as I burst through the front door, still gripping the hammer.

"Hello?" Timid at first, then again after having mustered everything inside me. "Hello?"

The walls and floors creaked hard as they settled.

I scanned the room, trembling, desperate to find my father.

"Hello?" Timid again.

I turned to leave but heard a noise behind me.

I whirled around and saw nothing.

Slowly, I took a few steps forward, scanning the shadows for any sign of my father.

A cold hand gripped my shoulder.

I screamed and spun around again, swinging my hammer wildly at nothing.

There was no hand.

And Dad was still dead.

But I convinced myself that I really was hearing my father on the second floor as I crept slowly toward the stairway.

The walls began to violently shudder and shake as books, candles, and other objects flew all about, hurling toward the ceiling and crashing back onto the ground.

I made it to the second floor, and the room swirled in chaos, shadows dancing ominously on the ceiling and walls, the air heavy with the sound of frantic movement.

I might have seen a lone figure trembling in the hallway.

I knew it was an apparition as I ran toward it, but the sight was a gallon of water down a parched emotional throat, so I raced toward the ghost that could not be, only to find that I'd run right into a closet.

The door slammed shut behind me, and I screamed.

I tried the knob, and sure enough, I was locked in.

After suffering several long moments of unadulterated panic, I finally recovered my breath.

Then lost it immediately as the acrid scent of smoke curled into my nostrils. Sudden and ominous, slithering through the walls and corners of the house to seep inside the closet, filling my every breath with another gust of fear.

Anxiety swelled in a tide as it threatened to swallow me, but then I found my breath again and gathered my wits.

I gripped my Husky 20 oz. ripping hammer. Brian had generously let me pick my favorite from our Home Depot haul.

The frantic chaos on the other side of the closet door kept getting louder and louder.

I had to ignore it. I raised my hammer and brought it down hard on the closet door, over and over until the wood splinted into fragments.

The door flew open, and for the length of a hiccup, I saw the source of that smoky stench — a roaring black dragon exploding into the hallway, its eyes glowing with menace and rage until it puffed away in a cloud of charcoal-colored smoke.

There was no fire-breathing dragon. There wasn't even a fire. But there was still an awful cacophony of shouting and rattling, along with a massive gust of wind blowing down the hallway.

I would have dealt with the fire-breathing dragon if it came with another look at my father.

I sprinted, my hair and clothes both whipping in what felt like gale-force winds. I struggled to keep my footing as the howling wind threatened to knock me off of my balance, trudging toward all that shouting and rattling.

I raced up the attic stairs and threw the door open to find Brian and Ariel standing side by side, their heads bowed in concentration, surrounded by candles, ancient artifacts, and intricate symbols drawn on the floor. No sign of my father or any other apparitions.

A stone gargoyle lay in the center of their circle, its fierce eyes burning with power. Wind whipped brutally around them, but they looked determined, locked in a battle against unseen forces, and determined to win it.

Their bodies tensed as they raised the gargoyle, hands and arms moving in rhythmic gestures. The air smelled of incense, burning herbs, and candles amid the tang of sulfur and brimstone.

The furious wind suddenly died as if strangled. The poltergeist was bound to the statue.

"That was a big one!" Brian exclaimed.

"A real fucker," Ariel agreed.

What have I gotten myself into? And the much louder and more dominant of my two thoughts: fuck yeah, this shit was awesome.

Chapter Seventeen

Mom was definitely going to kill me.

I was a grown woman who could go to Home Depot whenever I damn well wanted, and I could also go to a haunted house afterward if that's what I felt like doing. But I hadn't told her where I was going or that I was even going out, and if she looked in on me in the morning — hopefully, she had stopped checking on me during my sleep a long time ago — then Mom would know I sneaked out.

Even though a grown woman can't really *sneak* out.

I was just leaving without telling her.

Now, it looked like I would be staying the night at Darrow & Grimes, whether I liked the idea or not. Mom was an early riser, and it was already four in the morning, so if I went home now, I would just end up waking her for sure.

Besides, I was still wired from a midnight adventure that had stricken me with terror and buzzing adventure, my intrigue only growing as we left the haunted home behind us and took the gargoyle to Clarence, who was eagerly waiting to see what we returned with back at the lab.

I couldn't wait for him to explain what I'd seen because neither Ariel nor Brian was any help on the drive, both of them painting a picture of what I already knew because I had seen it with my own eyes.

But I found myself in the same situation while telling the story to Clarence in a chattering ramble.

"The wind was crazy, and I ran down the hallway, and my clothes and hair were whipping everywhere, and I kept tripping, and then I got to the attic where Ariel and Brian were playing Harry Potter, and there was magic and incense, and candles and the gargoyle's eyes were like totally glowing red, and the wind got even worse, and then they raised it in the air like Rafiki lifting Simba, even though it looked really, really heavy, and—"

Clarence had heard enough from me. "Nothing to it. It's all just matter and energy interacting."

"Fuck Harry Potter," Ariel said.

"I like Harry Potter," Brian admitted, then turned to Clarence. "So what do we do with the gargoyle now?"

Clarence had been convinced that anything less than a saltwater bath for the statue would leave them shy of getting the job done, but it was a two-hour drive to the ocean, so that would have to serve as Plan B if Plan A failed by morning time. Brian got a large vat, filled it with salt water, and let the gargoyle stew in it while each of us claimed a cot.

Clarence was the one who lived in the lab, keeping an eye on things, but by the looks of things, this was far from the first overnight at Darrow & Grimes for the gang.

Clarence turned Gnomey toward the wall, then explained what he was doing to keep me from annoying him with my next obvious question.

"I don't normally turn him toward the wall, but we all need to stay safe. Our outer wall is made from a special fireproof material, epoxy, and urethane layers."

"Sounds expensive," I said.

Brian nodded. "It was."

"Looks like we paid for a good night's sleep." Clarence handed me an extra pillow and surprised me with a grandfatherly smile.

We all laid down, but I obviously wasn't the only one of us not yet grounded. I kept tossing and turning. Ariel was wide awake, too.

"Why do you keep moving around?" she asked.

"How did you end up here, at Darrow & Grimes, I mean, with all of this stuff?" Even after three tries, I still sounded like the village idiot.

I couldn't see Ariel rolling her eyes, but the gesture was easy to imagine. "Snuggles. Obviously. If your favorite stuffed animal starts trying to scratch your eyes out, you get curious fast."

That wasn't much of a biography.

"You want to know more?" Then Ariel answered her own question. "I was Brian's first hire eight years ago. My parents were in the business, which is probably how my Aunt Mildred ended up in Snuggles."

"Tell her about how you like this stuff so much that you turned down all of those modeling contracts," said Brian in the dark. Obviously, he couldn't sleep either.

"No need. You just gave her the story she didn't ask for."

I actually liked knowing.

"Do you want to know how I got started?" Brian asked.

"I'm sure she can figure it out," Ariel answered for me. "Your name is on the door. Maybe you should tell her why you haven't gone bankrupt yet?"

"We're not going bankrupt," Brian argued.

"*Yet.*"

"She's right." Clarence was apparently wide awake as well. "This business started floating in the bowl back around the time Brian's daddy died."

Brian defended himself. "Our business model doesn't leave a lot of room for profit. We literally destroy our most valuable pieces."

"*Our* business model?" Ariel said.

"What about you, Clarence?" I asked since the scientist was obviously awake, too. I could totally understand that with all this excitement. What happened tonight was terrifying and exhilarating, but it left me with so many questions. Had that really been my dad? I looked over in the direction of the ghost phone, willing myself to stop thinking of such crazy ideas.

"I was studying an old arcane sword at Savannah State when a couple of young fellows came in and offered me a dream job," Clarence said.

"Darrow & Grimes?" I asked.

"William and Montague in the flesh."

"How long ago was that?"

"Fifty years," Clarence replied.

"And he still hates the words *magic* and *demons*," added Brian.

"Lies!" Clarence spat before addressing me. "How about you? It wasn't just that Dybbuk Box that brought you in here."

In the past few days, I have been wondering the same thing. I didn't believe that this could all be a coincidence. The Dybbuk box, the auction, ended up in the shop, not to mention my Uncle Kevin's trunk crashing through the ceiling.

"My Uncle Kevin," I explained. "Well, I was always

sort of a hopeless nerd, but my Uncle Kevin always got that I wasn't into school like my brother and sister and wasn't meant for a normal job." No one asked any questions, but I kept rambling right into an unnecessary confession about my father. "It wasn't just my Uncle Kevin. I also lost my father last year."

I held in tears. "I miss him so much. Maybe that's why I dropped out of college … I don't know. Since his death, I've felt his presence around me. Tonight, I thought I saw him and even smelled his cologne. Crazy, I know."

"Interesting," said Clarence, tapping a finger to his lips.

"You dropped out of college?" Ariel asked.

"It just didn't make sense to me anymore. And then, poof, I ran into you all. I was lost even before my dad died. But now… I feel like maybe I'm supposed to be here."

A long pause before Clarence spoke. "We're glad you're here." He sighed. "Now go to sleep."

But I couldn't, even after I was tossing and turning to a chorus of snoring. I kept thinking about Dad.

And that got me thinking about the ghost phone again.

Thinking about that was clearly an awful idea, with it literally across the room, so I turned my thoughts toward the job instead. It felt dangerous, and I loved it, but I also couldn't stop wondering why Brian had chosen me. I'd never even applied, and that made me wonder if I was really just a diversity hire.

Ariel probably thought so.

After counting backward from a hundred several times and still not feeling remotely close to sleep, mostly thanks to my incessant thoughts about the ghost phone, I finally sneaked out of bed and walked to the light glowing on the wall in front of Gnomey.

I thought about Dad again. About seeing him and

hearing him at the house just hours ago. Wondering if this was all crazy or if I was a basket case of nuts.

I looked over at the phone, knowing I shouldn't even be near it. I considered creeping back over to my cot and doing the right thing, but the impulse was too strong, and six seconds later, I was grabbing the receiver and pressing the ghost phone against my ear.

It felt cold in my hand. I had the feeling in my stomach that I had around other objects, except this was more direct and intense, and I almost dropped the receiver.

At first, there was only static, and I was too timid to even whisper for worry that someone might hear me and wake up.

"Hello," came a soft crackle through the phone.

I didn't dare answer.

But then I heard a second "Hello" coming from behind me.

I nearly jumped out of my skin, stifling a *yelp* as I slammed down the receiver and turned around to see an older woman lightly glowing. It could only be Beatrice.

"You're messing with things you don't understand," she said, gesturing to the phone. "Nothing is free. Not even in the spirit world. There is always a price you will have to pay."

My heart sank. "What's the price?"

She shrugged. "It's different every time."

There was a ghost, a real live ghost, in front of me. Or perhaps a real dead ghost. I was surprised I couldn't see through her, but other than the slight glow about her, she looked solid. Maybe I could throw something at her and see if she could catch it.

"What's it like … on the other side?" I asked.

"I'm sorry?" Beatrice snapped.

It suddenly felt like I asked if she was wearing any

underwear, not that a ghost would have the need. We'd have to play catch some other time.

"I've been watching you, and I must say it's nice to see a little culture around here."

I wasn't sure whether to be flattered or creeped out that I was being *watched*.

"Where's Clarence?" she added.

"He's over there." I pointed to his sleeping form. "He's the one that sounds like a grizzly bear rummaging through a trashcan."

Beatrice harrumphed and floated away toward Clarence.

I slipped back into bed, scratching a sudden yet unrelenting itch on the back of my head, fierce and demanding. I dug at my scalp for relief and gasped at the realization that I was holding a large clump of my own hair.

I woke up what could have only been an hour or two later. My hand flew to my head before I even opened my eyes. And yes, I was definitely missing a chunk of hair, so I rearranged myself to cover it up.

Everyone was awake and gone from the lab, including Clarence. I hoped that Beatrice hadn't told on me. If not yet, she still might. So, the best thing I could do would be to get in front of the issue.

I went out to the front of Darrow & Grimes to announce my misstep with the ghost phone, but two steps out of the lab, the stench of something terribly foul curled into my nostrils and nearly sent me falling to the floor.

"What is *that*?" I yelled to anyone who would answer me.

I looked toward the front of the shop to see Clarence, Brian, and Ariel all standing in a semicircle around Jackie. I could only see the top of Jackie's head, so I ran over to see what might be happening, even though the smell was a warning for me to stay the hell away.

On top of Jackie's desk was the severed head of a goat. Its eyes bulged, and its tongue stuck out with an expression of surprise. It looked like a demented jack-o-lantern with ooze seeping onto the spread-out newspaper it had been plopped on.

What the actual fuck?

Chapter Eighteen

THE GOAT HEAD WAS THE GROSSEST THING I HAD EVER SEEN or smelled. It wasn't a fresh kill because it was bloated and discolored, its eyes glazed over and milky with decay, its nose misshapen and twisted, skin carpeted in sores and sagging patches of putrid fur, emitting a reek that filled my sinuses, like sour milk and rotting flesh.

While the incinerator had made short work of it, the smell lingered, as well as the sense that something was wrong. The gang was unusually quiet, each lost in their own thoughts, watching the flames take away the source of concern.

"Could it be the poltergeist?" It would be so much better if this was a supernatural problem rather than a human one.

"That's not how it works." Brian's forehead wrinkled in concern. "That head was placed there by a person. A living person."

"Which means we've pissed somebody off," Jackie interjected.

"Nemicon? Monique? That dude at the Carnivale?" Ariel shrugged. "We naturally make enemies."

The group dispersed, ready to move on with the day. As hard as it was to leave the mystery unsolved, we didn't have much to go on.

"What now, Uncle Grandpa?" Ariel said to Clarence, even though he was neither her uncle nor her grandpa.

"We need to throw that statue in the ocean like I said fourteen times last night. We'll go out on a boat and sink it to—"

"Three times," Brian interjected.

"And on that last time, you were kind of an asshole about it," Ariel added.

"Looks like I needed to be." Clarence took a long sniff to prove his point. "I'm glad we waited until morning. Now, have fun on the boat."

"You're not going?" I asked.

Clarence shook his head. "I hate boats."

Even though Mossy Oaks was minutes from the Atlantic, I really didn't enjoy it as much as others did. All those creepy things swimming around your feet unseen freaked me out. Don't even get me started on how sand finds its way into everything — even a ham sandwich sealed in a plastic bag. Now, that's a curse worth looking into.

"I get seasick," I said. "Maybe I should stay here?"

Ariel nodded. "That sounds awesome. One day of puking is my quota for the week."

That made me *want* to go, just to prove I could be a good time. But I wouldn't be, and the odds of proving myself good at anything were best here at Darrow & Grimes.

I was hoping that Jackie or Clarence could help me

mend a few of my earlier mistakes, but I was determined to get Monique back on Team Darrow & Grimes and get the Mansions of Madness game back from Justin.

"Don't fuck anything up," Ariel said as she left.

I waited a whole five minutes after Brian and Ariel were gone with the gargoyle before approaching Jackie. There were only six days left. "This Justin guy is going to die if we don't—"

"You can't save the people who don't want to be saved," she interrupted, shutting me down before I started. "And that boy doesn't want to be saved."

"How can you even know that? Do you even know where he is?"

Jackie shook her head. "Brian calls the shots, and we do what he says. If he thought that boy could be saved, I'm sure he would save him."

I couldn't understand how they could be so heartless to let a kid die like that. If we didn't come to his rescue, who would?

Jackie was dusting the half-empty shelves. It seemed unnecessary because there wasn't anyone coming in to look anyway. I wondered if the shop was in as bad shape as Ariel and Clarence said. I had just gotten the coolest job ever, and I'd hate to lose it quickly.

Jackie was obviously not going to be persuaded using my current tactics, so I needed to try a different angle.

I picked up a rag and sprayed some Pledge on an empty shelf, then began wiping it down.

"Why don't you ever go with Brian and Ariel? You have so much more experience than me."

"That's for sure." Jackie laughed. "I was an agent for twenty years, ever since William hired me right out of college."

"Oh."

"Don't sound so surprised. I wasn't born to offer customers fudge, you know."

"What changed?" I asked, slightly worried that I might be offending Jackie without knowing it.

"I had a geriatric pregnancy a couple of years ago." Her eyes stared somewhere far beyond the walls of the shop. "Too many complications. After everything I've seen in the field…" She shrugged. "I decided it was safer transitioning to a desk job, with the occasional trip to a sale. It's so much calmer, running the front desk and selling trinkets to the community."

Jackie grinned at me. "But don't get me wrong. I'm fully trained and capable of protecting the shop should anything charge through that door." She nodded at the front as if a monster might ding the little bell above the door at any moment.

"You don't miss … the other stuff?"

"There's nothing to miss. Where do you think Brian gets most of his information?"

"From you?"

Jackie jabbed both thumbs back at herself. "That's right: me."

"Where do you get the information?"

"All over the place, but I've been chasing down stories about haunted objects on Reddit since 2004."

"I thought Reddit came out after 2004?"

"Exactly." She nodded. "If it wasn't for me feeding info to Brian and coordinating all the items he brings in so the demonic objects play well together, D&G would have gone bust years ago."

"This place obviously only survives because of you!" I kept buttering her up. "Brian is lucky. We all are."

"Well, thank you." Jackie smiled, seeming surprised.

"Where else do you do research besides Reddit?"

"My favorite place is a chatroom called Occult Connection. It was named back in the 90s," she explained, shaking her head as if disappointed. "You should see the URL required to get there."

"Can I? See the chatroom?" This was working even better than I had hoped.

"Sure!" Jackie seemed excited to show something to someone. "Follow me."

She led me back to her office, which was really just her computer by the front counter, where it felt like the painting of Montague Grimes in that saloon was keeping watch over us.

"You need an invite to join the chatroom." Jackie glanced at the screen. "They won't invite you, so I'll just show you around."

"Can we see if there's anything about Mansions of Madness?"

Jackie raised an eyebrow. "You aren't going to give this up, are you?"

"If I can save him, I have to try."

Jackie sighed. "Fine, but if you get yourself into trouble, don't expect Brian or Ariel to drag you out of it."

Jackie stared at me for a moment more and then started to type.

She clicked around for several minutes, but the only thing we saw was a single post about the ridiculous brawl at the storage auction. There was even a GIF to mark the occasion, with Darren and Brian tangled in punches.

Not a single post about Justin or anything to help me find him. He must not be connected to the arcane world at all. Maybe I should have been nicer to the guy, and this whole thing could have gone another way.

"Do you have any idea how to find this guy?" I was

getting desperate. The days were already counting down, and nobody seemed to be taking it seriously.

"Look, I lied. Brian ordered me to keep quiet." Jackie placed a comforting hand on my shoulder. "But clearly, you're not going to let it go. We do care about helping people, and your research was valid. I found him, and Brian went to see Justin yesterday morning."

"How did you find him?"

"The Vault."

"What's that?"

"It's what we call our database of everything arcane. Honey, we catalog everything. There isn't a collector or auctioneer in the state that isn't in our database. It was just a matter of greasing the right palms, and we got his name and address from the storage facility manager."

I held my breath, waiting for her to continue, even though the look on her face already gave away the ending.

"He didn't want to hear it. Said he loves the game, and there's nothing that would make him part with it."

My shoulders sagged.

"So we're just letting it go?"

"As I said before, you can't help people who don't want to help themselves. So do all of us a favor and let it go, Shondra. Nothing good will come of it, and you risk pissing Brian off if you continue chasing it."

I was disappointed to hear about Justin, but I would let it go for the moment. I turned my attention to the Monique problem that we could possibly solve before Brian and Ariel returned.

"Do you think we should look for any dolls?" I asked. "Since we're still on the site?"

"Good idea." Her fingers were already dancing across the keyboard again.

My eyes started to wander as Jackie was hunting. But then they fell on the painting, and I gasped.

It really did look different today. Montague had his shoulder turned outward, and his right arm no longer at his side turned ever slightly more toward the door. His new positioning wasn't gross like the goat head, but it was definitely creepier.

"I thought you already knew about Montague?" Jackie said, noting my shock.

"I guess I can really see it now. Doesn't that bother you?"

She shook her head. "Not a bit. Old Montague has been making small movements for years now. There's nothing to worry about."

"Maybe I could search the Vault."

"Absolutely not," she said sternly. "You aren't ready for that. You may never be ready for that."

"Oh. Okay."

"I'm sorry, honey. The Vault is tricky and can be dangerous if the wrong person is poking around it. But you can help us online. If you like to do online research, I can give you some sites to get you started. "She gave me a smile, followed by a lesson, along with a few logins I could use, though Jackie kept the one for Occult Connection to herself. Then, I spent a quiet afternoon doing research.

I was supposed to follow the various message boards to find new objects for D&G, both for immediate disposal and later sale. I was also supposed to be helping Clarence document his research on the earworm and how the gramophone responded to an ever-widening array of frequencies. But I obviously hunted for dolls more than anything, and whenever I felt reasonably sure that neither Clarence nor Jackie was going to look in on me, I investigated Mansions of Madness.

It was already well after lunchtime when I could finally execute my new primary mission and retrieve Justin's address from the D&G database. I had to wait until Clarence called for help with a particularly large cluster of fungi that had colonized the wall. He'd asked for me first, but I told Jackie I wanted to practice manning the shop.

The Vault was on a 1984 Apple Macintosh Model M0001. The original. A classic. The monitor was huge, and I noticed that there weren't any ethernet cords plugged into the back, which wasn't surprising since there was no port for them. I felt confident that it wasn't connected to any Wifi.

I was in charge until Jackie returned. I opened the drawer under the computer. Were they kidding? Did they leave the password taped there? I really needed to talk to these guys about digital security.

I looked around the desk for a floppy disk or a stack of them but came up with nothing. I was sweating, worried Jackie would return any minute. I turned it on, hoping for the best. Maybe I'd be lucky enough that they would have upgraded the old beast.

A monochrome Vault graphic appeared on the screen with a blinking cursor. I typed in SHADOWGATE1987. Whoever set up the system was old school. Real old school.

"Clarence wouldn't like seeing you doing that."

I almost leaped straight out of my chair.

"Beatrice, you almost gave me a heart attack." I looked to see her staring at me. I guess she was true to her word. She was watching me.

"Did Clarence or Jackie give you permission to be in the Vault?"

"Not exactly, but this is really important. Like life or death important. There is information here that can help save someone."

"That boy Justin you've been going on about?"

"Yeah. I need to convince him to give up the game, and everyone here has given up on him."

"They know what they are doing. They have been dealing with arcane objects for a very long time."

"They're wrong this time, Beatrice. If they fire me, fine, but I couldn't live with myself if I just let him die and I didn't do something."

Beatrice said nothing for a moment, and the next, she was gone. No smoke or ectoplasm, just gone. I wasn't sure if that meant she agreed with me or if she was talking to Clarence.

I pressed enter, and there was a C drive prompt with another blinking cursor. So, there was a hard drive in this thing, but how big? One of the things Dad and I shared was our love of technology and nostalgia. There were some old computers in our basement, which Mom hated but I loved. Dad's lessons on old-school computing were one of the things we did together, and it was ours alone. Once Dad passed, removing any memories of him in the house was one of Mom's first priorities, which meant the computers were hauled off. It felt like a betrayal, and besides, those old Macs and Commodores were worth something to collectors.

I strained my memory of DOS and entered a few commands. The number for the memory size couldn't be real.

100 ZB. Did computers exist on the market with disk drives with zettabytes of information? Who are these people?

I typed a few more commands, and the screen scrolled like I had just fallen off a cliff and the mountainside was passing me by.

Too many folders. I needed to narrow my search.

"You have about five minutes."

I jumped and knocked over a pencil cup full of markers without caps. Heathens.

"Beatrice, a little warning, please."

"Sorry. I bought you about five more minutes of time, so be quick about it."

I grinned, feeling I had my first real ally here, and it didn't even bother me that she didn't have a pulse.

I wrote down both Justin's number and address, as well as another phone number I'd been thinking about grabbing, just in case. Now, I just needed an excuse to get out of the shop and follow the trail.

"Thanks, Beatrice, I owe you."

Gone again.

Instead of going home to shower and change as I'd told Jackie, I headed to Justin's neighborhood. My research had turned up a game shop, the Anti-villain, not too far from his house, which would help me with part one of my plan. Plus, nerd math said that the odds of him having been inside the place multiple times were about as great as betting on him having seen at least one season of *Doctor Who*.

I tried to sound cute once I was inside the place. "I was wondering if you guys could help me?"

But the guys were nice enough without me having to dress up. I asked them some questions about Justin, first by physically describing him and then by using his online handle when that got too awkward.

"You know," I finished, "Dragonskinner69?"

There were three geeks, giving definite The Trio from *Buffy* vibes, each answered with a varying degree of actual help. Ricky, Tommy, Robby. Why did all their names have to end in a "y"?

"That dude rules," said Ricky with no elaboration. He

was lanky and thin, with long arms and legs, his neck like a reed, and his Adam's apple like a golf ball perched on his throat.

A second nerd, Tommy, had dark circles under his pale eyes and said, "He's alright."

And the smallest nerd among the trio, Robby, who had wire-rimmed glasses and pants that were a little too short, gave me something I could actually use. "His blog is pretty cool."

"What's it called?" I asked.

"*A Gamer's Guide to the Galaxy*," replied Ricky and Tommy in unison.

"I'll check it out." And since I was already here. "Do you happen to carry the Mansions of Madness game?"

"First or second edition?" asked Robby.

"First."

"We only have the second," said Ricky.

"It's way better," added Tommy.

Robby nodded in agreement. "More monsters, better storylines. Plus, they have this badass madness crate that's super hard to get. And we carry it."

"What's that?" I asked.

He threw his buddies a look: *Ha ha, isn't she dumb?*

"It's ridiculous," Robby declared.

"That doesn't really help me." I smiled, trying not to sound like a complainer.

"The crate is *amazing*." Ricky was suddenly very excited. "I spent an entire afternoon putting it all together."

"Took me like two hours." Robby was clearly a braggart.

"Worth every second." Ricky kept going. "The Engines are so rad. Worth every cent for one of my favorite games. You should totally buy it."

"How much is it?" I asked, already scared of the answer.

"Four hundred bones," said Bobby.

"Oh." That was like four times more than I was expecting. But if buying this game would help me to save a life and keep my dream job, then the expense would surely be worth it, eventually. "I guess I'll take it."

Chapter Nineteen

"I DON'T UNDERSTAND WHY WE CAN'T JUST GO TO A movie," Mom said.

I should never have stopped home. "Because I'm working."

"Delivering junk to someone's house."

"I'm not delivering junk. This game cost $400." Not that she needed to know where that $400 came from.

"Oh my." Mom touched her cheek like the news cameras were rolling on her right now. "Isn't it used?"

"You act like you're too good for a daughter who works at Goodwill."

"You act like your dropping out of college is helping you to achieve some sort of personal growth." She couldn't help but add, "And you're also acting like you don't work in a thrift store!"

She felt bad after that. So did I. We made it up to each other by making everything worse. I still couldn't agree to go to the movie, not with so much on my mind — all the crazy haunted objects, the ghost phone and my missing clump of hair, that house last night, with Dad's ghost or my mocking imagination, Kip thinking he's better than everyone, Ariel only barely tolerating me, no matter how hard I tried.

So, Mom took me on my errands instead.

She drove me to Justin's house first. I knew it was a mistake when we pulled up, thanks to the cinder blocks on my boots in the middle of a river feeling that settled into my stomach as Mom's Mercedes kissed the curb.

Something was off. A faint echo of the arcane that I was beginning to recognize. Like learning a new language and hearing it in the wild for the very first time.

I hauled the crate up to the front door, refusing Mom's help. It wasn't that heavy, and I didn't feel like looking ridiculous. I didn't even want her to get out of the car, but she insisted that it was important to support me in my new career in a tone that sounded mostly like derision.

Justin opened the door before I could knock, and I saw that my mission had already failed.

"Go away." He looked … different than before.

"I brought you a present."

"I don't want a present. I don't want anything from you." His eyes were wild and unfocused, his face gnarled into a scowl. He shivered in the doorway, his hair matted and disheveled … and growing down his face?

That seriously had to be my imagination.

"It's the special crate from Mansions of Madness, second edition."

"How did you find this place?" Justin radiated an aura of angry belligerence.

Mom stirred beside me, clearly uncomfortable and suddenly impatient.

Justin said, "This is my place. You don't belong here."

Mom touched my arm. "Maybe we should go."

"Maybe you should," Justin agreed, leaning forward so

I could smell his reeking breath, hot and rancid, laden with the sharp tang of bile. "How would you like it if I just showed up at your house?"

Looking and smelling like that? I would hate it.

"Shondra. We should go."

"I've got this, Mom."

"That's your mother? Why did you bring your mom to my house? You're here to take my MoM, aren't you?"

Mom was confused. "What's he talking about?"

"No, not at all. This is mother-daughter time," I explained to Justin, feeling as dumb as I sounded. "I wanted to bring you this crate."

Justin finally registered my gift. He glanced down at the crate, then back up at me. I felt a bloom of hope.

But he ripped the petal away. "It's the second edition. You know how I feel about the second edition!"

His accusing voice was a lashing whip. Why was he getting so worked up?

Mom squeezed my arm. "We need to go!"

I shrugged her away from me. "*You* need to go." I glared at her, gritting my teeth like a little girl. "I'll meet you at the car in a minute. I have a job to do."

"My MoM isn't for sale or trade," Justin snapped.

"Shondra, what is going on here? Are you trying to buy his mom?"

"No, mom. Just go to the car," I pleaded.

"Are you going to steal my MoM if I won't give it to you?"

"Shondra, I can't be involved in a kidnapping!" Mom said. "Is the thrift store just a front for some sort of slavery ring? I did a piece on a slavery ring not long ago."

"Mom, just stop. He's talking about a game. This game," I pointed at the crate. "It's called Mansions of Madness. M.O.M."

"Oh. Why didn't you just say so?" Mom asked. "Wait, are you going to steal his game?"

"Mom. Enough already. Nobody is stealing anything. I'll explain it all later. Please, go to the car."

Mom surrendered, turning around and walking back to the car in a perfect stride without another word, though I could feel her worry for me.

I looked back at Justin, straightening my shoulders and looking him in the eyes as I prepared to do what I came here to do.

"You too," Justin said.

It was hard to stand in the heat of his fury. Something was so energetically *off* about him beyond the reek and his furious scowl.

"I'm trying to save your life."

He laughed at me.

"You're going to die in six days unless you—"

"Are you threatening me?"

"I just said that I was trying to save your life! What the hell is your problem?"

Judging by the look of him, Justin was suffering from an untold number of problems. And right now, he clearly saw me as one of them.

"10, 9, 8…" He started counting, and I could see in his eyes that he would kill me if I didn't back down right now and walk away. "7, 6, 5…"

I couldn't surrender, but his eyes were filled with a seething rage, glinting with a willingness to destroy me.

"4, 3, 2…"

I felt suddenly small and vulnerable. In another second, even Mom wouldn't be able to help me.

"This isn't over!" I shouted, dragging my new $400 Mansions of Madness crate toward Mom's Mercedes.

"You have a very interesting job," she said as I

slammed the car door. "But I'm concerned about you stealing. If you just finished college, you'd have a good job and wouldn't need to resort to a life of crime."

"Can we just go?"

"Where to next, my little overachiever?"

I gave her Monique's address. Things couldn't possibly go as poorly there as they had at Justin's.

I had even more to prove now, and as she pulled up to the house, I finally acknowledged the truth. Even if I was loath to admit it, Mom's star power could really help me out here. Monique seemed like the kind of woman who would love a local celebrity.

"Do you want to come with me?" I asked when I could tell that she was going to leave the engine running.

"Oh." Mom was always so dramatic. "Am I allowed? Should I call my lawyer first to make sure he can bail me out of jail for being your accomplice?"

"If you want to come, then come. I don't want to play any of your games tonight."

I got out of the car, knowing she would follow me.

Lord have mercy. She did.

Monique opened the door and looked right through me. "Is that Joanna Henry I see on my front porch! It can't be!"

"Hi, Monique." I smiled. "I'd like you to meet my mom."

"Joanna Henry is your mom?"

This was already working.

"Would you like to come in?" Monique beamed at us. "I have eleven kinds of tea."

"Yes, please," Mom answered for us. "That would be lovely."

Monique was enough to inspire some genuine curiosity in my mother.

"What kind of tea would you like?" Monique said once we were all congregated in her small foyer.

"What are our choices?" Mom asked, even though she had been standing right next to me when Monique told us there were *eleven* kinds.

Monique rattled off choices like they were burning her throat. "Earl Grey, oolong, jasmine, green, white, black, and yellow teas, plus rooibos, peppermint, and a few herbal infusions."

Mom smiled. "Peppermint, please."

"And you, dear?" Monique said.

I bet she didn't even remember my name, though now, at least, she knew the last one for sure. I barely liked tea but felt obligated to play along.

"Oolong for me, please." I smiled, just like my mom.

"I'll put the kettle on, then I can show you girls what we've been up to!"

Mom tried to ask me what that meant once Monique left for the kitchen, but I shushed her because even if the lady of the house was no longer in earshot, one of her dolls might still be.

But Mom found out soon enough, and I was already spinning explanations in my head. Or I would have been if any came to me.

"It's a senate debate," Monique only sort of explained, articulating why the dolls were arranged in their room-sized diorama with a suite of miniature props.

I looked back toward the front door, longing to be on the other side, abhorring the conversation I would soon be having with Mom.

I seriously considered suggesting that Monique get a cat. Being a crazy cat lady had to be better than being a crazy doll lady at least ninety percent of the time.

Mom was about to burst with all of the questions inside her, but she somehow managed to keep them inside.

"You have quite a lovely collection," she said.

"*Family*," Monique corrected her with the cheeriest smile. "Radisson over there is playing Speaker of the House today, but she's been with me since the Clinton years!"

Monique laughed for a surprisingly long time.

Mom finally started laughing along with her, for entirely different reasons.

Then I was joining them, though there was a hysterical quality to the sound, a little too fast and grating. The mood wasn't about to get more buoyant than this.

"I'm really sorry, Monique, about what happened before. D&G really should have checked with you first instead of doing what we did to … you know. We were only trying to keep you safe. I would really love it if there was a way I could make it up to you."

"I've always wanted Robert the Doll."

"Robert the Doll?" Mom repeated.

I had done enough doll research to know all about Robert, one of the most famous supposedly cursed dolls in existence, dating back to the early 20th century when it was given to a young boy named Robert Eugene Otto, living in Key West, Florida. Robert was apparently possessed by a dark spirit and often blamed for mischief and odd events in the Otto household, including the death of the family's maid. The doll still lives in Key West, now as a museum piece.

"I'll explain later," I told Mom, then turned to Monique. "Getting Robert the Doll is impossible. He's in a museum."

"I know where he is!" Monique barked at me.

"Who or what is Robert the Doll?" Mom asked.

"Robert was made more than a century ago by an artist named Robert Eugene Otto. He's been haunted pretty much ever since," reported Monique.

"Haunted?" Mom repeated, incredulous.

"All of my dolls are haunted," Monique said, in a tone like *water is wet* or *fire is hot.*

"Oh," Mom replied, almost to herself. "You're crazy."

Monique ordered us out of her house, me for the second time in just a couple of days. I was an ace at making everything worse.

"I can't believe this shit," Mom muttered on her way to the Mercedes. "I think it's time for you to quit the thrift store for the criminally insane."

I didn't respond.

And neither of us spoke the entire way home.

Chapter Twenty

MOM THOUGHT EVERYTHING WOULD BE BETTER IF WE HAD dinner together. I stayed stoic and polite, complimenting her baked chicken and rice multiple times, smiling with delight, and using all of my manners.

"You can knock that off," she said.

I suggested that we watch *The Day at Night*, the news show that made her locally famous and had given her an unfortunate (for Mom) day off.

I heckled the reporter sitting in her usual seat. "You suck, Becky!"

Mom laughed, so I kept going.

"You should stop trying and go back to school."

Another laugh.

"I don't want to be a hater, but you suck hard and also smell bad."

Now, her laughter sounded polite.

So I tried too hard. "Hey, Becky, why don't you go back to the kitchen and make me a sandwich?"

Mom shook her head. "Not that one."

I hung mine. "Sorry."

"I wish days off of work weren't mandatory," said Mom.

"That would be great if you could work every day. Everyone else is total shit except for you."

"We can be done now." But Mom was smiling.

I left her on the couch and went up to my room, finally able to make the call I'd been wanting to make ever since sneaking that extra number from the Darrow & Grimes directory.

"Who is this?" Kip said.

"It's Shondra. From Darrow & Grimes."

I had to stop talking because he was laughing. At first, it sounded genuine, even if that hurt, but then it was clearly over the top and intended to hurt me.

"Will you please stop laughing?"

"I'm laughing with you," he said.

"Does it sound like I'm laughing?"

"You would be if you knew what I was thinking." He laughed again, a barely there rattle this time. "What do you want? Or is it okay for me to hang up now?"

"I have an idea."

"Did it hurt?"

"An idea that will make you look like a rock star in front of your boss."

"I'm not sure that rock stars really exist anymore," Kip said. "Can you name the last one?"

"Do you want to hear my idea or not?"

A mild chuckle. "Sure. I already paused my episode of *Warehouse 13*."

"I love that show," I said. Maybe I'd misjudged him.

"I wasn't really watching it."

Apparently, Kip couldn't say anything without making me feel stupid.

"Last chance. But you can't be an asshole. I have a

great idea, and you're going to thank me for it. Do you want to hear it or not?"

"Go on." Just two syllables, but there was more meaning and intention in them than anything I'd heard from Kip on the call so far.

* * *

Three hours later, Mom was asleep, and I was standing outside of Justin's house watching as Kip jogged up to join me.

"So," he said, "explain to me again how breaking and entering is a win-win for both of us?"

"The haunted first edition of Monsters of Madness is in that house as promised. We just need to get the game. Then you can take it back to Nemicon and be a big hero."

"I get what's in it for me. I want to understand the second win in this win-win scenario."

"I'm just trying to save that guy's life."

"Who is that guy to you?"

"Does he need to be anyone? The game is cursed, and there are only six days left. He's going to die, same as every other owner before him."

"That still doesn't explain why you're giving the game to me."

"Because I'm hoping Nemicon's clients will have ways of containing it."

"Darrow & Grimes has ways of containing it."

"I can't ask anyone at D&G. They are seriously content to let this guy die, and they've already specifically told me not to pursue this."

Kip grinned at me. "So you're a rule breaker?"

"Only sometimes. Are you in or out?"

"I *am* standing here past my bedtime."

"You're a big boy," I said. "You should consider staying up later."

We sneaked into the house together, Kip leading the way as if he broke into places all the time, going straight to the darkest part of the home and working a few windows until one flew up with barely any effort.

Kip helped me to climb inside.

He followed me into the bathroom, then down the hall and into the kitchen. Justin lived in a perfectly normal house, but given the circumstances, his place still felt creepy. Quiet, the rooms shadowy and dark, the atmosphere thick with escalating tension and unease behind all those drawn curtains.

Kip's breathing sounded heavy beside me.

"Are you okay?" I asked.

"I'm fine. You?"

My throat was too dry for an answer. Faint light bleeding out from under the basement door cast an eerie glow across the hallway, the darkness broken only by a rhythmic ticking from an old clock on the wall.

"I'm fine," I whispered. "Where do you think he would keep the game?"

"Down there," Kip whispered back, pointing to the closed basement door. "Are you ready?"

No. But I nodded. I could feel the dark energy seeping up through the floorboards and every crevice in the house. Dread clawed my brain. The feeling was much stronger than it had been when I first encountered Mansions of Madness at the auction. There was a hunger tainting the air that made me feel as if I was in the mouth of some large starving wolf.

Kip took a step, then another, and suddenly, there was a loud *snap* from under his foot that might as well have been an explosion, detonating the silence.

I pitched forward, startled.

Kip tried to stop me from falling, but I dragged him

down on top of me when I went crashing to the ground. Our noses touched, and we were eye to eye.

Oh, no, no, no, Mr. Kip. I'm not going to be drawn into those eyes.

I pushed Kip off, and pain brought me to my senses. Even without the lights on, I could easily do the math. The floor was littered with mousetraps, their metal jaws snapping shut as we moved and rolled.

Darkness closed in around us, and so did the agony. Everywhere on my body, and surely Kip's. There was a long and pregnant moment where I could hear our hearts beating, and I could almost smell what was about to happen before the lights flicked on to prove me right.

An older lady was looking down at us.

She smiled wide, enjoying the sight of us caught in her literal trap. Or her son's. "Justin! You caught something!"

A cacophony came loudly from down in the basement.

I jumped to my feet, and so did Kip, more mousetraps snapping shut on our skin as we scrambled out of there. The woman was cackling like a mad witch stirring her cauldron.

We raced toward the front door amid the sound of Justin thundering up the stairs.

He appeared like a demon from nowhere, exploding out of the basement, blocking our way until Kip grabbed me by the wrist and yanked me around him.

I had to ignore what I saw. It was too much to consider the reality while running into the night, clutching hands and trying our best not to lose each other.

We sprinted four blocks without stopping.

Even after we finally did, I could barely catch my breath.

And only then could I think back to that flash of Justin and truly wonder: had his ears really become pointed?

Chapter Twenty-One

"WHAT THE HOLY SHIT WAS THAT?" KIP FINALLY ASKED.

"Attack by mousetrap?" I offered.

"I don't even mean that. I mean ... did you see him?"

"Yeah, I saw him." Though I really wished that Kip hadn't asked me.

"Win-win, my ass."

"I'm sorry."

"I'm sure you are."

"What do we do now?" I asked.

"You're telling me there's no contingency plan for getting chased by a dark elf?"

"I don't think he's a dark elf."

"Of course, he isn't a dark elf!" Kip snapped at me, too loud in the otherwise silent night. "Dark elves don't exist! But what the hell was that?"

"A guy named Justin. At least, I think it was Justin."

It wasn't just his ears. His hair was stringy and looked like patches of it were missing. His skin was pale, almost a blue-gray color. It had deep lines in it, like he had aged fifty years since I had seen him earlier in the day. The curse must be acting quicker than I thought. What would he look like in a few more days?

We were in over our heads. I had been so stupid to think after just a few days of hanging with experienced arcane object experts that I'd be ready to go at it alone. Kip was as green as I was, and so he was just as freaked out.

"I think we should go to D&G. We need help," I offered.

"You work there, so have fun. Why would I want to go?"

"Because I think those mousetraps might have been haunted, and Clarence can help us if that's the case."

The mousetraps bit us like mouse-eating piranhas and wouldn't let go of our skin until we had made it out of the house. Not natural.

Kip sighed, but he didn't argue.

We each walked back to our own cars — parked a block away from Justin's house but in opposite directions — then agreed to meet back at the shop.

It took us less time to get there than for Clarence to finally open the door after the two of us stood outside, banging like the pedal on a bass drum.

"Do you know what time it is?" Clarence asked when he finally answered.

"I think we might have a haunting." I showed him one of the mousetraps, its metal clamp still bloody from where it had bitten into my skin.

"Consider rephrasing that," Clarence said.

"I think there might be something abnormal about these mousetraps, and I'm sure that your knowledge of science and wizardry with its application will be the solution."

Clarence opened the door and impatiently gestured us both inside.

I was going to be in *so much trouble*, but at least no one else besides Clarence was around. Beatrice made a quick appearance in the corner for my benefit, arms crossed and shaking her head with disapproval.

"Why is he here?" He nodded at Kip. "You scared, too?"

Kip shook his head. "Not at all."

Clarence told us to wait right there. This time, I didn't comment when Kip's eyes turned to his father's painting above the counter. He had moved another small fraction since the last time I'd looked.

Clarence returned from the lab a few moments later with some sort of Geiger- counter-looking device (no dangly bits on this one). He ran the device across both of our bodies before doing the same thing to our actual injuries with yet another device, then finally declaring, "Congratulations, you were both dumb enough to get bitten by a bunch of mousetraps."

"They're not — violating science?"

"You want to create hybrids of two different species through genetic engineering? *That's* violating science. What we have here is a failure to understand the basics of energy."

"I understand the basics," I argued.

Kip looked like he was biting his tongue.

Clarence glanced at one of the mice traps in admiration. "Victor m156 Metal Pedal Sustainably Sourced FSC Wood Snap Mouse Trap. Doesn't get more classic than that. A simple, straightforward design for a clean, instant kill. Made from FSC Certified Wood, harvested from responsibly managed forests."

"You sure know a lot about mousetraps," I observed.

"Do you own stock in that company?" asked Kip.

"I know about a lot of things. Now, how did this all start?"

Kip and I jockeyed for control of the reply, talking loudly and over each other.

Me: "Kip didn't look where he was going and stepped on a mousetrap, and then he pushed me, and I fell into a bunch of mousetraps right as the lights came on, and this vintage grandma was looking at me like she was trying to burn my body with her eyes, and she yelled for her son, and then her son tried to chase us."

Kip: "Shondra calls me up out of nowhere tonight, acting all cloak and dagger. I asked her for more information, and she said she would 'give it to me when I got there.' But the only thing she said is that we were supposed to break into this guy's house, a guy I never met, and steal his Mansions of Madness game."

Clarence eyed us both as we finished.

I knew that this was all my fault. Again. I just couldn't bear to think about that, and it felt so much better to blame the situation on Kip.

"So this is all about the game you were specifically told to ignore?" Clarence tried to clarify.

"I was trying to help."

"There is never a shortage of things to do around here. I suggest the next time you're looking to lend a hand, you try and find something that needs doing."

"Like saving a guy's life?" I exclaimed.

"We're in the business of saving those who want to be saved."

"How do you know he doesn't want to be saved? Maybe it's just the game forcing him to refuse our help."

"Did he look like he wanted to be saved when he was chasing you out of his house?" Clarence asked.

Kip shook his head. "He did not."

Fuck you, Kip. I was so onto him. "He's up to something."

"Yes, that is why you brought me here. Because I'm up to something."

"I say we use the earworm and see what he knows," I suggested.

Clarence raised his eyebrows, looking into my eyes to see if I was kidding.

"That's a bit too far." He shook his head. "And not what we do here."

I already felt bad as the words were leaving my mouth, Clarence's tone made me feel worse, and seeing Kip looking over at the painting of his father stuck in a saloon and only able to move millimeters in months, I felt like the jerk I probably was. Why was I acting like this? Sure, Kip was annoying and cute, which was even more annoying, but why would I suggest torture?

"I reckon the two of you should just stay here and wait for Brian to sort all of this out until morning."

"Sort what out?" Kip said. "I don't want to sleep here. I don't *have* to sleep here."

"Then I don't want to sleep here either."

Kip shook his head. "I should never have followed you."

"It's late, and there are empty beds just a few feet behind me. You're both tired, and I'm sure you'll fall asleep before you even—"

"Fine." Kip was already walking past Clarence on his way to the lab like he knew the place inside out and had every right to be there.

Like he should have my job.

Clarence moved Gnomey, so he wasn't looking at any one of us while we slept. The big new crack in the plaster on the wall prevented him from pointing in that direction again. Then he told Kip not to ask him any questions; his slumber had been interrupted, and if there was anything either of us wanted to know about the garden gnome, he would be happy to answer them in the morning.

I fell asleep fast, just as Clarence predicted, but I was only down for an hour or so before I was suddenly wide awake, worried and upset, feeling even more awful about myself than usual.

I was in a dark room, curled into a ball, with tears streaming down my face, thinking about my dad again. The vacuum of his absence was too much for me, the weight of something so empty nearly unbearable.

Memories came in a wave, too many precious moments shared threatening to drown me. Knowing Dad was gone from my life forever was a dull ache, I wished there was some way to bring him back and be whole again while feeling so alone in that room with the three of us.

I would have given anything to hear his voice again.

I rolled over and saw a soft glow, the light from Beatrice's form coming from the shop into the lab. Clarence said she'd been keeping watch after what happened with the goat head, but it looked like someone was dragging a night light across the floor.

I peeled back my covers just a second after considering the ghost phone, and my heart was pounding as I bounded up to it.

I only hesitated for a beat once inches from touching it, remembering my hair and wanting to touch the bald spot.

But I have plenty of hair, and whatever I lost could grow back. I needed my father's voice to make me whole again.

I sat in Clarence's chair and lifted the receiver, thinking about Dad harder and more on purpose than at any other time since he died. I thought about him like I had a job to do. Grief-stricken and overwhelmed, fixated on the memories as they came at me, staring them down without blinking despite the pain because if that would bring him to the other side of this line, then every second of agony would be worth it.

"Hello?" I said several times before my voice turned more demanding. "Hello?"

"Hello," came a cracking voice in reply several times because I guess it couldn't hear me yelling back until it finally whispered, "It's coming."

But the line didn't go dead.

There was a terrible shrieking and screaming in my ears until I hung up the phone, slamming it down like I had a grudge against the base.

It was then I realized the price of that call.

This time, it wasn't my hair.

I was frozen in place, unable to budge so much as an inch from my spot.

Gnomey was directly across from me.

And he was staring at ME.

Chapter Twenty-Two

I WAS AWAKE FOR MAYBE TWO SECONDS BEFORE I SAW Beatrice, her ghostly face hovering in front of me.

I realized she was holding my hand, though I don't know why I didn't notice it immediately — her skin was like a block of ice. I was surrounded by the gang at Darrow & Grimes, with Kip added to the mix for max humiliation.

Beatrice vanished, but everyone else was still there.

My forehead felt like it was already split down the middle, about to crack wide open. Clarence was scanning me with yet another device, this one with a long and purple nozzle that felt like it was giving me a dirty look.

"She's clean," he said to everyone before turning to me with the identical message. "You're clean."

"Thank you?" I was tempted to smell myself.

"Nothing attached itself to you in the night," Clarence explained. "But that doesn't mean that there isn't internal damage."

"From Gnomey," Brian added like I hadn't understood.

Brian and Clarence started talking, but I was already

tuned out, trying to rewind to the last thing I could remember before it was lights out in front of Gnomey.

The sudden paralysis. My heavy and unresponsive body was struck by a numbing cold. A wall of apprehension and dread I couldn't get over or under.

The knowing of something lurking in the darkness, waiting to pounce on me.

At least I could finally move again. I lifted a hand and rubbed on a patch of something wet that had been irritating me throughout the few seconds of my recent awareness.

Blood. Dripping from my nose and down the front of my sweater.

I noticed Clarence and Brian's tone for the first time.

The scowls I'd seen on their faces as they came into focus were finally registering for me.

Everyone was pissed.

I didn't know why, but of course, it had to be about me.

Brian and Clarence stopped talking and turned to Ariel in unison. She looked like she was trying not to shake her head at me.

The tension was sharper than a shard of glass against my skin, and I was stirring up enough courage to interrupt by asking what I had done to make everyone so mad. But I never got the chance.

A sudden commotion out front split the moment and scattered the group.

Everyone started walking toward the shop, except Ariel, lagging behind to hand me a wet rag.

"Here." Then she followed the gang to the front of Darrow & Grimes.

Beatrice reappeared, nodding sadly at the ghost phone. "I warned you!" she wailed, seeming to take my indiscretion as a personal affront.

I ignored the apparition while cleaning myself with the rag, in a hurry to finish so I could see what all the ruckus was about.

I finally stumbled out to the front of the shop to find the place packed to the rafters with middle-aged women, many of them yelling.

One woman — I could practically smell her hairspray and perfume from where I was standing — waved a flyer in the air and bellowed at Jackie. "There's supposed to be a book signing with MC Beaton!"

"Does she mean the woman who wrote the Agatha Raisin series?" I whispered.

"Mmm hmm," replied Jackie.

"I'm pretty sure she died a few years ago."

"Mmm hmm ."

I scanned the shop, "Is she…here?"

Having the ghost of MC Beaton would be cool, no doubt, but the idea of one more entity watching me creeped me out a bit.

"Nope."

"Then why do they think she's here to sign books?"

"Don't be daft, girl." Hairspray Lady must have overheard me. "Every true fan knows she isn't dead. That's what *they* want you to think. We have known for years that her death was staged."

I was about to ask who *they* were, but Jackie's frown and head shaking made me reconsider.

"And we were promised pies!" roared a woman who was surely over six feet, her sweater fashionable but much too small for her broad shoulders.

"And half-price antiques!" added a woman with her hair in a tight bun, wearing a floral blouse and a long skirt that looked like it might have been hemmed an inch per year for a decade.

"What's happening?" I dared to ask Clarence, still standing at the periphery, using the wall to hold me upright and letting everyone else take care of the chaos. "What can I do to help?"

"If you can make yourself invisible, do that." Clarence went back to watching the show.

Jackie loudly declared that everyone was welcome to free fudge for as long as it lasted and that all inventory in the shop would be seventy percent off for the next three hours.

The shelves were all bare by the time D&G was empty again, but the customers all left happy, and happy customers led to a thriving business.

"Not at seventy percent off," Brian strongly argued.

He was right. About that and everything else, now and for the rest of time. I would agree with anything. I just couldn't take how furious he was with me.

Brian had given me a chance even if I was only his second choice, and he might have hired me for the wrong reasons. But now he couldn't even look at me.

"I'm really, really, really sorry."

He shook his head. "Saying it three times doesn't make it better. It's not like rubbing a magic lamp."

"No such thing as a magic lamp," Clarence huffed. "No such thing as magic."

"This is definitely not my fault." I waved a hand around the pillaged shop.

"No, the ad placed that drove those women in is clearly not your fault. But everything else you *chose to do* is."

"I didn't mean to touch the ghost phone." Though, of course, I had *meant* to. "I should never have done that."

"Did you mean to break and enter? Should you have done that?" Brian retorted. "Touching the ghost phone was just icing on the cake."

"But you broke into that haunted house!" I argued. "We all did! Aren't we supposed to do stuff like that if we're trying to save people? I was only—"

"Jackie set up the de-haunting, Shondra. We didn't just have permission to be there; we were at that house by invitation. We were supposed to go in and clear the place for the realtor who was trying to sell the place. A house with an angry haunt isn't easy to sell. The owners didn't know about our involvement but were delighted to no longer live with a poltergeist."

"Please don't fire me!"

"I should fire you, Shondra!" He looked seriously pained. "Lone wolfing it like that will only get us all hurt or killed. This is a hard enough job with everyone following the rules. I hate to say it, but I really don't think you can be trusted."

"Of course, I can be trusted!" I was protesting, but based on what? I had shown exactly the opposite. "I'll prove it to you. I just need you to give me a chance."

"I have given you a chance, Shondra."

He kept using my name. So he was for sure going to fire me.

"I think I need to let you go."

"You *think*?" I repeated the word but filled my voice with hope as I said it.

"Give the girl a chance!" Beatrice appeared out of nowhere, standing in between Clarence and Brian. "There's something to this one."

She nodded firmly as if her word was beyond question.

"I'm sorry." Brian shook his head. "I can't keep her."

"I agree with Beatrice." Clarence surprised me by coming to my defense. "There is something to her. Scientifically speaking."

So, now I had two possible allies. There was hope yet.

"Fine." Brian looked relieved that someone had made the choice for him. "I do enjoy her enthusiasm." He kept talking about me like I wasn't even there. "And she does remind me of myself, once upon a time."

"Because she's had plenty of chances?" Clarence said.

Brian ignored the silent jab at nepotism but agreed to keep me on. For the time being. Assuming I didn't cause any more problems.

I couldn't tell if Ariel looked happy about the news or not.

"I will need to stick you with some of the grunt work for a bit," Brian informed me. "It's only fair."

Ariel smiled.

"Cool," I said, happy to still have a job. "Should I help Jackie clean up out front?"

"I'm sending you to another auction," Brian replied.

I was living to be around the arcane stuff, dangerous as it was, and it felt like there were answers inside some of the mysteries. A link connecting me to Uncle Kevin and my father. So yes, that sounded great to me.

"Just point me toward the haunted objects."

"No," Ariel interjected.

"No haunted objects," Brian clarified. "Just a regular auction to restock the shop." He gestured around at the empty shelves again. "Those Agatha Raisin ladies cleaned us out."

Chapter Twenty-Three

BUYING CRAP WAS ONLY FUN IF IT CAME WITH AT LEAST A remote possibility of the crap being haunted.

But Brian sent me on a mission to "fill the shelves like stupid fast," so I was on parade from one storage auction to another, attending each of them alone.

I supposed mindless work would be better than obsessing over the situation with Justin. Sure, he looked like a deranged elf and had set a trap ... correction ... *traps* for us, but I still thought he was redeemable. The curse was twisting him, but I was stumped about what to do short of swatting him and telling the dispatcher that the weapons and drugs were inside the Mansions of Madness box.

And they were all so *boring*. The bidders arrived early to stake out their spot, and an auctioneer arrived and set up his podium and mic. Bidding wars erupted between strangers and rivals, competition got fiercer and fiercer until people were bidding on items they had no use for, simply for the sake of winning the battle.

There was a lone hint of excitement at the second auction when the auctioneer announced that he would be bringing out a few "secret items," but it turned out that secrets weren't loudly declared in front of a crowd and that the reveal of a vase that was over two centuries old was a lot less impressive when the owner had superglued it back together.

"Welcome to the storage auction for Unit 23!" And so started my fourth auction that day. "We will start the bidding at a dollar. Do I hear seventy-five dollars? Yes? No? One hundred dollars?"

This one promised to be just as boring as the first two. Jackie had checked and cleared every location before sending me in to represent D&G, so there wasn't even a remote chance of finding something haunted here.

And as much as I did want to work at Darrow & Grimes, old crap didn't excite me so much as old crap with ghoulish potential. Everything felt more like labor and a lot less fun when everyone was mad at me.

But I bid on what I knew would make Brian happy, the same as I had at the first three auctions, and ended a long-ass day with two units full of crap.

This second one was much better than the first.

I carefully cataloged everything before loading it all into the D&G truck. I would be returning to Darrow & Grimes with a lot of junk and a handful of treasures.

There was definitely some trash to get rid of, but I was sure that Brian and Jackie would both be thrilled with my haul. Ariel would still roll her eyes at me, and Clarence would care about as much as I did.

I separated everything that wasn't already boxed up into three categories: potentially valuable, interesting, and why would anyone pay to store this?

In the potentially valuable category, we had a set of pearls, a Peugeot bicycle, a finely crafted rocking chair, an antique sewing machine, a box of cufflinks, a porcelain vase with a hairline crack, an old statue, a suit of armor from Peter Jackson's *Lord of the Rings* (I think), a set of 1920s dinnerware, a box of china with a picture of the *Titanic* in black and white on the lid, and an oil painting of what appeared to be a married couple, ready to murder each other.

In the interesting department, I was bringing back a box of antique buttons, a full tank of helium (maybe that was valuable?), a collection of Victorian pornography, a second rocking chair (with a broken back, but it could probably be fixed), a trunk full of letters, a wooden toy boat, a box of black-and-white photographs (the people were all really ugly, and I felt terrible for thinking so), plus a big box of assorted baseball cards from the 80s in rubber-banded stacks with some Garbage Pail Kids mixed in.

The old letters and pictures might need to be thrown away, but I didn't want to assume. I was sure that Victorian pornography would have value, maybe even an uncomfortable amount, but I didn't understand why anyone would pay to store a book on how to make bumper stickers or a pair of stuffed animals that looked made out of melted crayons when they weren't even haunted.

The pictures and letters got me thinking about Dad again, not that it took much to stir those memories. They seemed to be right on the surface these days. But then that put me on a path to considering my life over the last few months and my steady downward spiral.

I had gone from dropping out of college to clearing out people's old junk.

Maybe Mom, Rashida, and Malik were right. Maybe this was stupid, and I was literally chasing ghosts. Maybe the best thing I could possibly do for myself would be to go back to school and finally get on with my life.

Like Mom kept saying, I could end up like Uncle Kevin if I wasn't careful.

Of course, I didn't want that for myself, even if I didn't actually know what happened to Uncle Kevin in the first place.

I sighed, taking another fleeting glance at all the junk before closing the back of the truck.

But then I stopped. Swallowed. Clenched and unclenched my fists without meaning to. Felt a tickle inside my nostrils as a familiar scent lifted me onto my tiptoes before I was suddenly paralyzed again, frozen as the memory fixed itself onto me.

The scent of my father's aftershave.

I swallowed again and climbed into the truck, following the scent to a box in the corner. I opened it up, and the aroma bowled me over before dissipating into a reek of musty dust.

I blinked, barely able to believe my eyes.

I was staring down at an exact replica of Robert the Doll. Large and crude, chipped paint and stitches visible along its seams.

Its vacant eyes seemed to follow my movements.

It couldn't possibly be the real Robert, but I took out my phone and checked anyway, looking to see it even though I had just recently been reading about the real thing. Sure enough, he was still safe and sound at his Florida museum. And people were still posting *SORRY ROBERT* every few hours on his Facebook profile, hoping to break the curse they believed he'd put on the world at large.

This Robert the Doll was fake, but that didn't mean it was entirely useless.

And if I wanted to do something with it, now was the time. Before I took the haul back to Darrow & Grimes.

I couldn't ignore the coincidence. Monique said that Robert the Doll was the one way for me to get square with her, but I had considered that request an impossible feat. Maybe one Robert was as good as another. He could still join Monique's family as one of her babies, and she could still dress him up as Othello or whatever.

I had to wonder if Dad had led me to that box in my hour of need. Was I really just supposed to ignore a sign like that? Of course not.

So I took Robert the Doll out of the box, carefully, because my heart was beating fast and a replica might still somehow be able to hurt me. I closed the box and set the doll beside my bag. Looked at it for a long minute before taking a deep breath and closing the truck.

My interest in the plan was already dimming. Monique wasn't dumb. She wouldn't believe that I had Robert the Doll and might be insulted by my trying. Maybe there was no point in pretending unless I wanted to piss her off even more than she already was.

"What do you think, Dad?"

There was obviously no answer, but I knew what to do as I climbed into the truck and then considered my plan on the drive back to D&G.

Maybe I was overthinking this.

Maybe Monique really was gullible.

Maybe it would be easy to convince her that I had Robert the Doll because that was what she most wanted to believe.

Monique would be looking for reasons that her greatest wish had come true.

I was still unsure by the time I got back to the shop, and Dad still hadn't supplied any answers, but I tried to put it all out of my mind as I parked, still trying as I started unloading.

"I'm glad you're back." Jackie didn't sound especially glad. "How was it?"

I tried to make my day sound more interesting than it had been, but my efforts weren't necessary. Jackie was barely listening, obviously still mad at me, just like everyone else.

We unloaded the truck in silence.

"Can I help with anything else?" I asked when we finished.

"I'm good." Her smile looked tired. "See you tomorrow."

"See you tomorrow," I repeated, feeling rejected but doing my best not to show it.

I drove home, feeling low and tired of messing up in front of everyone all the time.

I made it to my bedroom without Mom making me feel bad about anything, so that was a modest victory.

I rode the glory while falling asleep, giving myself a pep talk by repeating the mantra, "Everything will be okay … everything will be okay…"

In and out, the thought along with my breath.

I had messed up too many times.

But I could do better. And I would. If the gang was really done with me, then I would already be gone.

Beatrice and Clarence still wanted me around, and that was something for sure.

It was time to give this my all. Time to make this work. Even if I had to buy boring units for weeks, I was determined to work my way back to the arcana that fascinated me.

I fell asleep with the ghost of a smile.

But a few hours later, I woke up screaming, with live mice skittering all over my body.

Chapter Twenty-Four

I WOKE UP EXHAUSTED, MY EYES HEAVY AND SCRATCHY, MY limbs leaden. It felt like I had been running nonstop for days, but in reality, I was on fumes because two nights ago, I'd helped de-haunt a house, the night before last had been spent in the direct eye line of Gnomey, and last night had me trapping mice.

I could still feel them all over my body. Little dark bodies wriggling and squirming as they darted over my arms and legs. Tiny claws scratching at my skin, leaving a trail of red welts that hadn't stopped stinging even hours later as I waited for the exterminator to finally arrive.

I needed him to get rid of any mice that might have escaped my bedroom — Mom would have seven strains of shit fit if she found any critters on the loose.

"The traps are all set and baited, ma'am."

"And none of them are in sight?"

"I didn't see any mice, and all the traps are hidden away, just like you asked, ma'am."

The exterminator smiled at me, even though I had asked him the same question four different times now.

I smiled back. "Thank you."

But I felt uneasy about everything.

I drove to work in silence, considering my entire situation.

It had been six days since Justin made the mistake of bidding on the lot with Mansions of Madness. Only four more days until his demise.

Adding to my stress was trying to figure out where the mice had come from. Were they even real? Or was I losing my mind? The exterminator had been just a little too patient with me.

The bites and scratches on both of my arms said they were real. Maybe the mice had come from a haunted object. Maybe the traps had been cursed after all. Or maybe it was the replica Robert I had taken out of the box and then sneaked home with me. Clarence hadn't scanned it, but I didn't get the feeling I usually did around haunted objects. But how accurate was that? I didn't even fully understand how I could feel the haunted objects.

Or maybe Justin had released the rodents into my house as a way to get back at me. But how would he have done that? Or even know which room was mine? Just because he had used mousetraps before didn't mean—

Kip! He was caught in all of those mousetraps because of me. Last night could have been his revenge. A grown man's total asshole version of toilet papering someone's house. Kip must have moused me.

But I couldn't say anything to anyone at Darrow & Grimes. Not about the rodent invasion and not about my Robert the Doll replica. I still intended to fix my fuckup with Monique, and I needed time to do that. I knew if I even breathed a word about it, Brian would forbid it. I only hoped my theory of Ariel being able to read minds was nothing but my overactive imagination. She'd rat me out in a minute.

The ice was already cracking when it came to my place at D&G. One more upset, even one that wasn't my fault, and I would be locked out of the most interesting job I could ever hope to land for the rest of my life.

The bell dinged above the door as I entered, and Jackie looked over at me. She almost smiled. I approached the counter, hoping that everything could be cool like it had been on my first day when Jackie seemed to like me automatically.

I glanced at the empty glass case and wished that I'd thought to bake a batch of replacement fudge. Or, who was I kidding, buy some at Costco. That might have been a slam dunk for getting back on her good side.

"That's a pretty blouse," I said, complimenting Jackie with the first thing I could think of and definitely mean.

The blouse was light blue, with intricate embroidery in white. Delicate and feminine, hanging loosely from her frame, capturing just enough light in its soft folds to lend a delicate sheen to her skin.

"Thanks," she said. "Can't wear this at home with the damn baby. He'd probably puke on it."

I almost told Jackie she looked luminous, but there was no way that wouldn't sound weird, even though I really did mean it.

I glanced at *Saloon at the End of the World*. The change in Montague was more dramatic this time. He was turned to face outward in the painting, and his arms had noticeably moved. I felt a thrill ripple through me, glimpsing through the veil into this secret world.

"What can I do to help?" I asked.

Then, the bell dinged above the door. We both looked

over to see a pair of police officers entering, one right after the other.

"Can I help you?" Jackie was on alert, her posture fully upright.

I fell an instinctive step back, pressing against the glass case.

"We're looking for Brian Darrow," said the first officer, Shepherd, according to his badge.

"He's not in," Jackie told him.

"Will he be back soon?" asked the second, Nichols.

She shrugged. "I'm not sure of Mr. Darrow's schedule today."

"I suggest you find out." Shepherd gave Jackie a threatening nod.

"We're going to have a look around," Nichols said, turning around and starting toward a row of empty shelves.

Shepherd said, "We have it on good authority that this shop is the front for a drug lab."

Great, someone had beat me to the chase and swatted us.

Jackie looked around and dared to smile at him. "You've got to be kidding."

"What's back there?" Shepherd nodded toward the lab.

"Why don't you ask me again when you have a warrant?" She grinned at him. "I'm guessing you don't have one of those."

I felt so nervous standing in between them, but Jackie was a badass, staring this officer down without flinching.

Nichols abandoned the shelves and returned to his buddy. "It's awfully suspicious that you're not just letting us have a look."

"You can shop all you want. But we're pretty picked over right now."

Nichols gestured around the shop. "Doesn't seem like you have enough inventory to stay in business."

"We had an unexpected rush." Jackie had an answer for everything. "Normally, I'd offer you some fudge, but we sold it all in that rush I was just telling you about. I think we have some Triskets in our private employee lounge if you'd like any of those. I wouldn't want you to think I'm being inhospitable just because I refuse to let you invade my boss's privacy."

"Do you really think your boss would prefer that we make this a bigger deal than it needs to be?" Shepherd, trying again. "Officially closing your doors for as long as it takes for the investigation to—"

"Are you threatening me?"

"No, ma'am, of course not."

"Did you hear him just try to threaten me right now?" Jackie asked the room.

"Yes," I answered.

"I'm not threatening you," Shepherd said.

I joined the conversation. "It was definitely implied."

"Sorry, boys." Jackie shook her head, not apologetic at all. "It's a warrant or nothing."

The officers left after another short round of impotent grousing, and I wanted to give Jackie like a hundred high-fives. It was easy to see that she would have been a formidable agent and surely excellent at the auctions as well.

"Lock the doors," she said when they left.

I locked the front door, turned the window sign to *CLOSED*, then joined Jackie and Clarence in the lab.

Beatrice was glowing a few feet away from Clarence,

who was holding his lab coat and waving yet another wand across the fabric, this one bright yellow with a short nozzle.

"What is he doing?" I asked Jackie.

"Playing with the energies."

"I'm not playing with anything!" Clarence snapped. "I'm running tests. Trying to see if I can alter the lab coat's energy signature to turn Beatrice corporeal."

She glowed a little brighter, almost like she was blushing. And hell, if Clarence wasn't practically giggling right back.

It was the first time I had ever really noticed them like that before, the two of them clearly in love. Not unrequited, but for sure undeclared. Maybe the fact that Beatrice was haunting his lab coat was declaration enough.

"Can I help?" I asked Jackie, pointing to the latest cluster of mushrooms growing on the wall. "I could clean those off if you like."

"You don't even have to ask."

I went right to work, thrilled to be useful.

I carefully moved Sylvia's vessel to another shelf all the way across the room before I started scraping the mushrooms, but once I got going, I didn't stop, moving slowly and steadily across the wall, scratching at the clusters of darkly sprouting fungi. Their spongy, rubbery texture seemed to fiercely cling to the wall as I gently nudged them off and tossed them into a pile on the floor, quickly removing each piece without damaging the surrounding surface or leaving any mushrooms behind.

But the entire time, I felt a tugging behind me.

A new vase sat on Clarence's desk, clearly drawing me toward it.

The haunted object was silently begging me to pick it up.

I couldn't even help myself, turning away from the wall

to see the dark porcelain, thinking it was the most beautiful thing I had ever seen.

I lunged for the vase but bumped into the nearest shelf and knocked Sylvia's vessel to the floor.

There was a sharp gasp, I wasn't sure who from, but the entire room was suddenly frozen.

The worst curse ever invented (supposedly) had just fallen to the floor. The room exhaled, seeing that Sylvia's vessel had dropped without breaking. I thought I had moved it before I started cleaning? What was wrong with my brain? I was making so many stupid flubs, and my dexterity was severely impaired. I needed to roll a saving throw for sure.

Clarence cleared his throat. "I think it's time for you to go home."

"But it's still early. And I just started."

"It's time for you to go home, anyway." Clarence looked angry.

Beatrice looked disappointed.

I'm not even sure who else was in the lab. Not then as Clarence stared back at me and I wanted to die of shame and embarrassment, or as I turned around and ran from the lab, then out of Darrow & Grimes.

Chapter Twenty-Five

IT WAS HARD TO FEEL LOWER THAN WORTHLESS.

But after running out of the lab as I had, there were clearly some even darker depths to explore.

I was hanging onto my job at D&G by a thread. And that was more than I really even deserved. I'd messed up enough times to lose count. Everyone was either embarrassed, ashamed, or making excuses for me. Maybe my job was already gone since the Sylvia's vessel incident, and nobody had bothered to tell me.

I was tired of feeling like this. I was spiraling out and had become a one-woman wrecking crew. A true menace — and I hadn't any idea why. I wasn't normally like this. My previous employers loved me, and I was often their favorite employee. So why was I such a fuck-up now?

Tired of feeling like I wasn't even good enough to clean mushrooms without getting snared by stupid arcane objects.

Tired of—

Wait. How I had been feeling under the vase's spell was

probably exactly what Justin had been going through with Mansions of Madness?

It wasn't his fault. Yet, he will die nonetheless.

I needed to understand him instead of stewing in my anger at him. So I searched for his blog, A Gamer's Guide to the Galaxy, and clicked over to a gallery of articles:

• 10 Killer Board Games to Hunt For If You Are a n00b

• Ultimate List of the Top 10 Rarest and Most Valuable (and KICKASS) Board Games

• Straight-Up Advice For Novice Collectors (How to Get Started)

• 10 Bucket List Board Games (I Have Four of These!)

• The Thrill of the Hunt: Finding Rare Board Games

• Bored of board games? It's YOUR Fault.

• How to Spot a Fake or Reproduction (Has This Happened to You?)

I clicked on the Ultimate List article. Mansions of Madness wasn't even one of the Top 10 Rarest games or on Justin's bucket list. More surprising (although I guess saying this makes me a jerk), he was a terrific writer. His articles were fun to read, even if I didn't really get all of his references. I considered myself a sometimes-gamer and full-time nerd for sure, but this guy specialized in board games and actual old-school RPGs.

And the site itself was cool. Justin included some incredible art with each of his posts. I didn't know if he drew it or sourced it or what, but I found myself staring at each of the articles longer than I meant to and reading one of them in its entirety twice about how to tell the difference between editions of a game, with a rather long winded but rollicking side tangent about expansion packs.

A Gamer's Guide to the Galaxy also had eighty-four pages of images with painted figures. According to Justin's

About page, he loved board games more than life itself. That didn't surprise me, considering how he had come off when we met. And this was me being a jerk again, but I did blink a few times at the number of comments on some of his posts. All of those likes and retweets.

It wasn't about the board games; it was about Justin. These people were serious fans of his work. Someone named SmileyTime44 seriously seemed to like him. Like "like-like" him. However, by his responses, he seemed oblivious.

I clicked through the articles, from one to the next, until I had seen them all at least once. But I still didn't have any of the clues I needed, so I started clicking through to individual comments, which led me to other blogs. One of them was written by SmileyTime44, and she had two separate posts about how great she thought the blog was. Oh boy, Justin, someone has a crush on you, bad.

I was probably just wasting my time, but I could also be getting closer to gold, and if so, then I needed to stay in the mine.

Justin was worth reading. The rest of this, not so much.

I made my way through a myriad of new articles and comments, following a trail of blogs down a winding maze, falling deeper and deeper into a subgenre of gaming I was caring less and less about.

I wanted to know more about Justin, or Mansions of Madness, or any of the possible ways I might be able to get through to him before it was too late. The seemingly endless labyrinth of websites, podcasts, and forums dedicated to analyzing everything from the latest developments to minutiae the mainstream stopped caring about a long time ago eventually led me nowhere.

My eyes were getting more tired.

I had to read everything twice.

My elbow slid off of the desk, and I was jarred wide awake.

That was the second time in the last few minutes. It had been a long time (hours now?) since I'd last seen anything useful or useable, but I still wasn't ready to surrender.

I only had four days to save Justin from himself and from the situation I had gotten him into.

That four might as well have been three, considering it was after midnight.

I couldn't afford to sleep, regardless of my exhaustion.

I needed to stay up and keep going.

Just another few minutes, and…

Trying to stay awake was hard, and my blurry eyes incessantly blinking, barely able to focus on the forum posts as I forced myself to keep reading through a fog of fatigue and mounting frustration, following a meandering path through an endless forest of content that only led me to nowhere and offered zero answers to the urgent questions flying like flocks of wild birds in my mind.

I had never been more tired, but I told myself just one more page…

I woke up to the sound of scratching at my door, like someone (or something) walking back and forth along the hallway on the other side.

But I knew the sound of my mother's footsteps, and that wasn't her walking. Nor was it Rashida or Malik. These footsteps were light, clickety-clackety, and not at all like an adult's.

I was on full alert. Wide awake. Ready to battle whatever darkness was revving to hurt me. I was even more scared than I had been at the haunted house or at Justin's place when he'd shown up all pointy-eared and angry, but I knew I had no other choice. I had to swallow my fear and take a look.

Slowly, I opened the door, poking my head into the hallway.

I glanced up and down but didn't see anything there.

Then I cast my gaze to the floor and stared at the dark shape sitting like an evil idol on the carpet.

I knew what I was going to see before I flicked the light on. So I bit down on my bottom lip to prepare.

I tasted blood, but that was better than screaming at the terrible sight.

Replica or not, Robert the Doll was on the floor and staring right up at me.

Oh, hell.

Chapter Twenty-Six

EVERYONE SEEMED TO BE HATING ME JUST A LITTLE LESS BY the time I arrived at work the following morning. I was emptied out and running on vapors, but Jackie smiled like it was still several days ago when I dinged the bell above the door.

I had the replica of Robert the Doll tucked into the bottom of my oversized bag. The secret cargo hung like a fifty-pound bag of rice from my shoulder. Would Ariel sense I was carrying it? Or Beatrice with all her *watching*? I felt like coming home late as a teenager and trying to slip by my parents' room so that they wouldn't smell the booze on me or grill me about why I was late.

I couldn't tell anyone. Not yet. Not until I had more of a handle on things. I knew how Brian (and everyone) would feel about me lone-wolfing it like I was — that's what kept getting me into trouble, over and over and over, after all — but I couldn't just blurt it all out. I was hoping to explain what had happened, everything from finding the replica Robert in yesterday's haul (and no, I should not have taken inventory purchased by Darrow & Grimes home with me), then the mice and the creepy footsteps and … everything.

But now wasn't even close to the proper time, with all of the stress in the shop and Jackie having to field incoming calls from the police.

"Again?" I said as the phone rang.

"It might be a customer this time," Jackie said on her way to answer the call, but I could tell by her voice that she didn't really believe it.

"Darrow & Grimes?" She tried to sound polite, but a second later, Jackie was back on the defensive and snapping into the phone. "Just because you still don't have a warrant doesn't mean you get to harass us … no … yes … I understand that, Officer Shepherd, but it's not my fault that someone smells sulfur coming from the shop."

Jackie looked irritated, waiting for whoever was on the other end of her call to finish their interruption before she started on her list, presumably of things that could possibly smell like sulfur.

"How about natural gas, or a skunk, or old eggs? An iron left on for too long, or an engine in need of a tune-up?"

A long pause, then Jackie again. "I look forward to your next call."

She hung up with a scowl, looking very little like the woman who had offered me fudge just a week ago.

"Is there anything I can do to help?" I asked.

"What do you think?"

I wanted to tell Jackie that I thought it felt impossible for me to get anything right. Instead, I gathered enough courage to approach Brian in his office.

He seemed open, his eyes surprisingly warm as I entered, and his air relaxed as he gestured toward the empty seat in front of him.

I sat down and dropped my bag on the floor right beside me.

"You look serious," Brian said.

"I have something to tell you."

"Sounds like I should be glad I'm already sitting."

I pulled the Robert replica out of my bag and set it on my lap, feeling like a ventriloquist holding her demonic little dummy.

Brian raised his eyebrows. "Is that what I think it is?"

"Only sort of." I shrugged. "Maybe."

Then I told him all about going to Monique's house with my mom and how Monique said that she wanted Robert the Doll more than anything else in the world right before I found him just sitting at the bottom of the box looking up at me. The doll had to be haunted, right?

Brian was patient, even through the more panicked parts of my story, but he didn't seem the least bit concerned after I finished. Neither did Clarence when I repeated my story for him or after he was waving a ruby-colored wand across what he and Brian both swore was a completely normal replica.

"There's no energy signature on this doll whatsoever," Clarence announced.

"Someone must be fucking with you," added Brian.

"So, the doll is for sure not haunted?" I had to double-triple-check.

"Doesn't look like it," Brian replied.

Clarence gave me a dirty look.

"Could it be Kip fucking with me?"

"No." Brian shook his head, emphatic.

"How do you know?"

Brian opened his mouth to answer me, but his phone rang and got his attention instead.

"Yeah," he answered after looking down at the screen,

walking out of the office while falling into an easy-sounding conversation with whoever was on the other end of his call.

"Jackie!" I heard Brian call out once back in the shop. "Where is Ariel?"

I scurried behind him, curious to know what might be happening or about to happen, arriving in time to hear Jackie deliver Ariel's possible whereabouts.

"She was checking out that stuffed banana dog toy. I'm pretty sure she's still there."

"Dog toy?"

"Every dog that gnaws on the toy develops narcolepsy and falls over," Clarence explained. "Ariel said that she thought this particular curse sounded tragically hilarious and was interested in seeing it firsthand."

"Give her a call and tell her to meet us at the farmer's market," Brian told her.

"And you can't do that because…"

"Because we're going to the farmer's market. Come on, Shondra. You're coming, too."

"Why are we going to a farmer's market?" I asked once we were about a block away, and it was much less likely that Brian would decide to change his mind and leave me behind.

"Pastor Villalobos will be there."

"Oh." Brian had said the man's name like I should have known it since childhood, so I kept the question to myself. "Cool."

I wondered if "farmers market" was a euphemism for something much darker — I was picturing a possible swap meet full of black-market arcana — but by the time Brian pulled into the parking lot, I knew it really was just a cordoned-off lot lined with stalls full of colorful fruits and vegetables, surrounded by an array of tents and booths selling artisanal goods.

Shoppers bustled about, perusing the offerings and savoring the fresh, fragrant aromas, but there didn't seem to be any haunted objects in sight.

I smelled fresh produce and blooming flowers, warm bread, and roasting meat wafting from the various stalls. Sweet scents mingled with earthy aromas, and the faint whiff of wood smoke hit my nostrils as the sound of chattering shoppers drifted into my ears.

The hum of voices and the clanging of metal pots and pans, the shouting of vendors shilling their goods amid the occasional barking dog breaking through the din.

It was all so perfectly normal.

Until we got to the enclosed bit all the way in the back, past all the colorful tents to a short row of ten or so brown and gray offerings, each one filled with arcane objects, even the simplest stall many times more interesting than all of the tents out front added together and multiplied times two.

The energy tester in Brian's pocket started screaming, so he had to take the device out of his pocket and mute the thing.

"We're going into that second to last one." He pointed down the row toward a tent that loomed a foot taller than the others and the darkest by far.

It was hell, walking by all of those other tents with only a fleeting glance inside, wanting to go into each one and run my hands over all of the mysterious items. But the second to last tent belonged to Pastor Villalobos, and there were more than enough arcane objects behind the flaps to wow me.

"Young Darrow," said the man as we entered.

Brian nodded in greeting. "Pastor. This is the newest member of the family, Shondra."

Those words felt nice, even if he didn't really mean them.

"Shondra." Pastor Villalobos offered me an acknowledging nod. He was old enough to border ancient, but still with all of his hair, thick and silver, full as his heavily lined smile. The man was garbed in simple yet slightly tattered robes, looking at me with piercingly thoughtful eyes.

"You are here for what is new, I presume?"

Brian gave him a nod. "Always."

"Don't touch anything," warned the Pastor as he ran his own hands over the first item in his presentation, a haunted first edition of *The Great Gatsby* that caused its reader to become obsessed with a narrative that honestly didn't have all that much going for it.

The Pastor moved with a measured, deliberate pace as he reached into the depths of his tent, producing a series of intriguing objects, each one more interesting than the one before it.

A collection of strange crystals, one ancient scroll (the Pastor whispered its details in Brian's ear), and a brass statue that he claimed could cure loneliness or drive a person to suicide, depending on the weather.

I was transfixed even before I found The Smoke and Mirror.

"Don't look into that for more than a few seconds," the Pastor warned me as I stared into a beautiful, beveled mirror. "And don't touch. I promise you won't like what happens if you touch that glass."

I had never looked more beautiful, but my reflection began to smoke, and I wondered if that was really my face.

"I told you," said the Pastor as I flinched away.

"What is this?" Brian asked, picking up what looked like an oversized sewing needle with overgrown interest.

"That's the Phantom Needle," the Pastor explained. "It can cut through anything."

Brian eagerly nodded, seemingly satisfied. "How much?"

The haggling started.

But only barely, before Ariel came striding into the tent, her face marred with the usual scratches from Snuggles, I had to assume.

But just behind her, I saw Kip and Darren Dupree. Plus, their boss, Rudolph Branson.

They had a large cart loaded to the gills, and now they were barging into this tent to claim even more arcane objects for themselves.

Chapter Twenty-Seven

TOO MANY THINGS WERE HAPPENING AT ONCE.

In addition to the Nemicon gang, I also saw a flash of what had to be Justin on the other side of the tent flaps.

Was he here looking for me? Should I be scared? More than I already was?

Or — and this felt infinitely more likely — was I just imagining things because I felt guilty that I couldn't save him?

Right now, I couldn't think about any of that, not with the Nemicons suddenly sharing the Pastor's tent.

I wondered how Kip could be around Rudolph, knowing that the man might be responsible for what had happened to Montague, directly or indirectly casting his father into the *Saloon at the End of the World* and trapping him inside.

I wanted to say something when the three of them barged into the tent, but I was here to be a team player. If Brian wanted to call Kip out on his loyalties, then he would have surely done so already.

My job right now (and all the time, even if I hadn't been great about doing it so far) was to follow Brian's orders.

In this instance, that meant standing back and listening to Rudolph and Brian starting to spar out loud while Darren began to browse. Kip stood off to the side with a smirk, like he was hiding something, same as always. With all the cursed items lying about, someone surely was going to get punched in the nose.

Rudolph sneered at Brian. "It's too bad that even the early bird won't be getting the worm in this instance. Your thrift store budget is no match for ours."

"We have plenty of budget!" Brian retorted, talking over his adversary. "You should see the shop right now! Our shelves are all empty because we sold out of everything."

Rudolph made a face. "I'd really rather not. I have a very sensitive sense of smell."

Kip smirked again. And again, I wondered about all of the many things he must surely be hiding.

And I might have seen another flash of Justin walking by the tent. Maybe.

"Gentleman." Pastor Villalobos was suddenly in between Rudolph and Brian, trying to make peace between the men, even though it also seemed like a part of him might have been enjoying the quarrel. My money was on Brian throwing the first punch. Spirit energy hung in the air like thick smoke. "Please. I'm sure we all know that arcane objects often find their most appropriate owners."

What was that supposed to mean? Didn't objects usually go to whoever could afford to buy them? That was probably just the Pastor trying to keep his customers from killing each other and his inventory moving.

Another smirk from Kip. I want to change my bet — I was going to be the one to throw the first punch right into his smug face.

"What are you hiding?" I snapped at him. "There must have been some reason that you left—"

"Why are you even here?" Brian shouted at Rudolph, drowning my voice out with his. "I don't see any art you can hang."

"—Darrow & Grimes in such a goddamned hurry!"

That definitely got to him. Kip looked almost worried, shifting on his feet as a hand involuntarily flew up to touch his neck. A nervous tic, for sure.

But he didn't respond.

Brian and Rudolph were now barking back and forth at one another.

I kept yelling at Kip. "I should stick you in that Cray-Z-Boy over at The Carnivale Arcane — that will get you spewing the truth!"

Brian and Rudolph each slammed into a verbal wall, ceasing their arguing and turning to stare at me in unison.

Rudolph: *Interesting …*

And Brian: *What the fuck, Shondra?*

That sinking, sickening sense settled back into my stomach. An old lesson still not learned. I'd opened my big mouth again, accidentally informing Rudolph — the owner of Nemicon, and therefore D&G's numero uno enemy — of something he might not have otherwise known. He didn't seem like the kind of guy that attended many Carnivales, but I bet he would now. *Damn it, damn it, Shondra!*

The questions were coming, but before either Brian or Rudolph could say anything, I saw a third flash of Justin outside the tent.

But this time, he wasn't just passing by; he was hanging out at the end of a stall, clutching a shopping bag under his arm, the Mansions of Madness game poking out of the top. The little bastard was taunting me! I was trying to save his life, and he was playing games with me — literally.

I could no longer question my eyes with Justin fifty feet away from me.

Though he barely looked like Justin now, hunched over, with pointed ears and a wild nest of matted hair. Even from inside the tent, I could see his sunken eyes, the way they seemed to glow with malice.

The creature looked like a grotesque, inhuman version of Justin, a dark reflection of the man he used to be.

Neither Rudolph nor Brian had responded to my blurting about the Cray-Z-Boy yet. The moment was pregnant, as if neither one of them dared to open his mouth before I broke the silence.

Justin locked eyes with me, and I didn't know what else to do. So I yelled his name, and he darted out of sight.

I raced after him, ignoring Brian calling out after me as I pursued the hulking, inhuman beast through the crowded farmer's market.

His long, lanky limbs moved with unnatural speed and agility, leaping over tables and stalls as he fled the scene. He only turned back once, seeming to glare at me with his glowing eyes.

I ran faster, ignoring the insistent stitch in my side, fueled by a fierce sense of determination, desperate to stop him from dying.

"Justin!" I yelled.

"Shondra!" came a bellow from somewhere behind me.

It took me a beat before I realized it was Ariel.

Justin had doubled back toward the Pastor's tent and was now barreling toward it. Brian and the Nemicon Trio were waving their arms, all four of the men unified in wanting me to stop as Ariel screamed their wishes out loud behind me.

"Shondra! Stop!"

But I had to keep running because Justin was getting away, and if I gave this last little burst of effort, draining the rest of my energy while giving me everything I needed to—

Nope.

Justin darted off in the other direction at the last second with incredible grace that left me no time to maneuver. I had rolled a 1 for a dexterity check. It was going to be bad.

I crashed into the Pastor's stall, rolling over onto and off a table, knocking his tent full of wares to the ground in a jumble of merchandise and battered wood, tarnished metal and smashed glass vases, shattered ceramic statues, and vintage bottles now in shards.

Errant glass lashed my skin on its way to the ground, its impact dulled by pounds of colorful fabric.

I was disoriented, momentarily blinded by the rush of noise and activity. But then I looked around, blinking in wide-eyed horror and surprise.

I was covered in broken glass, and people were running and screaming everywhere.

But not Pastor Villalobos, the Nemicon gang, Brian, or Ariel, now finally caught up and shook her head in disappointment at me.

Then I saw the reason that Ariel would hate me forever. Her hand had been fused to the mirror Villalobos had warned me about. She must have accidentally grabbed it — or tried to bat the mirror out of her way — when everything in the tent went flying.

When *I* sent everything in the tent flying.

Ariel scowled, her expression twisted into something even worse with all of those giant boils suddenly erupting all over her face.

Chapter Twenty-Eight

WE WERE DEBRIEFING BACK AT THE SHOP, BUT IT WAS obvious from looking at the gang's collective expressions exactly how little scrutiny there needed to be.

It was obvious that everything that had happened at the farmer's market was entirely my fault, even my first misstep that no one had even mentioned: delivering information to the enemy.

Brian finished catching Clarence, Beatrice, and Jackie up on my latest misadventures. Jackie looked disappointed down to her toenails, and Clarence seemed even more done with me than before. Only Beatrice had any apparent sympathy for my situation, not exactly smiling at me, but I could still see her glowing face pinched with concern more than frustration.

"It's all her fault!" Ariel jabbed a finger at me with none of her usual composure.

"Come on," Clarence said, gesturing for her to follow him back to the lab. "Let's get to work on you."

It only took ten minutes for him to get the mirror off of Ariel, and she didn't have so much as a hickey left to remind her of the unfortunate incident. But all was *not* well that ended well. Clarence ran a lavender-colored wand across the mirror once it was off of her body, shaking his head in a way that made me feel even more worthless than I already did.

"It's ghost energy. Not spirit energy." Clarence nodded at the Dale & West incinerator, and Jackie used a pair of tongs to toss it inside.

I didn't even offer to help. I was lucky they were still letting me stand around to see the show. Maybe they'd forgotten I was still in the room.

"Am I done?" Ariel asked.

"Do you think you're done?"

She looked up at Clarence, pouting, sounding almost defeated. "No."

Ariel knew what to do, heading straight to one of the cots and laying down so that Clarence could cover her face with an oxygen mask.

Brian walked over to the wall next to Ariel's bag, planted his back against it, then slid down to the floor and hung his head in between his knees.

"You ready?" Clarence asked.

Ariel slowly nodded. "I really hate this part."

"It hates you too." He zipped a big white body bag around her, then started pumping sage smoke into it.

"It's just ten minutes this time, right?" she asked, her voice barely intelligible coming from behind both the bag and her mask. "Five?"

"An hour," Clarence told her, in a tone that suggested it was an old answer patiently delivered. "And then you'll be fine."

With Ariel lying there, Brian still dejected against the wall, and Jackie avoiding my eyes, I figured I might as well climb right on that giant elephant in the room and ride the beast out of there.

"Can I help sort through the new merchandise?"

I wanted to sound brave, confronting what I had done and offering to help, even if nobody wanted me around right now. By "new merchandise," I meant all of the items from the Pastor's booth that Brian had to put on his (surely maxed out by now) credit card.

No wonder he couldn't stand to look at me.

"You can help me," Clarence replied when no one else did. "We're going to catalog it, then destroy anything that isn't whole."

I glanced at the table full of pieces and shards.

Brian was still on the floor next to Ariel's bag. He finally looked up, his eyes gleaming with defeat more than anger.

"We need to talk," he said.

"Of course!" I sounded way too chirpy and really needed to knock it down a peg or two. "Let me just help Clarence."

"Now."

Everyone was staring at me. I might as well have been naked. I was dying to melt on the floor.

"In your office?" I had to hope. Whatever was about to happen, I really didn't want it to go down in public.

"Here is fine." Brian sounded so tired, and I was the one who had done that to his voice. "I think it's time to—"

"I KNOW I CAN DO BETTER!" Then softer, less manic. "I'm sorry for everything that's happened so far. It's all an honest mistake—"

"MISTAKES!" came a mumble shout from behind Ariel's oxygen mask.

"—and I'll never, ever make another one. You have my word!"

"I think you can appreciate how little your word actually means around here by now." Brian looked pained yet relieved to have finally spoken the truth to my face. And boy, did that hurt, despite every word being fully deserved.

"I was trying to do the right thing!" I declared one last stab at keeping the gig, regardless of my dignity. "It could have happened to anyone."

"You're always trying to do the right thing," said Jackie.

"And no," Brian disagreed, "this could *not* have happened to anyone."

"But all of those smashed arcane objects, that has to be a good thing, right? Even if we had to pay for them, we just destroyed an object with ghost energy." I nodded to the Dale & West. "Remember the mirror?"

Like anyone in the lab could forget.

Brian shook his head and continued to admonish me. "You haven't learned anything. You're still just thinking about yourself."

"I promise I'm not." Even if I lost my job, I couldn't stand anyone at Darrow & Grimes thinking the worst of me. "All of this happened because I was trying to save Justin's life. That's not about me!"

Brian shook his head again. "I'm sorry you can't see that it is."

Jackie, Clarence, and Beatrice kept looking at me. Ariel said something I couldn't decipher.

Then Brian dropped the hammer on my toes.

"I think we need to put this to a vote."

No! Not a vote!

"All those in favor of keeping Shondra on, please raise your hand."

Singular. And Brian was right. Because only Beatrice raised her arm in the air. Until she motioned for Clarence to join her. After two long seconds, he reluctantly did.

"Those in favor of letting Shondra go?" Brian raised his own hand before he finished his sentence.

Jackie didn't look happy about any of this, but her hand followed his just a beat or two later. It still was a tie.

Ariel actually took the time to unzip her bag. I had no idea if that would reset the clock on what she obviously saw as an abominable experience, but it was apparently still worth the additional discomfort even if so.

Just so I could see her with a puff of smoke curling around her crown in a halo.

Ariel raised her hand.

"Ay," she said, loud and clear, even though Brian never requested that anyone say anything.

Now, the moment was broken. And my future was inevitable. My old boss turned back to me and made it a fact.

"Sorry, Shondra." No, he wasn't. "But you're fired."

Chapter Twenty-Nine

I GOT HOME, WENT STRAIGHT TO MY ROOM, COLLAPSED ON the bed, and sobbed. I stayed that way for a long while, minutes into hours, then hours into sleep.

The bed was a mess of tangled sheets and pillows as I tossed and turned, unable to find a comfortable position or any sort of comfort at all, haunted by a procession of terrifying nightmares, vivid images, and soundscapes coming in mounting waves, consuming me with despair.

Leaving me restless and disturbed.

No REM and maybe two hours of sleep, then it was morning, and even with both of my eyes pried wide open, I could still barely function.

I had ruined everything, and now my life itself was a curse.

I never got the chance to be great at the job, or even good, but my short-lived gig at D&G had been something I cared about, so I would have been great at it eventually. I really liked everyone. I felt like I understood them, and they seemed to understand me. Most importantly, and way better than anything I ever got at college, my eyes had been opened to a new world. Everything in it fascinated me.

Now that I could see into some of the world's many hidden colors, how could I return to a life of black and white?

Was I destined to live the rest of my time on this planet as a sad sack, with the only haunting in my life being the kind I leveled upon all of those message boards I would be spending way too much of my future time stalking, following leads from the sidelines, or the bleachers?

Oh my god, was I going to turn into Monique? Obsessive and creepy, gathering information in the hope of D&G castoffs?

I longed for a conversation with Dad to dull this incessant pain inside me.

My usual ten minutes under the hot water tripled to a half-hour shower. I spent twenty minutes staring into my closet before deciding to get back in my pajamas.

I had cereal for breakfast, but I searched for the right kind, poured the bowl, and filled it with almond milk, all in slow motion. I watched several shows on TV for more than three hours, though the only thing I could remember a few hours later was an old episode of *iCarly*.

I turned the TV off and ran upstairs when Mom's car pulled into the driveway. She shouldn't be home right now, and I didn't want to talk.

So I returned to my room, trudging up the stairs with the weight of regret hanging low on my shoulders. Yes, I was wallowing in self-pity, retreating from the world as I languished in bed, pulling the covers over my head, consumed by the heavy drag of inadequacy.

I had to stop flopping around and feeling sorry for myself. I gave myself a pep talk.

You still have a life to live, Shondra. And you can't do anything good until you stop feeling bad about yourself.

You have to get up. Get out of bed. Grab your laptop and get to work on your résumé.

Pick up the pieces. You can and will get past this.

You have to be strong. Have hope.

Suck it up and…

I started sobbing.

A few moments later, my door swung wide, and Mom rushed into the room.

"Oh, honey." She didn't even ask what was wrong, just pulled me to her chest and started petting my head, stroking my hair in long and loving strokes until I finally stopped crying.

"Do you want to talk about it?"

"Yes!" I cried out, then laughed at my own sense of release.

I'm not sure exactly how much I spilled because it all came pouring out of me so fast, but I told her a version of everything, starting with how excited I was to get the job at Darrow & Grimes and explaining it in a way where I felt like she was actually hearing me for the first time, and ending with what happened yesterday at the farmer's market.

Or, more to the point, afterward, when everyone ganged up to fire me.

"They didn't gang up on you," Mom said, though that was the first time in my entire story that she had disagreed with anything. "It sounds like you had plenty of chances."

I wanted to agree with her, but the tears would start again if I did.

Another hug kept me from crying.

"I can't pretend like I don't think this whole thing is insane, Shondra, but I am really very proud of you."

"Why are you proud of me?" I sounded like I was accusing her of something, like maybe lying to my face.

"I'm always proud of you. Even when I want you to reach higher." She offered me a knowing smile. "Or when I don't understand something as well as I should yet. But I've been impressed with how wholeheartedly you've gone into this job. Enthusiasm might be your fatal flaw, but it's also your superpower."

"Thanks?"

Mom was quiet for a moment. "Do you remember when you were a little girl and insisted on learning to ride a bike?

One of my best moments. I was six, and it was Christmas. Santa had brought Malik a bike, and I wasn't having it.

"I insisted on getting a bike."

"'Insisted' is saying it mildly. You were obsessed. Day and night, you worked on my nerves until I gave in."

Telling me "no" only lit a fire in my little kindergarten heart.

"You didn't exactly give in; you told me I had to teach myself to ride Malik's bike."

Malik had been pissed.

"I thought that would deter you like it would a normal child."

Normal? Me? I wouldn't have done it if it weren't for Dad's smile. Dad always had my back. Boy, could I use his smile right about now? The smile that said he believed I could do anything.

"I watched you get on that bike again and again. I wanted to go out to stop you, but your dad wouldn't let me."

I laughed. "I didn't have any skin left on my elbows and knees."

"It wasn't funny, Shondra. I was horrified."

I didn't cry. I wouldn't cry. I just got back up and tried again. Malik tried to get his bike back from me, but I gave him the "I dare you" stare.

"Your brother begged me to make you stop. You were denting and scratching his new bike, but again, your dad stopped me. He said, 'Watch, she's going to do it.' Oh boy, was he right. I could have killed him."

Dad was there for me the whole time. His head poked out between the curtains. No words needed to be spoken — his smile was enough.

I got on again, and this time, I found the balance I needed, and the bike moved down our street. I was going faster and faster. The intersection came up fast. I had mastered balance and momentum — but not braking.

I woke to Dad's face. His eyes looked red and puffy; he leaned down and hugged me tight.

"It wasn't that big of a deal. You were so dramatic about it."

"Are you kidding me? You almost died. I tried to warn you, but you insisted on riding a bike. I'm not sure Mr. Williams ever got over it. He came by every day for almost a year checking on you."

Malik seemed less worried about my untimely demise and more about his bike having been wrecked. Dad reminded him that bikes could be replaced, but I couldn't be, and that he should be nicer to me while I was in the hospital.

"I didn't even have a broken bone. I just had a bump on my head."

"Shondra, you were unconscious, and your father did CPR until the paramedics got there. They said you stopped breathing on the way to the hospital."

"Sure, but they said it was just a concussion. Again, you're being dramatic."

I touched my face and could feel the little piece of gravel that was still there. Thankfully, the scarring from the asphalt burn was minimal. Two days later, when I was allowed to go home, Santa apparently made a special delivery before the new year. Two bikes with bows stood propped by the tree.

"While I appreciate this trip down memory lane and all, is there a point?"

"Yes, two points. First, you never shied away from anything in your life. While it has resulted in more gray hairs than a woman of my age should have, I have respected you for it."

I'm not going to cry. I'm not going to cry.

"And the second thing?"

"Your father loved you. I know parents should never play favorites, but you were his. You were his heart. And I know if he were here, he would be extremely proud of you." She pulled me into yet another hug.

"Thank you." I tried to catch my breath, surpassing the grief that filled every recess in my being. "I needed that right now."

"Do you feel better?"

"A little."

"Is there anything that might help you feel a lot better? Maybe something else you still want to tell me?"

After a long pause, where I didn't feel rushed at all, I said, "I just feel so bad about this person that I want to help, but I can't help him on my own."

"Why not?" Mom asked.

"Because I need Darrow & Grimes to help him. I actually can't do it myself."

"I'm sure you could."

"I mean literally, Mom. Clarence has equipment that could save this guy's life, but I can't get them to use it."

"Why not?"

"Because they only help people who want to be helped. But I'm the one who got him into this, so I'm the one who needs to make sure he gets out of it!"

"I hope you're not trying to get your job back, Shondra. Even though I'm proud of you, it does feel like it's time to move on from them."

"No." I shook my head. "Yes, I want the job back, but I don't need it. I just need D&G to do what I can't."

Mom nodded, looking thoughtful as if she was seriously trying to help me figure out what to do.

"You need to give them something they want," she finally said.

"Like what?"

"Something they need."

"Like?" That wasn't really helping.

"You would know that better than me, Shondra! But if you figure out what these Darrow & Grimes folks need more than anything else, I imagine that will give you the fastest path to having them help you out."

"Thank you, Mom!"

"Sounds like you have your answer."

"Not yet. But at least I know what to do next."

Mom didn't ask what that might be, probably because she didn't want to know. She left me alone after another long hug.

She closed the door, and I practically dove for my laptop. The one thing D&G always needed more than anything else was research, and I was aces at that.

I might have removed one helpful source in alienating Monique, but maybe I would become a new asset. I would dig as deep as I needed to go, for as long as it took to get there.

I started at A Gamer's Guide to the Universe. Justin's blog hadn't been updated since before he brought Mansions of Madness into his life (before I brought it into his life), but there were definitely more comments than the last time I was here, with many of them sharing some flavor of *Are you okay, man?*

Even though I had been through the entire site just a couple of days ago, I went through every page again. When I didn't find what I needed on Justin's site, I started backtracking through every thread and board I'd been on in the past, retracing my history back to that first night after my encounter with the Dybbuk Box when I'd gone through Uncle Kevin's trunk.

After hours passed without finding anything new or useful, I returned to where it all started, closing the laptop again and walking over to the trunk.

I opened it up and began rifling through Kevin's old treasures, glancing at pictures and letters, lightly fondling the various objects as I moved them around inside the trunk, desperately searching without knowing what I was looking for, going through his many papers in a fit of mounting frustration, scanning each one before setting it gently down and moving onto the next.

Once everything was out of the box, I noticed a rectangular shape on the bottom of the trunk. I ran my fingers across it. They were seams. I pushed around it, and there was a click, and a small compartment popped open. Inside was a small leather-bound journal with handwritten entries.

I flipped through it, and I suddenly saw something that stopped my heart.

I had to breathe through the moment. Recover my

breath as the pieces of this puzzle began to assemble themselves.

I read Uncle Kevin's entries word for word, and my heart somehow managed to pound even harder and faster with every new sentence.

The picture pasted on the next page terrified yet delighted me. I finally had something to give Darrow & Grimes, though it wasn't good news. Uncle Kevin had given our resident mushroom-growing garden gnome a new name, but one a lot less friendly than Gnomey.

The entry referred to the haunted object as *The Harbinger of Doom.*

Chapter Thirty

It had been nine days since Justin was first cursed by the Mansions of Madness game. But even going on as little sleep as I was, I still opened my eyes, ready to conquer the world. Or at least confront my reasonable fears that everyone at Darrow & Grimes really, seriously hated me.

"Hi." Jackie gave me a strained smile, looking over as I alerted her to my presence with the jingling bell.

I approached the counter with confidence, surprised to see that she wasn't alone. Clarence was up front instead of in the lab for once, standing on a ladder, screwing a fresh lightbulb into a light fixture just a few feet from the register. He looked half-naked without his lab coat, draped over the back of an adjacent chair.

"I have something important," I announced.

Clarence stopped screwing in the lightbulb and turned to look at me.

"Something for all of you," I clarified.

"I'm sorry, honey." Jackie found her compassion. "But you really need to go. We can't—"

"You're going to want to hear this." I straightened my

shoulders and firmed my voice, repeating the message but now with my full voice. "Everyone at Darrow & Grimes."

Clarence and Jackie traded a nod, then disappeared into the lab together, leaving me standing out front in the shop all alone.

I couldn't imagine that they would be gone for long, but each minute without answers felt like it was trying to murder me, so I killed that time right back by browsing the cluttered shop, looking at everything wistfully since it was the last time I would see any of it.

Surprising how much bric-a-brac Jackie had managed to get her hands on in the last couple of days, with a solid assist from me. One of the few things I'd done right.

Amid all the clutter of trinkets and knickknacks, I felt a swell of nostalgia I didn't deserve. I'd barely known this crew for more than a week; there was no logical reason for me to feel so attached, not to them and not to this place. And yet, while running my eyes along the shelf in front of me, already full again, now with ceramic figurines, fragile vases, and an old wooden clock, I saw the place as the second home I would never have, and the D&G gang as the second family I apparently didn't deserve.

Yes, I was devastated, but if Clarence and company could help me save Justin's life, then my excommunication would be worth it.

I bounced on the balls of my feet, still waiting but doing my best to stifle a rising tide of impatience.

I turned my attention to the *Saloon at the End of the World* and was startled again at the painting, even though I was used to the sight of Montague moving around in there.

He was facing almost fully forward, his arm and hand floating up like they were reaching out to me.

The image was both arresting and haunting.

I felt swallowed up by the picture, standing perfectly

still as I stared at it, unable to move as I wondered about this man, Kip's father, and whether he would ever finally make it out the saloon door.

What might happen once he reaches the other side?

It killed something inside me to think that I would probably never know.

Jackie finally came back out of the lab with Clarence in tow, holding a device he'd used to sweep me once before. The one with a translucent nozzle.

Brian and Ariel stood just behind Jackie, all of them looking somber while waiting for Clarence to finish the job.

"No new negative energies," he announced once done with his sweep. "She's clean."

"Is Gnomey still back there?" I asked.

Clarence looked agitated. "Of course, Gnomey's still back there. Where else would he be?"

"I have some important information — and a request."

"You're not getting your job back!" Ariel declared.

"I'm not trying to get my job back," I told them, hoping that might settle some of the tension that hung like humidity inside the shop. "I just want your help with something. But I'll tell you the information first. This isn't an exchange. I promise. Just two things that should be brought to your attention."

The doubt was clear on everyone's faces.

But Brian gave me a slow nod. "Go on."

"I found some information about Gnomey in my Uncle Kevin's old trunk."

"How do you know it's the same garden gnome?" Clarence asked.

I pulled out the leather-bound journal, flipped it to the page I had marked, and pointed at the image. Grainy as it was, you could clearly see the hole in his hat and the missing right ear. The gang moved back into the lab so I could hold up the image next to Gnomey and see the match.

I had finally earned the room's attention and for the right reasons.

"The gnome is a portent."

"Of course it's important!" Brian declared.

Clarence snapped his head over to the boss. "She said *a portent*."

He nodded for me to continue.

"According to my uncle, the garden gnome was originally a decoration for a family of five living in Hawaii. Garden gnomes are more of a rarity on the island, but the children loved him and spoke to their garden gnome all of the time. They even took him on picnics every once in a while. But then it started to move on its own. All three of the children thought one of the others must be messing with them, even though none of them could explain the mushrooms that kept growing all over the walls."

Jackie and Clarence traded a look.

"One night, the oldest sibling woke up in the middle of the night to find Gnomey staring right at him while his brother and sister were still sleeping. The sight of it frightened him something fierce, enough that whether his siblings were playing with him or not, he felt an urgent need to get rid of the garden gnome. So he took it deep into the jungle and left it at the base of a cluster of palm trees. His home was engulfed in flames by the time he got back, and the garden gnome was glowing in the firelight."

"A bit dramatic," Ariel said when I finished.

"The point is, there was a trail to follow after the family in Hawaii, hopping to three different islands before making its way to the mainland, across four states. That's where my uncle's research ends because he lost track of it. But that's Gnomey, I'm sure of it. And according to that asshole's history, he only shows up when something big is about to happen. Something *bad*."

Everyone was listening, leaning forward, even Ariel.

"And the bigger the mushrooms get, the closer the danger. I think that—"

BOOM!

A deafening explosion tore into the lab from the shop. Thick plumes of smoke billowed in front, followed by the slow lick of spreading flames.

I didn't stop to think. My body was already in motion, on its way to do what I had to do, darting around the fire and racing back into the shop.

Even if Kip was a jerk, I couldn't let the guy lose his father.

I dashed toward the counter and the painting hanging behind it. I lifted it off the nail, then sprinted back to the lab.

The lab door slammed behind me the second I reached safety.

A beat later, I heard a second *boom* thundering from the shop and rattled the door in its frame, but it held.

"Are we safe in here?" I asked while gasping for air.

"Remember, the walls are reinforced. The exit doors are reinforced steel from an underground bunker we acquired," explained Clarence. "We are quite safe."

I turned around to see Gnomey's back to me, his deadly gaze fixed on the door.

Chapter Thirty-One

WE WATCHED THE DISASTER FROM A MONITOR AS sprinklers came on to douse the fire. Brian was in tears, hugging me, clutching me, actually shuddering with gratitude before letting me go.

"You saved the painting." He shook his head, then clarified. "You saved *Montague*. I can't believe you would run into a burning room for a man you didn't know."

"He's family." I shrugged, feeling awkward, but the room got several degrees warmer when the words left my mouth.

The gang closed in around me, like a blanket over my shoulders on a chilly night. A tight huddle shielding me from the unbearable isolation that had been swallowing me. Finally, a sense of camaraderie.

It barely lasted a moment.

"My lab coat!" Clarence shouted, then he ran back out into the blackened shop where his lab coat had been draped carefully over a chair.

Beatrice.

We all heard him cursing before we got there. The

neighbors could probably hear him too. He was irate, already pacing while waving a fist in the air.

His lab coat had been incinerated, which meant Beatrice was no longer haunting it.

"She's gone!" Clarence lost his resolve, all of his regular stoicism having melted like icebergs in the future. "Beatrice is…"

The rest was just mumbles and tears.

I could barely believe it. Beatrice had been the one supporter who had stuck with me through all my mistakes. She had seen something in me nobody else had, and now she was simply gone.

The gang traded desperate looks, torn between their own sadness and the need to comfort Clarence.

"It's okay." Jackie was by his side, standing on her tiptoes and reaching up to put an arm around him.

Brian clapped Clarence on the back. "If there's anything I can do, just … you know."

"Fuck." Ariel jockeyed in to give him a hug.

"I was … I was…" Clarence drew a deep breath, and every part of him seemed ready to finally make his confession.

But he didn't get the chance before there was a gagging, hacking cough as Beatrice visually blurted into the room, appearing in her usual ethereal glow.

"You were what?" she asked, a huge grin on her face that made her glow even brighter.

"Beatrice!" Clarence could barely believe it. He ran over to her, clearly wanting to hug her, but was unable. He swatted at the air. "We thought we'd lost you!"

"Looks like I'll be living in between the here and there for a little longer." Beatrice beamed at him. "Good thing I'm not sick of you yet."

Clarence was overjoyed. So was everyone else in the

room, whooping and hollering with little hallelujahs of joy until the commotion settled. Then Clarence stepped away from the huddle, looking over at the combusted chair that had once held his lab coat with concern. It seemed whatever had started the fire in the shop had begun at the chair. Black marks emanated from it from across the floor, and the heat had been enough to melt the metal of the chair, leaving it looking like a bent-over skeleton. But that wasn't what Clarence was concerned about.

"What is it?" Brian asked.

But even I knew the answer to that before Clarence said it out loud.

"If she wasn't on my lab coat, then what else could she have possibly been attached to?"

Nobody knew everything in the lab was now suspect.

Clarence started taking inventory, recruiting an extremely willing Jackie and Ariel into his mission while I shuffled my feet in uncertainty, and Brian shifted on his, waiting to interrupt them through an awkwardly painful few minutes.

"Um, guys?" Brian cleared his throat when no one responded. "We need to get out of here."

"Where are we going?" asked Jackie.

"Wherever we can regroup," Brian replied, sounding almost like a leader. "We have Montague, thanks to Shondra, so I suggest we leave out the back."

"Why?" Ariel asked. "The fire is out."

"Do you want to go in there?" Brian looked back at the shop. "It's not like we're abandoning the place forever, but we need to figure this out, and I'd rather leave through the lab door. Secure the place before the fire department arrives."

Brian nodded toward the rear exit.

I didn't disagree. The fire had burned fast and fierce,

swallowing several shelves before it went out. The air was still thick and warm. Water mixed with ash and gave the appearance of black ink dripping from everything. The smell was a mixture of charred wood, plastic, and a hint of burnt hair that was eerily reminiscent of the smell of corn chips. Leaving out the back sounded great to me.

Ariel nodded. "Great. Easiest problem we'll be having all day, I'm sure of it. Next one up: Where are we going to go? I would ask you all over to my place, but I don't want to hear you all bitching about Snuggles."

But no concern about what Snuggles might be doing to invite the bitching.

"Brian's apartment above the shop is now full of that putrid smell, in addition to it still being decorated like an adolescent boy growing up in the 90s. So, twice as many reasons to stay away."

I'd heard Ariel loudly joking about the state of Brian's apartment before, cluttered with posters for Mudhoney and Screaming Trees, plus the Lakers and Pokémon.

"We could all go to my house!" I offered before dialing back. "If you guys want to."

"We're not all guys," Ariel said.

"I'm sure your home is lovely." Jackie smiled, the first fudge-worthy one in days. "But I need to stick around until the fire department takes their report."

Clarence nodded. "If we're going to go, then let's go."

"Now you're sounding like me." Ariel turned from Clarence to Brian. "What are we doing with Shondra? Is she back in? Can we go to her place in suburbia?"

"It's, like, a few minutes from here," I said.

Brian sighed as he looked at me, but the gust was from fatigue with the world more than me this time. "You're back in, but no more thinking that you can do your own thing. Literally, never again. This means you have to tell us everything and hide nothing."

Ariel nodded. "We want all the dirty details."

Brian shook his head. "They don't have to be dirty."

I tried not to squeal. "Thank you!"

"This is your last chance," Brian warned me again.

"I understand. I swear, I won't let you down."

Ariel looked at the group. "So we're all going to be honest with each other?"

"Of course." Brian nodded.

"Starting now?" Ariel pressed.

"Yes. Starting now."

"Great." Ariel clapped. "Then maybe it's time that you tell Shondra what you've been hiding."

Brian looked shifty, his eyes darting around before he reset himself. "I think that's better as a show and tell."

"Then start showing her," Ariel said.

Brian took out his phone and started talking into it moments later.

"It's me ... yeah ... I need you to meet us at — hold on." He turned to me. "What's your address?"

I gave him the address, and then Brian repeated it to the receiver before ending the call.

"What's happening?" I asked.

"We're having a council of war."

Chapter Thirty-Two

I COULDN'T STOP PACING MY LIVING ROOM AS WE WAITED for our mysterious guest to arrive. I watched minutes tick by on my living room clock, anxiety and anticipation churning more by the second.

It wasn't the visitor that was making my muscles tight with knots. We had one day — one day — to help Justin, or he would die. It was a cinderblock on my chest, making breathing difficult.

The room was silent and still, though it shouldn't have been. Nobody wanted to talk because everybody was afraid I might ask the wrong question, or they would say the wrong thing in reply.

So time passed, with only ticking to break the stillness.

Until the front door swung wide, and I felt a swell of hope that Brian's pending revelation was here.

But instead, it was Mom, Rashida, and Malik.

All three of them paused in the doorway.

Malik spoke first. "Look what Shondra brought home."

"Jerk." My sister nudged him with her elbow. "Hi there, I'm Rashida."

"You must be Shondra's friends." Mom smiled at everyone. "Welcome to our home."

I introduced the group, and even Ariel could not have been nicer. Once everyone had traded names, Mom invited the gang to get even cozier.

Mom smiled. "I'd be happy to whip up a little dinner if you're interested."

I smiled back. "We're interested, for sure. Clarence and Brian will actually be staying over if that's okay. They're kinda homeless right now."

"Not homeless," Brian overcompensated. "Our building went up in a blaze."

"Of course!" Mom barely batted an eye. If she was performing, then bravo. "I'm happy to have you both!"

"And a ghost?" Beatrice waved, but Mom couldn't see her.

Though the way Clarence glared at me, I felt a deep need to acknowledge her.

"And a ghost," I repeated.

Mom held her smile but shook her head. "Unless your ghost needs a helping of dinner, I don't need to know that part," she clarified. "I don't *want* to know that part."

She got started on dinner, and I went to help her. Mom was a performer to the bone, so there was no way her unexpected guests would be leaving without a memorable meal, even if she was "a prisoner of whatever she had in the fridge."

Mom asked me to prepare a small platter of appetizers while she started on the pot roast — a standard thick beef stew with carrots, potatoes, and green beans, but she made hers extra special with a caramelized mess of onions reduced with rosemary and thyme.

I loaded the appetizer tray with vegetables and dip,

plus a cheese plate full of fruits and meats. Crackers, butter, and three jams completed the charcuterie.

The aroma of her roast was heavy in the air when there finally came another knock on the door, this time from our mystery guest.

I went from excited to mortified in a blink as I opened the door and found myself staring into Kip Grime's smirking face.

I wanted to slam the door and whirl around to give Brian my dirtiest look. Instead, I stayed there and stared him down.

"Aren't you going to invite me in?" Kip could not look more smug.

"Are you a vampire? If I don't invite you in, will you go away?"

Brian was there by my side. "It's okay," he assured me, gently nudging me away from the doorway so Kip could enter my home. The soul-sucker.

"We're all friends here," said Kip, and I was totally wrong about him not being capable of elevating his smirk to yet another level.

"Now, do you get the show and tell?" Ariel asked.

Brian closed the door. "Kip has been acting as a double agent."

Wow. If that was true, and of course, it had to be, then I was even more of a big-time jerk.

Kip shook his head. "He makes it sound like a spy movie. But really, I've just been clocking in at Nemicon and reporting to Brian."

"You two were hired at the same time," Brian explained. "But Kip went to work at Nemicon because I needed eyes on whatever Rudolph is doing."

"He's been planning something for years," Ariel added.

"But we don't know what it is or when it's going to happen."

"It's Rudolph's fault that my father is trapped in the painting. So…"

Kip stopped, and his face flooded with panic at the realization that the *Saloon at the End of the World* had been at Darrow & Grimes when the fire started.

"The painting! The fire!"

"It's okay!" Brian clapped his apparent buddy on the shoulder and pointed to the painting, leaning against the corner wall. "Shondra rescued it."

Kip turned to me, and either I saw him differently, or his smirk was all gone. One second later, I was wrapped in his arms, even though I would have never asked to be there.

I did have to admit it was nice once I was.

He finally pulled away and addressed the room. "Rudolph is definitely up to something serious."

"Like what?" I asked.

"I don't know, but I've also lost his trust."

"What do you know?" I said. I felt like everyone had read the book, while I'd only glanced at a pamphlet.

"He's working with someone."

"How do you know that?" Brian's question, so maybe some of this was new.

Kip shrugged. "A lot of secretive phone calls. Schedule changes, evasive answers, weird names batted around that I've never heard. Lots of reasons."

"Are any of those reasons named Justin?" I asked.

"Good question," Ariel said.

I loved the warmth of her sun.

"I'm not sure there's a connection," said Kip.

"He's the most likely candidate for having started the fire. Don't you guys agree?"

Clarence shook his head. "I don't think we can know that. Not enough evidence."

"There was one name I've heard them talking about the last few days. Justin."

"What? Are you serious?"

My heart was pounding.

"I heard Rudolph talking about that game you were after and that they wanted it for themselves."

"And?"

Spit it out, man. Stop dragging it out. The clock is a-tickin'.

"After I returned from the farmer's market incident, I heard Rudolph talking on the phone to someone. He said he had located Justin and that they would have the game soon. He told the person on the phone that they had a way to secure it and avoid the curse."

This was it. If Nemicon knew a way to defuse the curse bomb, then we needed that information pronto.

"Maybe we need to lean harder on Rudolph to get some answers," I suggested. "Stop lurking in the shadows."

"We can't use the earworm on purpose," Brian cut me off. "That goes against everything we stand for."

"That's not what I'm saying." I shook my head. "Remember the Cray-Z-Boy at the Carnivale Arcane?"

"Of course," Ariel said.

"We already saw how to use it," I said, then explained to everyone. "When people in the chair were guided toward questions they didn't want to answer, that person's time with the chair usually ended with them blurting the truth."

"You heard him!" Clarence barked. "That's not how we do things!"

"I don't want to hurt anyone. This is just a matter of

getting Rudolph to tell us the truth." I turned from Clarence to Ariel. "You saw the chair — tell him!"

"Even if we were willing to use this chair, we don't actually have it," Brian interjected.

Ariel added, "The owner said it was his best earner. If he wouldn't part with that stupid doll, then there's no way he's parting with this."

"So we steal it." Now, I felt bold.

Brian shook his head. "We don't steal."

"Okay," I said, changing tactics. "We *liberate* the recliner. Does D&G *always* do the right thing? Well, today, that means getting that chair. Not just because it would help us with the Rudolph situation but also because we saw how the Carnivale was using it. We break into the Carnivale, liberate the chair, then feed it to the old Dale & West once it's done."

"I don't know…" Brian said. But he was hedging.

And if Clarence had any objections, he was keeping them to himself. I chose to see Beatrice's glow as her ghostly form agreeing with me.

Ariel said, "I think that if we're not willing to play a little dirty, then more innocents will get caught in the crossfire."

"She's right about that." Brian was talking to everyone but clearly trying to convince himself. "Nemicon never cares about innocents."

"Confirmed." Kip nodded, but the gesture was a lot less annoying than it usually was.

"So, are we going to *Ocean's 11* this or what?" I asked.

"I don't think it will be that complicated," Brian replied.

"More like *Ocean's Six* or *Seven* if Beatrice is coming."

"Thank you," Beatrice glowed, grateful for the acknowledgment.

All we had to do was break into the Carnivale, find some way to get the Cray-Z-Boy out of there, use it to question the evil owner of Nemicon, and then hopefully leverage whatever we found out to save Justin's life.

And we only had one day to do it.

Chapter Thirty-Three

THE ADVENTURE WAS GETTING UNREASONABLY EXCITING, even if not everyone wanted to hop on board. Clarence was too old for this shit. He actually said those exact words out loud.

Brian got a call from Jackie while we were making plans. He needed to get to the shop asap because the firemen and police were both demanding access to the lab for different reasons, and he was the only one who might possibly manage to keep them at bay.

So it was me, Ariel, and Kip breaking and entering. I curled my toes to give my giddiness somewhere to go without anyone noticing.

"Calm down," Ariel told me.

We agreed to reconvene at my house later (and yes, I loved that my home was a sort of unofficial headquarters and that it made me more like part of the group), then the trio headed to the Carnivale and went to the truck.

We were on the way when it struck me that this same truck had just been filled to stock a shop that already needed to be stocked again, and still with no profits in the register. It really did feel like a curse.

We would have to restock later. First, we needed to end the curse and rebuild the shop.

We. It felt so great to say, even if I was only saying it silently to myself.

Ariel stopped in front of the Carnivale, and just as I'd imagined, the place was even creepier at night. Dimly lit and more sinister, shadows yawned across empty pathways and loomed over a darkened parking lot.

She killed the lights, then the engine, and we all got out of the truck.

Ariel stopped cutting through the fence, setting her bolt cutters on the ground to properly look at me. "You sure you're ready for this?"

I must have looked like I'd peed myself, but I was seriously excited and couldn't wait to creep through the empty Carnivale, even though I was the teensiest bit scared.

We wove through the unsettling displays, stalking shadows toward the haunted recliner in the back. Antique lamps shown dim yellow light around the warehouse. Left on for whom? Or what?

It didn't take long for the answer to be obvious. The Cray-Z-Boy was not the only haunted object in The Carnivale Arcana. Apparently, this place came alive at night.

A taxidermy beaver waved at us while his buddy, the rabbit, just glowered. A pair of mannequins lurched awkwardly our way, though their jolting motions were easy enough to outrun.

The wax hand grabbed a handful of my hair and yanked me back until Ariel mashed it to goo with the bolt cutters. More hunks of hair were lost. Great. The wax should be a joy to get out.

We were nearly to the Cray-Z-Boy when the haunted

suit of armor attacked, clamoring toward us with its iron-shod fists swinging.

I darted out of the way, and its fist crashed into the wall, coming back covered in drywall instead of my blood.

Ariel swung the bolt cutters at the armor, but it batted her weapon away. They went flying to land with a terrible clanking thud on the ground.

She charged the armor empty-handed, but it batted her away.

Kip nudged me aside and ran forward, tackling the armor and pinning it to the ground while I kicked at its empty helmet. We both waited for Ariel to retrieve her bolt cutters and turn the haunted armor into scrap.

Our quest became ever so slightly easier after that.

At least, I thought it would. But then we reached the recliner, and even without any more haunted objects or beings to stand in our way, there still seemed to be an impossible wall in front of us.

The recliner was much too heavy. Even with all three of us hefting, we could barely lift the thing, let alone carry it.

So we each grabbed an edge of it and sort of pushed/dragged/heaved the recliner back the way we came, past the empty suit of armor.

The Cray-Z-Boy didn't exactly have the same effect as if any of us were to be sitting in it, but it did give our entire trio a vicious case of the giggles, followed by some wildly out-of-control hiccups, then weird burps that echoed through the air and gave me a weird taste in my mouth.

The physical sensations got increasingly worse as we continued dragging the recliner.

I spent too much effort even thinking about it and needed a moment to rest.

"Hold up for a second ..." I panted through my

giggles, then hiccupped into a burp, terrified that I was going to fart.

We set the chair down, and that's when I spotted Dollie staring, clearly judging our thieving.

But I wasn't afraid of Dollie or anything else right now.

"Maybe we should take the doll, too," I whispered to Ariel. "As a peace offering for Monique."

I felt proud of myself for not just taking the doll, lone wolfing it as I would have in the past. Although thieving wasn't normally my style. Maybe it was the chair releasing my inner pirate.

"It can't hurt." She looked down at the chair. "We've already done the crime."

Kip shrugged, clearly just wanting to get the hell out of there with the chair. "Whatever helps you guys."

"I'll be right back," I said.

Then I sneaked up and carefully lifted Dollie from its case. She seemed lifeless, so maybe I'd been wrong about it. I felt the pressure of spirit energy form all around me, so it was difficult to determine its exact source. I could have sworn she had moved her head last time.

I held the doll up in triumph, proudly displaying my prize for Ariel and Kip, or probably Kip and Ariel.

Though if the doll wasn't haunted, Monique might not even—

Dollie opened its eyes and *shrieked*!

I dropped it, but only for a moment, grabbing a handful of its hair before the doll hit the ground, which was apparently a recipe for making it shriek even louder.

Dogs started barking.

A chorus of alarms started screaming, one right after the other.

The barking got closer, followed by the sound of heavy footsteps pounding the concrete from somewhere nearby.

"Stop right there, or I'll shoot!" bellowed a familiar voice.

We all stopped dead.

I dropped Dollie on the ground. She stopped shrieking, fully content once away from me. She seemed to smirk up at me.

This was all my fault.

"It's not your fault," Ariel whispered as their pursuer came into view.

The owner actually smiled when he saw us. And that loud barking had turned into happy panting from the two excited mastiffs flanking him on either side. Their toothy grins were friendly as slobber dripped from their mouths.

"Good thing I recognized you," Parker grunted, though his mood sounded breezy. "I was about to put a serious hurting on you."

"You don't have a gun," Ariel observed.

He shook his head. "I don't believe in them."

"But you just said—"

"I believe in the concept of fear," Parker cut Kip off. "Now, which one of you wants to tell me what the hell you're doing on my property after hours, dragging the Cray-Z-Boy off like it belongs to you?"

"We came here to steal your haunted recliner." Ariel was honest and blunt. "But it's a bitch and her sister to move."

The owner laughed. "If you want it that bad, you can have it. But you'll need some help getting it to your truck. I assume you brought a truck?" He shrugged. "The three of you look ridiculous dragging this thing."

Kip eyed the owner in suspicion.

"Why?" Ariel was always more direct. "You refused to sell it the other day when we offered you good money. So why just give it to us now?"

"Because I don't need good money." Parker laughed again. This guy sure seemed to be in a phenomenally good mood compared to the last time our paths crossed. "I got great money. Rest of my life, money. 'Fuck you, money,' as they say. Well, more like 'To hell with you, money,' but whatever."

He gestured around at the Carnivale. "I sold the whole kit and caboodle."

"To whom?" Kip asked, and his appropriate grammar was less annoying than it should have been.

"Nemicon." The owner nodded. "And, yeah, they're total assholes, but you can take the chair thanks to their generosity. That Rudolph dude didn't even bother to look around this place before signing. I can't imagine he'll even notice the recliner missing. Enjoy, and thanks for patronizing The Carnivale Arcane."

I had to bite my tongue to keep from smiling, imagining us using the Cray-Z-Boy on the very man we were stealing it from.

"Thanks for your help," Kip said, getting right to business by squatting down and positioning himself to lift the recliner.

The owner got on the other side and started to lift as well, followed by Ariel.

But I glanced down at Dollie and held onto my streak of bold behavior. "Do you mind if we take the doll, too?"

Parker was instantly sober, his humor all gone like I'd insulted his family. Then, he stated what he saw as the obvious.

"It's not The Carnivale Arcane without a haunted doll."

What a strange, strange man.

Chapter Thirty-Four

IT WAS A BUMMER TO LEAVE THE CARNIVALE ARCANE without Dollie, but Parker was a prince once I stopped pressing the issue, heaving with both legs and shoulders to get the Cray-Z-Boy into our truck. He asked if we wanted to get an early breakfast at Waffle House.

"That place is a public restroom that serves breakfast," Ariel said.

Parker didn't argue. He just gave us the address in case we changed our minds and told us that he planned to get his hash browns smothered and covered.

"Okay," Ariel told him.

Something was off with Parker. Before he threw us out without blinking. Now, he acted as if we were best friends. Had Nemicon done something to him?

"Damn it," Ariel exclaimed when she turned the truck on.

My heart jumped. "What?"

"Now I'm hankering for waffles!"

A couple hours later, we arrived at my place but left the chair in the truck. Kip was in a good mood, or at least he seemed to be considering the number of compliments he kept giving me, not getting the hint that it was embarrassing to talk about my bravery around running into the fire, even though I loved the positive attention.

"What took you so long?" Brian asked as we entered. Ariel texted him right after they finished loading the chair, but before Parker started going on about Waffle House.

"We had to make a stop," Kip explained.

"With the truck?" Brian raised his eyebrows. "Where?"

"Ariel wanted waffles," I said.

"And she wanted Waffles a la Mode over on Lexington," Kip elaborated.

"Sorry, I wasn't in the mood to eat a plateful of shit," Ariel didn't really apologize. "Guess I'll see you guys later."

She almost sounded sorry to go.

Kip left with Ariel so they could share a ride back to their respective cars unless there was something funny going down between the two of them. But why should I care if there was?

Maybe I cared a little.

Clarence and Beatrice were sitting side by side on the couch like they were watching TV. Once Kip and Ariel were gone, they turned toward one another and began to whisper like Brian and I weren't even in the room.

He took that as a sign and nodded at me, gesturing toward the stairs. I led the way to my room and then closed the door for some more debriefing. Brian wanted to hear all the stories he'd just heard in the living room again, quietly now with just the two of us.

I could actually feel him respecting me.

"Is that your Uncle Kevin's trunk? Where you found that journal?" Brian nodded at the behemoth sitting by the foot of my bed, surely knowing that it had to be. "I often wondered where that journal got to. My dad was always going on about it."

"You knew my Uncle Kevin?"

"Of course! That's one of the reasons I wanted to hire you." He glanced at it again. "Kevin Henry. I didn't know him personally, but he and my dad were friends."

"Do you want to see?"

"Are you kidding me?" Brian grinned like a kid with a big bag of gummy bears. "I'd love to."

Brian started looking through the box, telling the story about how Darrow & Grimes came to be, prompted by an article about a coffin convention he found in the trunk.

"This is where they met!" Brian exclaimed, waving the article like a prize. "It was an arcane convention, but the front was filled with coffins. Creepy enough to keep looky-loos out, and objects could be stored in the coffins for potential buyers to review. The event itself was boring until my dad and Montague struck up a conversation and realized they had similar goals. I still have William Darrow's first arcane purchase. A nightlight that runs away screaming and blinking when you unplug it."

Brian laughed to himself. "They found Clarence shortly after that. And once they had their scientist, the rest was history!"

"So, you are telling me that my uncle was a founding member of Darrow & Grimes."

"Yes, but then…"

"Then what?" I was sitting on the edge of my seat.

"There was a falling out between Montague and him. I don't know the details. My father would never tell me. But he had a ton of respect for Kevin and your dad."

I stopped breathing.

"My dad? He was a part of Darrow & Grimes, too?"

"Maybe? I'm not sure about that. I only heard my dad

mention him once before he passed, and a little about you."

"What about me?"

"That someday you would step into the shop and that I needed to take you in. You were owed a place because of how they treated your uncle."

"So that's why you hired me? Not for my massive skills?"

Brian laughed. "Do you really want me to answer that? Only Clarence knows this story, so please don't share it with any of the others."

"Lips are sealed." I made a motion of locking my mouth closed. "So ... were you really firing me?"

"Absolutely. I agreed to give you a chance, not to give you a free pass."

That was fair.

"But you have proved yourself worthy of one last chance."

I took a big breath. While I loved hearing the D&G origin story, the past seemed less relevant when the present felt like a haunting.

"I have a theory about the attacks on the shop," Brian said.

"Go on."

"Kip didn't say anything about Nemicon trying to burn us alive. And I don't know, it almost feels like that goat head would be beneath them."

"So, if not them, then who?"

"I think it's Justin."

Color me shocked. Now, he was paying attention to Justin. About time.

"He really wasn't happy with me that day I tried to help him. The goat's head, the fake ad, then the mice, and the footsteps were one thing, but someone started that fire.

We know the game has cursed him, and that changes people."

"And he's turning into something else." I shivered, thinking about what I had seen. But then I shook it off, exhaling anxiety to ask the question that had bothered me most. "Is Justin savable?"

"Depends on what you mean by 'savable'?" Brian replied.

That wasn't the answer I was looking for.

"If he really is turning monstrous, and that's not my imagination…"

"I don't think it's your imagination." He shook his head, but that didn't comfort me. "I was at the farmer's market."

"Then does that mean it's too late to save him? If Justin has really turned into something else, is it even possible to turn him back? We are running out of time. Tomorrow it's all over."

"I don't know." Brian shrugged. "I had never seen the Mansions of Madness game before this, so I don't really know anything about it. Curses aren't like socks or earplugs. There is no one size fits all."

He shrugged again. "But I imagine the curse will have something to do with the way the game works, and as for saving him…" A third and final shrug. "Sometimes we can save people. Just not always."

"But we're going to try?"

"You bet your ass we are." Brian nodded, his voice stronger and clearer. "We have to stop Justin either way. He's the likely candidate for whoever is coming after us. If we help him, great, but I honestly just care about making sure that Darrow & Grimes is safe."

"What about Rudolph?"

"We need to keep the game out of his hands, especially

if he has figured out a way to bypass the curse. In the process, we need to figure out how we can fuck with his plan once we know what it is. And then we stick to doing what we do best."

We were still both too wired for sleep, but it was time for us to settle down anyway. Brian made himself a cozy spot on the floor of the hallway, with enough pillows and blankets to build himself a fort.

"I love sleeping on the floor!" Brian declared when I protested that it wouldn't be comfortable enough for him. "That's the most natural way to sleep. It's better for your back. It grounds me. Great for my spine."

Even if I didn't think that he meant it, I believed that Brian wanted me to be happy with the situation, and that warmed me more than the blanket.

I drifted to sleep almost immediately.

But not long after, I was woken by an awful commotion coming from downstairs.

I sat straight up in bed, scrambling to my feet after another deafening crash, already panicking that Justin was inside my house, worried about Mom, both what might happen to her and how much she was going to yell at me about the noise later on, no matter what else was happening.

Brian was wide awake, too, the soft dawn streaming through the window like a wash of light on his tension.

I gasped as I entered the living room to what had to be several dozen small, black bats swirling and fluttering about.

Clarence was already frantically waving a broom in the air with one hand and swiping at the airborne vermin with a blanket using the other. Beatrice was trying to help but obviously couldn't, waving her arms through the bats while shouting out encouragement to Clarence.

Brian ran into the fray, waving his naked arms into the cloud of loudly screeching bats weaving through the air all around them.

I could hear Mom waking up in her bedroom.

Great. Her getting all pissed off would be even worse than the bats.

Chapter Thirty-Five

MOM WAS FURIOUS. RAGE BUBBLED UNDER THE FAÇADE OF calm, but she was certainly planning to murder me in icy cold blood later, waiting for our guests to leave.

I had never been more grateful for my new friends.

The final bat fluttered out the window, and we exhaled in collective relief, wiping sweat from our brows and looking around at the chaos — broken furniture and shattered belongings, the stench of guano already ripe in the air.

"I'm sure you'll clean this all up before you go back to bed," was all she said.

I did, with Clarence and Brian's help, plus Beatrice wishing us well until dawn was long behind us. No time to nap, but I made us all coffee. Then we stopped at Roasters on the way to Home Depot because Brian said he was still thirsty, which was a nice way of saying my coffee was weak or bitter or whatever. I didn't really know good coffee from bad.

I didn't need any more caffeine. This was Day Ten for Justin, so I was plenty awake. We had been hatching our plans while cleaning up, then again through all of the coffee breaks. We were ready, gearing up to confront Justin as a group. I think as friends, but I wasn't going to ask.

Friends or not, we were working as a unit to make sure that Justin didn't die on the day he would be otherwise doomed to. I hoped we could save him from his fate, but even if we couldn't, I was determined to stop Nemicon from getting their hands on Mansions of Madness and hurting any other innocents.

I didn't know what to expect, and so I had a whole string of obviously dumb questions that erupted from me. Were curses magic? Could we use magic words to break the spells? Did we need unusual magical weapons to combat the curse?

As Clarence kept insisting, there was no such thing as magic. So technically, and regardless of what it might look like, Justin wasn't *really* under any sort of spell.

"His energy is tied to the Mansions of Madness game," Clarence explained.

Brian clarified their plan out loud. "So we essentially need to untie that energy by getting Justin to agree to give up the game."

"Or we sever the connection," Clarence reminded him.

"And we do that by taking the game by force?" I asked.

"Right." Clarence nodded, unapologetic as could be. "It'll hurt the kid something fierce, but we also don't have many options."

"How will it hurt him?" I wasn't sure I wanted to know.

"As I said, the game is tied to his energy because it's using that energy as fuel faster than his body can replenish it. That's why he's dying."

"That's—" Horrifying. "It's eating him?"

Clarence nodded. "When we try to take the game away from him, it's going to eat faster."

"Shit." I would have been happier by not asking.

"You said this would help him. Could forcing it away from him kill him?"

The group looked at one another, but no one answered. By the expression on their faces, they didn't need to say anything. There had to be another way. We just needed to figure it out.

Ariel and Kip met us at Roasters, and then we all went over the plan together. I wasn't one hundred percent onboard, but I agreed to it for the moment. There was still some time to figure out a better one.

We would be starting the mission at Justin's house, breaking into his house (again) to get the game.

Kip was going to lure Rudolph to my house, where we had the Cray-Z-Boy still sitting in the truck. We decided not to unload it until we knew for sure we could get Rudolph to my house.

We already had a backup plan in the event that we couldn't get anything out of Rudolph, even after holding him down in the chair. Thanks to a little sleight of hand suggested by Brian, we were going to put the Phantom Needle inside my replica of Robert the Doll. We wouldn't fool Monique long-term that way, but the doll would read energetically as an arcane object, and Clarence would do his best to convince her that our Robert was indeed the real deal for long enough to find out what she might have heard about Rudolph's plan or how to manage the curse on the Mansions of Madness.

I didn't love that little strategy since I was the one who had cost D&G the relationship, to begin with, and this felt an awful lot like striking a match and tossing it onto the bridge.

"We don't like working with her anyway." Brian shook his head vigorously, obviously trying to reassure me.

"She has no respect for the branches of knowledge she is tapping into," Clarence said with disdain. "She's just another amateur playing peek-a-boo with a hungry lion."

Beatrice nodded. "Her energy is dark."

"She says that she doesn't have the time or space to compost!" Jackie chimed in, sounding like she wanted to contribute and like that little nugget of discontent had been irking her for a while.

"She's a weirdo," added Ariel.

But weren't we all? This was the biggest group of weirdos I had ever been around in my life. That's what I loved about being around them so much. They made me feel less weird, not because they were weirder than me, but because our varying levels of weirdness were okay.

Brian grew up in the arcane business and had been running Darrow & Grimes to the best of his limited abilities for a decade now. He was clueless, but I had to give the guy credit for trying. I had seen him reading three different books on leadership in the short time I'd known him. CEO seemed like an awfully big acronym for what Brian did around D&G, but I respected him more by the day. His heart was in the right place, for sure.

But what made him weird was his genuine obsession. He hadn't just grown up with the arcane. Brian had never grown out of it.

Ariel was a badass bitch who obviously didn't like anyone, especially me, coming into her space, even though she had eventually warmed up. She was competitive and liked to win. She also seemed to enjoy her role as the only agent in the field since Jackie moved into an office role. Brian barely counted.

But Ariel was weird because she grew up in this business, the same as Brian. She still kept her haunted teddy bear, despite the fact that she regularly woke up with scratches and the occasional bleeding wall.

Kip was another second-generation weirdo and nothing like the man I had cast him to be. Jackie was even weirder for choosing this life. Like me, she had come in from the outside, actively seeking answers to some of the world's darkest mysteries. Her baby would be like the rest of them, though, born to this world.

Clarence was the only person in the world (though surely there had to be more of them) that I knew who was equally enthralled with arcane objects and with the scientific explanations behind why everything worked as it did. That was a mathematically wonderful kind of weird.

Beatrice was automatically weird on account of being a ghost.

"Ready to gear up?" I asked my friends.

Following a rousing chorus of hurrahs, we were off to Home Depot.

Ray was excited to see us again and bent over backward to help. "Sounds like you're making some homemade weapons." He nodded in approval. "Mind if I make a few suggestions?"

"Please do!" Clarence sounded delighted, curious to see Ray's ingenuity.

Ray grinned. It seemed like he'd been waiting his entire life to deliver his list of handcrafted armaments and weapons of minor destruction. Not sure how I felt about that. Impressed and a little terrified seemed about right. He talked for a minute without stopping, then finished with, "Sound good?"

"Sounds great!" Clarence declared.

"Give me fifteen minutes." Then Ray was gone,

zipping around Home Depot like a modern-day black-smith arming us for battle.

It took him longer than he said, but almost an hour later, we had a club fashioned from a baseball bat and two metal pipes; a sword made of plumbing pipe and sheet metal; a whip fashioned from a chain, the handle from a car jack, and a roller skate; a dart gun made from a blow gun and a bicycle pump; a bow made from a fishing pole, string, and a piece of wood; a spear made from a dowel rod and a utility knife; a mace made from a sledgehammer, some chain, and the spikes from a lawn aerator; and a nail gun turned crossbow. All were Husky brand, of course.

I wasn't sure where the baseball bat, skate, and blow gun came from, but I felt it wise not to ask Ray too many questions, or I might find myself rubbing the lotion on my skin before I got the hose again.

"How about that?" Brian asked, pointing to a plain old crowbar.

"This baby's good as is." Ray stroked the metal bar, then slashed it through the air to demonstrate its power.

Clarence agreed. "Give me a lever long enough and a fulcrum on which to place it, and I shall move the world."

"I'll just stick with the hammer?" I struck a blow through the air like Ray had, but my weapon wasn't impressive. I was also in charge of the duct tape.

"Kick their haunted asses!" Ray cheered us on, taking his break in the parking lot as we donned our duct tape and armor.

"No such thing as haunted," Clarence grumbled, disappointed in his new friend.

Chapter Thirty-Six

WE WERE BACK AT JUSTIN'S HOUSE, BUT THIS TIME WE were ready. It was midday, and the sun was high in the sky, shining its bright light all over our home invasion, so we had zero minutes to waste.

Justin's mom opened the door after a single knock, seeming grateful to see us and not in the least bit suspicious despite our dubious appearance, complete with duct tape armor and handcrafted weapons. She must have thought we were LARPers playing some sort of game and didn't seem to recognize either Kip or me. Of course, the last time she saw us was only for seconds amid all of those mice traps and our screaming.

"You must be here to see Justin." She sounded so grateful and seemed to be actively avoiding giving our getups too much attention. "He's just down there." She nodded toward the basement with a sigh. "He's *always* down there."

She made it another few steps before abruptly stopping and turning back to them. "I was hoping you could do me a favor?"

"Anything!" I answered without thinking, desperate for this all to go well.

She leaned toward us and lowered her voice as if Justin could overhear her whisper from down in the basement with his pointy ears.

"I was hoping you could convince him to shower." She looked down at the floor for a long moment before turning her gaze back to them. "He's starting to smell ... it's really bad ... you'll see."

She turned back around without waiting for an answer and walked to the door, then finished her thought in a whisper before opening it. "*I'm sorry.*"

The reek hit us immediately.

"I told you," she said, still hanging her head as we filed past, trying not to gag.

A pungent, acrid stench filled the narrow stairwell, thick and overwhelming. The scents of sweat and urine, rotting food, and human funk bloomed from the basement where Justin was lurking.

The raunchy aroma clung to my clothing and hair as we descended the stairs.

Things were worse at the bottom. The world down there didn't just smell off; it *felt* off. The dark spirit energy gave me an immediate migraine and threatened to empty my breakfast from my stomach- up or down.

The basement was dark as expected, dank with cracked walls and lined with shelves full of books and creepy figurines. Cluttered furniture and eerie relics, a pair of old rocking chairs, plus a table of dusty chalices added to the creepiness. The floor was littered with moldy rugs and scattered detritus. But the arrangement of everything was deliberate, with menacing corners and winding pathways.

Mazes, I realized, along with everyone else, as we gasped together.

Justin had arranged the cavernous room like a real-life Mansions of Madness game, full of dark objects and perhaps unseen traps hidden in the deep shadows.

Mansions was a dungeon crawling, horror-mystery experience that focused on clue acquisition, puzzle solving, and battle against monsters called Eldritch Terrors. One of the most fearsome was Cthulhu — a monstrous, tentacled creature rising from the depths of the ocean, with scaly green skin and glowing red eyes on a massive writhing body, seeking to impose its will upon the world.

"Welcome, brave adventurers," said a voice crackling through a speaker somewhere in the gloom. "To find me, you must play the game and traverse my maze. Don't delay. Terror awaits!"

We couldn't be sure Justin was even down here. It could be some elaborate trap like the mouse traps, but we had no choice but to play his game if we had any chance of finding him.

I walked toward the bookshelf to get a closer look at a cluster of figurines and recognized several of them from the second edition because, of course, I'd been playing with the crate. It was badass. I picked one up as I heard someone (or something) making a strangling noise behind me.

I turned around to see a Crawling One — it looked half-snake and half-frog if the snake was made from an intestine and the frog from a nightmare — rising out of the floor behind me as if it was made out of water.

One three-fingered hand with talons took a swipe at my head, but I ducked. Kip took a massive swing with his improvised sword, and Brian was right behind him with the crowbar.

The Crawling One spit a mouthful of worms at us.

"Don't let them crawl inside your nose or mouth!" I

shouted at the clueless non-nerds. The little fuckers did damage once they got inside you.

Beatrice rushed in and tried to distract the Crawling One to give Kip and Brian some time to recover, but it simply reared back, passing through the ghost.

Kip staggered back and spat a worm out of his mouth as Brian frantically brushed them off his face. Ariel yelled for Brian and me to duck as she lashed at the Crawling One with the chain whip.

That was all I needed, climbing around to wrap the chain around its neck and yanking it down until the creature's face hit the ground.

Brian started whacking it with the crowbar.

A taloned hand smacked into me and nearly knocked me over.

I screamed, smashing at the hand with my hammer.

Clarence lunged, grabbing me hard but still like a grandpa and yanking me back while Brian kept clubbing the Crawling One over and over until Kip finally buried his sword in its side.

The creature gave a final heave, then twitched three times before falling still.

"Freaking Lovecraft," Brian spat.

The Crawling One flickered out of existence like a hologram, but my hand was still sore from where its claw had slammed into me.

Everyone looked at me.

"What did you do?" Ariel asked.

"It's a Crawling One." I held up the statue. "It's an Eldritch Terror from the Forbidden Alchemy expansion."

Crickets. Crickets.

I had out-nerded the non-nerds.

"I think the monster might have been triggered by our presence."

"What triggers them in the game?" Ariel asked.

"Exploring the mansion."

"Great," she said.

"Do you know the best way to go?" Brian asked.

"Nope." I shook my head. "There are monsters everywhere you go in the game. Still don't think this is magic, Clarence?"

"They're interesting, for sure. Most likely a sort of mass hallucination brought on by…"

But everyone ignored him, moving carefully through the maze of furniture. The smell was horrific, and the environment was claustrophobic. I had to keep reminding myself that Justin couldn't help it, that this was all because of me.

We were walking between a bookcase and a dresser when a man in a hooded robe suddenly appeared, the hood obscuring his face.

"Where is Justin?" Brian asked him.

The hooded man slowly raised his hand and pointed at them.

"He's a Dark Druid!" I yelled as dark shadows bloomed from the floor to engulf us.

We were swinging at shadows, none of us connecting, each of the thick clusters of foggy darkness like dry ice as they touched our skin.

"How are we supposed to fight these?" Ariel yelled.

Then Brian: "We should have brought a flame thrower!"

"The whole place would go up!" Clarence retorted, sounding defensive. "And these aren't spirits!"

He had one of his many devices out, this one with two separate nozzles, each a different color, and he was doing his best to scan them, but he dropped the device once engulfed by shadows.

I was crouched on the floor, batting at the shadows with my hammer, screaming because it felt like every inch of me was freezing while on fire.

An intense pink glow began to fill the room.

I looked up to see the rest of the group flailing, but Beatrice was floating overhead, her arms open wide as she whispered, drawing the shadows to her glow, absorbing them.

It was clearly a strain on her. Pink light flickered, and her face pinched in agony, but the relief was dizzying as we struggled to our feet.

"Are you okay?" Clarence asked a haggard-looking Beatrice.

"I'm fine," she replied in a raspy whisper. "I just need to rest for a bit."

"Thank you for saving—" I didn't get to finish before Beatrice flickered out.

And Clarence looked twisted with worry.

"We've only moved four yards through this mess; there has to be a better way to reach Justin," Ariel said, frustrated.

Hmm. The maze was shepherding us through this and was set up in a way that forced the group into every trap, so we needed to reach him without going through the maze.

I jumped up on a dresser, quickly looked around, then jumped onto a coffee table. It wobbled a bit before I caught my balance, then I looked around again. Nothing happened, so I stepped onto the seat of a chair. It creaked but held my weight. And still no monsters.

I looked at the gang with a grin. "The floor is lava."

Ariel grinned back at me and then jumped into another chair.

Everyone else followed.

Kip posed heroically on top of his chair, raising his sword up in front of him like King Arthur pulling Excalibur from the stone.

"Where do you think Justin is most likely to be hiding?" Brian asked.

I pointed. "Probably up in that little nook past the water heater."

He was clearly a coward, and that was the farthest spot from the door.

We worked our way over by jumping from one piece of furniture to the next and had almost arrived when Brian stepped onto a rickety sideboard that collapsed under his weight.

Clarence and I both lunged to catch him, but Clarence missed, and I got pulled down with him.

We scrambled to our feet and jumped up on an adjacent table, but it was already too late.

A shimmering in the air coalesced into a naked woman with horns and a long devilish tail right in front of Kip.

He looked down at her. "We don't want to hurt you, miss, but—"

The woman brayed like a goat and grabbed his ankle with a clawed hand, yanking Kip to the floor.

He dropped his sword, flailing as he fell.

"Goat Spawn!" I yelled. "From the Call of the Wild expansion!"

"Is that relevant right now?" yelled Ariel.

I couldn't remember this monster's power, but there wasn't time to ponder.

Now, we were all fighting the Goat Spawn while trying to stay off the floor.

Clarence got knocked down trying to pull Kip away from the Goat Spawn and get him up in a chair where he couldn't trigger any more monsters.

Brian attacked the Goat Spawn with his club from the front.

I moved in with my hammer from the side.

Ariel jumped to a dresser behind Goat Spawn and looped her chain around her neck, then yanked back hard, strangling her while Brian smashed her forehead in.

Ariel let go of the chain from one end, and the Goat Spawn dropped, then flickered from existence.

I was exhaling hard, feeling lightheaded and scratched.

"Why can't I feel my leg?" Kip moaned.

Blood was oozing from his ankle into his pants.

And only then did I remember the Goat Spawn's venomous claws.

Clarence tied a tourniquet around Kip's calf under his knee to slow the poison moving through his body.

"Is anyone else hurt?" Ariel asked.

I showed them the tiny scratch on my forearm. The flesh around it was numb, but I could feel the rest of my limb, so maybe it didn't get me that much.

We told Kip to stay put and that we would come right back for him, but even after we managed to make it to the partially obscured nook behind the water heater without anyone else falling and activating a trap, Justin wasn't there.

The voice had only been a recording. No computer, no boy-turned-monster, and not a single solitary clue beyond the note lying on an empty desk.

I'm coming for you. I'm coming for your little store. And I'm coming for every single one of the secrets you're hiding inside.

Chapter Thirty-Seven

THINGS GOT EVEN WORSE AFTER WE GOT OUT OF THE house. It wasn't hard to sneak out because Justin's mom was in the living room with the TV on extra loud, determinedly watching a sitcom with canned laughter. Probably to drown out the sounds of hearing us die in the basement.

Once outside, we piled into the truck, and Ariel took the wheel, peeling out of the driveway the second we were all inside. I almost fell out again, trying to close my door.

We barreled through a yellow blinking light before it turned red as Brian frantically swiped at his phone. He had to be calling Jackie back at the shop.

"Change of plans!" he shouted into the phone. "Get the chair to the shop! Keys are on the table. We'll meet you there!"

So he must have been talking to—

"Thanks, Joanna!" My mom! He was calling my mom. To help solve an arcane issue. That was weirder than any hallucinatory creature I'd just seen.

Kip had called Rudolph before our siege on Justin's playhouse and asked him to meet him at the shop. Kip told him that D&G had stolen the Cray-Z-Boy, and he knew where they were hiding it.

We didn't have to run any lights, but we did cut it close a few times. My palms were slick when we pulled up in front of the shop.

I wiped them off on my pants and hopped out of the truck. Everyone followed except Kip, who was pale and shivering. I hoped Clarence had some kind of antidote for him.

And maybe for me. The numbness in my arm hadn't spread, but I was still feeling light-headed. I hoped it was just the adrenaline. It would have been helpful if Justin had left some healing potions alongside the monsters.

But there wasn't time to worry more. Rudolph was walking down the sidewalk, right toward where the Cray-Z-Boy Mom and Jackie were just settling onto the sidewalk.

Kip gained speed and limped to Rudolph, grabbed him by the arm, and shoved him down onto the recliner.

Rudolph looked up at him in wide-eyed surprise, followed by an immediate beat of horrified realization, before he swallowed hard enough for his Adam's apple to bob up and down as he tried to choke on the coming admission.

But Ariel and I were ready for this. We had even practiced on the way over.

"What are you hiding?" we shouted in unison.

If I hadn't known Rudolph Bramson to be a wretched man who had ruined more than one life that I knew of for sure and clearly had no qualms about ruining plenty more, I might have felt sorry for him.

Still, it was hard to watch. He twitched and spasmed uncontrollably, desperately trying to throttle the truth before it escaped him, chomping on his bottom lip until blood started gushing, his body twisting into a pretzel of panic as the Cray-Z-Boy attempted to wrest the confession from him.

"How do we end the curse on Mansions of Madness?" I shouted.

His face contorted in pain and fear with his final valiant effort, but then he paled even further and sank down into the seat cushion. His wild eyes finally settled, and a single word puffed through his lips.

"Lulu."

Rudolph plugged his ears and started laughing loudly, hard guffaws coming like chuckling thunder from somewhere deep inside him.

Damn. His defenses were excellent.

Ariel narrowed her eyes at Rudolph, then turned to me with a curl of her lip. I knew what she wanted me to do and felt a shiver as she said it. "Go get the earworm."

"No, wait," Brian called out, but he didn't have an end to that sentence.

Clarence was nodding, encouraging me to do what needed to be done.

Jackie joined him, and even accounting for Brian's objection, I wouldn't be lone-wolfing it at all.

So I turned and ran, racing around the corner toward the D&G rear entrance, coming to a dead stop when I heard an unwelcome sound behind me.

Sirens.

I ducked behind a mailbox and saw the cops. Shepherd and Nichols pulled up at the curb. They must have a warrant now. It probably barely took a phone call after the explosions. If the shop already suspected of cooking meth, then the cops would only be more certain by now.

I stayed in my hiding spot, observing the scene as the D&G gang was forced to back off of Rudolph. Emboldened, their former prisoner shot to his feet and aimed an angry finger at the people who had accosted him.

"These people stole this chair from me!" Rudolph yelled.

The officers looked at the Cray-Z-Boy but clearly didn't know what to make of Rudolph's accusation.

Though they did recognize him.

"Aren't you Rudolph Bramson?" asked Shepherd.

"It is Rudolph Bramson!" Nichols answered for him.

"Did you hear me?" Rudolph looked from one to the other. "These miscreants stole my chair."

"You're on my property!" Brian shouted. "It looks like you're the one trying to steal it!"

"Miscreants?" my mom repeated.

Again, I was paralyzed with indecision.

I didn't know what I should do.

I was caught between the rock of wanting to do the right thing and the hard place of being forced to lone wolf it yet again.

"Are you going to arrest anyone?" Rudolph asked.

"If today is a good day, then yes," Shepherd nodded.

"But not for sitting in your chair," Nichols clarified.

"Stealing my chair!" Rudolph shouted.

The officers told him to scram unless he cared to involve himself with the illegalities happening at Darrow & Grimes, specifically in regard to cooking meth.

"There are no illegalities!" Brian protested. "Especially not meth!"

"Especially?" Nichols repeated, now doubly suspicious.

I still didn't know what to do. The cops were playing it cool because they held the cards, biding time until they could get inside the shop. I couldn't do anything to help Brian, Ariel, Clarence, Kip, my mom, and Jackie with the police right next to them, but I did know the plan.

I just didn't want anyone to get mad at me for doing my own thing like usual, even if I was only doing it on behalf of everyone else.

But then Brian made eye contact with me. First, a smile, followed by a nod, and I knew that he wanted me to sneak into the lab, lift the replica, slip away with Robert the Doll, and initiate Plan C: take the doll to Monique and bribe her for information on what Rudolph was up to, and Gods willing, a way to break the curse.

The first and second parts were easier than they should have been. But that was just fate prepping me for the rotten surprise awaiting me on the other side of the doorway.

I smelled Justin before I saw him. Fetid and rank in his ultimate monster form.

Justin's hulking body loomed in the alleyway, the Mansions of Madness game tucked like a prize under his arm.

I could smell the stink of his breath as he threatened me with a growl. "You're dead."

And then—

Chapter Thirty-Eight

JUSTIN LUNGED TOWARD ME.

I darted out of the way, falling several steps back into the street.

He had gone Full Monster. A hulking behemoth with heaving muscles on a bestial form, his mouth twisted into a snarl, eyes feral, and breath stinking of rot.

He took two lumbering steps toward me, then pounced.

I fell another step back with my hands raised, palms out, trying to pacify him.

"Please!" I ducked to the right, then circled around and raced into the lab.

I ran to the other side of the lab, still trying to talk calmly to Justin as he loped inside and slammed the door.

"Be careful!" I warned him. "Most of the things in here can hurt you. And I don't want to see you hurt!"

I shook my head to reassure him.

For a moment, he paused, but then his growl was even louder.

Justin lurched forward.

But this time, I held my ground, even though I was trembling down to my toes, and the stench of his breath was making me sweat.

I held his eyes, red and sagging with a demonic fatigue.

"You don't have anything to be afraid of." I shook my head again, then held his eyes, still terrified that they would lose their focus at any second and Justin would swipe me with something that now looked less like a hand and more like a paw. "Not from me, and not in this room."

He grunted and gnashed but didn't move forward.

"It's not magic," I told him in my very best Clarence. "It's only energy. If we understand that, then we can channel it."

He was actually looking at me. As if he could actually hear and understand what I was saying. Like Justin wasn't just some beast who couldn't be pulled back from oblivion.

"I get it." This time, I nodded, still scared but standing straighter. "You don't feel valued or seen. Nobody listens to you, so of course, you feel alone. No one cares as they should, or—"

Justin snarled, then retreated with what seemed like an involuntary step backward, pounding his crown with both fists as if punishing himself for being a coward.

I had no idea how much of the monster was in control, but as long as I could still see Justin behind that disfigured skin full of festering sores or sense his soul behind those bulging eyes of malice, I had to keep trying to reach him.

"I'm sorry for not taking responsibility sooner and for being manipulative and trying to trick you. I shouldn't have tried to get what I wanted from you in the way that I did."

His drooling mouth opened to reveal teeth that had twisted in his bloody gums. He roared at me, but still, I refused to budge.

I had been the one who turned him from a basement-dwelling board-gaming blogger into the feral monster in front of me.

The beast who obviously thought I deserved to die. The only thing keeping him from attacking me was him clutching the Mansions of Madness box.

Justin snarled again, but that one barely had any air in it. Nothing was landing. He wasn't the one in control, and I was still just a girl in his way.

His body tensed, and I knew this was the end of it. I couldn't believe that the cops hadn't come into the lab yet, but a minute from now, they were going to find the shredded meat sack version of Shondra.

I did the only thing I could think to do.

"Alexander!" I shouted the name of the game's original owner.

That stopped him cold.

"I know who you are." I swallowed and kept right on going. "Not just Justin, but *you*, Alex. I know how lonely you were and that if you couldn't play the game, then you wanted to live it. So, do you want to play Mansions of Madness with me now?"

He leaned his head back, looking like he was going to howl, but then he simply nodded like a puppy ready for his walk.

"Open up in there!" The cops started pounding loudly on the front door. "We're knocking the door down!"

So, we played.

I put on a pair of Husky brand gloves that Ray had given me first. Clarence, are you watching?

At least Justin was occupied now. Breathing more like a human and less like a monster. The person inside Justin was trying even harder to connect with the person inside me.

And still, the police kept pounding on the door. It kept

getting louder and louder. They would be on the other side any second now. The officers were seriously incompetent for still being stuck outside the lab.

I kept my cool, talking calmly to Justin like we had all the time in the world.

"I love your blog."

His ears perked.

"The Gamers Guide to the Galaxy." I laughed. "Do you like Douglas Adams?"

He nodded.

"Me too. The man was a master at making the absurd sound reasonable. And he made sci-fi funny."

Justin looked like he wanted to smile, so I added one more.

"He made the mundane hilarious."

Justin broke into a grin, and I noticed how much he had changed.

His twisted and deformed body had mostly reformed, scales and fangs receding. Eyes that had been glowing red and menacing now looked full of warmth and understanding.

Alexander's demonic spirit was getting sucked back into the game where it belonged as we played. As if each time one of us touched one of the pieces, a little bit of the curse energy went into it. The police hadn't succeeded in breaking down the door, and now I knew they wouldn't. Clarence had built this lab to last.

For an hour, we simply played. Soon, he began to talk about the monsters in the game, but then other things: painting figures, the smell of a new game, the delight in painting those images I'd see on his blog. And bit by bit, the monster receded until it was finally one hundred percent Justin sitting across from me.

I folded up the game and carefully returned it to the box as he watched me.

I was watching him, too, all the way to the Dale & West incinerator.

The police had put a drill to the door out front. Metallic screeches and high-pitched whirring accompanied muffled thuds and grunts.

I looked at the monitors to determine how long we had before they breached the door. But the police weren't banging on the door, but the brick about five feet to the right of it. No one could be that oblivious. There was obviously something else happening here, whether Clarence would use the word *haunted* or not.

I tossed the game into the incinerator and watched it burn as the drill whined louder, receptive and urgent, punctuated by a beat of boot heels against brick.

Something was definitely going on.

I looked at the monitors again, and that's when I saw it. I spun around to see Gnomey facing the door. Mushrooms were growing around the door inside and OUTSIDE.

Realization slapped me in the face along with the pungent, earthy scent of fungus. I knew exactly what was happening here and would have wondered what had taken me so long to realize, but the answer was obvious. The wall of fungi was dulling everyone's senses, and that was even truer for the officers outside.

My mood changes. My clumsy, erratic behavior. The gang's intense, emotional responses.

I had spent hours scraping the stuff, and even though I was wearing a mask, it was still affecting me and everyone else. And now it was warping the reality of a squad of police outside.

"Naughty, naughty, *wonderful* Gnomey."

Gnomey was the silent type. Silent but deadly.

Kip appeared in the open rear doorway as if to prove my point.

"How did you get here?" I asked.

He shrugged. "I ran. The police are barely paying attention. It's like a *how many cops does it take to screw in a lightbulb?* joke out there, watching them try to open up three feet of brick and reinforced concrete."

"How many cops *does* it take to screw in a lightbulb?" I asked.

Another shrug. "I guess it depends on the size of the bulb."

"One to screw it in, and the rest to stand around and look intimidating with their guns," Justin said.

Kip smiled, relieved to see that Justin was back to being a dork. The men shook hands, awkward but friendly.

"Let's get out of here," I said. I grabbed a few face masks from Clarence's worktable. "Wear these, and hold your breath."

Kip pointed to the wall of mushrooms on our way out the door. "Those would totally make an epic quiche of death, right?"

Justin shrugged, obviously not getting it.

Kip threw his hands in the air and gestured at me to acknowledge his joke.

But I didn't. Or couldn't.

"Agatha Raisin! Quiche of death! Like the ad that brought all those women to take over the shop? Come on, it's a good joke!"

"Did you place that ad? The one that sent them all here?"

"No! Double agent, remember?"

I looked over at Justin.

"It wasn't me. Not even Hyde me."

"Can you help me get Justin home?"

"Sure. But what about you?"

"What about me?"

"Are you enacting Plan C?"

Even though the Justin crisis was solved, without anyone dying, I might add, there were still questions about what Nemicon was up to. At least Mansions of Madness was now clearly out of their reach.

I nodded. "Absolutely."

"Just point the way."

Chapter Thirty-Nine

ONCE JUSTIN WAS SAFELY HOME, KIP AND I MADE A BREEZY conversation on the way to Monique's. We were both still processing because neither one of us seemed eager to talk about any of the weirdness. I didn't even ask the question that was burning between my ears.

Was I ever going to get used to this?

A Robert the Doll replica was sitting on my lap, and that didn't even feel weird.

But having grown up not knowing anything else, Kip probably wasn't the right person to answer that particular question.

Our talk was small, but even in miniature, it seemed like there was more to it. We talked about the weather, but only in relation to how it might affect the weekend, and traffic patterns only in regard to dinner time. Our favorite books because that was an easier segue than getting into the family, which is where the conversation almost went before I realized that his father was stuck in a painting, and mine was my most personal downer.

"Do you know how long you'll be?" Kip asked when we got to Monique's. "I'm happy to stick around."

"You don't have to do that. But thank you. I'll meet you back at my house."

He smiled. "That sounds nice." And it really, actually did. "I'm just going to walk you to the door."

I rolled my eyes but didn't stop him from getting out of the car.

Monique was standoffish when she opened the door. I could feel her on the other side, making us wait.

But then her eyes fell down to Robert the Doll, and she swung the door wide.

"Would you like to come in for some tea?"

I waved Kip off and followed Monique inside, same as last time, then made myself comfortable in the same seat while listening to the same choices and selecting my same oolong like last time, then waited while perusing the same shelf of mysteries that had sort of intrigued me before.

But a title jumped out at me that had missed my internal library of references the first time. I snorted laughter at the sight of it: *Quiche of Death*.

So, Kip had the same taste in books as the crazy doll lady. Though that was better than being a cat lady, not that she could ever be a cat lady, considering her found family. Claws and dolls did not go together.

But did she have a cat? There was a big bag from the pet store sitting over in the corner, so maybe there was a feline in hiding somewhere.

A very terrified cat.

Monique returned with a tray full of tea and two slices of cake. Her offering looked like a stock photo used to sell something related to feminine hygiene.

"It's lavender cake, iced with a light lavender frosting and decorated with fresh lavender flowers," she explained.

"Mmm ... lavendery."

"I know that's not the real Robert." Monique nodded at the replica. "But it is a stunning reproduction. The best I've ever seen."

I was surprised that Monique didn't seem mad in the least.

Not only was she friendlier than I expected, but the lavender cake also wasn't bad. Rich and buttery, with a soft, moist crumb that melted in the mouth and floral notes perfectly balanced by the sweetness of the frosting. Damn, Monique.

"So, are we agreed?" Monique asked.

But the shift in conversation was so sudden that I had no idea what I was agreeing to.

"I'm sorry, I—"

"Let's let bygones be bygones! It was all a mistake. We can be grownups. And friends." She filled her mouth with a forkful of cake. "Friends share delicious things, am I right?"

"You're right." I nodded, almost done with my piece of cake and already wanting more. "Have you heard anything about Rudolph Bramson? Nemicon?"

"That's a very general question." Monique almost sounded like she was scolding me. "I've heard a lot of things about Rudolph. A woman keeps her ears to the ground."

"Anything recently. That you think might be interesting to everyone at Darrow & Grimes."

Monique slowly nodded in thought. Then she finally lit up as if plugged into the wall. "Yes! Yes, I have something I can tell you about Rudolph."

I sat up straighter — this was exciting!

"Can you go and get Dorothy out of the doll room for me first? I have so much to tell you, but I need Dorothy to do it." She sighed. "I've been running around all day and … could you, please?"

"Okay!" I hated the idea of going to the doll room alone, but I wasn't about to argue with a sure path to exactly what I came here to get.

"She's all the way at the back!" Monique called out as I walked toward the hallway.

But my heart skipped a beat as I crossed the threshold into the doll room and saw that Monique's entire "family" was arranged as if they had just finished having a tea party without me.

"Do you see her?" Monique called out.

Oh boy, did I see her — staring back at me. It had to be Dorothy, with eyes made of plastic and vacant of expression, burning with a malevolent desire to see me dead.

I plucked Dorothy from her highchair and ignored what was either a snarl or more of my imagination — hard to tell while bobbing just offshore of Nightmare Island in that room.

Monique called out again. "Can you get Lulu, too!"

"Which one is—"

I stopped, swallowing a fat lump in my throat as I remembered what Rudolph had involuntarily blurted while sitting in the Cray-Z-Boy despite some rather furious efforts to contain himself. He had said *Lulu* too.

Someone was pounding on the front door.

I turned toward the hallway, but the doll room door slammed shut in front of me a beat before I got there. I turned the knob and yanked on the handle, but the door was locked.

And I was now firmly on Nightmare Island, trapped with the dolls.

"Monique!" I yelled.

But it was no use. The pieces of this puzzle were slotting neatly into place, and I realized what I should have seen a long time ago.

Maybe the mushrooms had been making me stupid.

MC Beaton fans at the shop.

Creepy doll footsteps at my house.

Bags from the pet store, in a house that didn't have a place for cats, probably for all of those mice and bats. I shouted accusations like bullets through the door.

"Did you do all that?" I yelled at her. "Did you, Monique?"

"No," she finally answered in an infuriatingly petulant voice.

"Did you do it with Rudolph?" I clarified.

"I'm not just some idiot who's going to confess everything!" Monique yelled back at me.

But really, she just did. The thing I didn't understand was — why?

And why me?

I sighed, considering my next best move. All of the shit that had been happening to me and to all of us, it hadn't been Justin. It had been Monique, with a near-certain assist from Rudolph.

So—

I froze.

Suddenly terrified — and getting so much worse.

Because the dolls had all moved. Every single one of them was posed as if ready for tea when I entered the room, but now they had their hands raised in a gesture of attack, dozens of beady little eyes bolted onto me.

I dared not blink.

I tried to draw my hammer, but the dolls were too fast.

Dorothy came alive in my hand, suddenly thrashing, jostling its little body around enough to yank my arm in its socket. I'd have to wonder where the weight was coming from later because a second doll — maybe Lulu — pounced on me, and then the rest of the room played follow the leader, leaping onto me one after the other until they had toppled me down to the ground like Lilliputians strapping Gulliver to the sand.

It was almost creepier for the lack of sound, just the swishing of their plastic limbs as their mouths gnashed open and closed without any sound leaving their assembly line lips.

I thrashed and flailed until they were off of me, and then I pried the Phantom Needle out of Robert, destroying the doll while cutting through the webs of thread holding me down.

I slammed the back of my heel as hard as I could onto Dorothy's head, and I could swear I heard a little puff of what sounded like genuine life leaving that plastic body for good.

I grabbed my Husky brand hammer and started busting down the door. It took a lot of blows.

I slammed the head into the door over and over, fierce and steady, sending splinters of wood through the air until the door was punched through with holes. Dolls were swarming my feet again; I could feel their teeth scraping at my shins and had to stop to swing my hammer at one that began to climb me like a tree.

Finally, the door splintered, and I shoved my face through like I was Jack Torrance.

Monique shrieked when she saw me.

She tried to run, but I was on her like a lion on a gazelle.

The front door burst open.

Kip, coming back to "rescue me."

He was panting. Doubled over for a full beat before catching his breath.

"That front door was *not* easy to bust through," he said.

I glanced behind me, wishing that Kip could see what was left of the doll room door. He finished recovering his breath and pointed to the bookshelf as he righted himself.

"Agatha Raisin," he explained. "My joke. Justin didn't get it. So Monique must have been the one terrorizing you."

I rolled my eyes. "Yeah, you're a beat behind there, Grimes. But anything to redeem your crap joke, I guess."

Kip just grinned at me. "It still looks like I was right."

Chapter Forty

LIFE WAS FINALLY AS GOOD AS I HAD BEEN WANTING IT TO be and getting steadily better. Darrow & Grimes was on the upswing, and that went for the entire gang, including Kip, who was officially one of us.

Us.

We were moving back into the lab now that the store-front was getting rebuilt. Insurance money is a wonderful thing. Kip's dad had insured the shop down to the nails in the floorboards. Perhaps he had foreseen the day something catastrophic would happen.

There would be nothing drab about the shop now. Jackie was planning to paint the place in bright colors and adorn the area with stylish lighting fixtures.

Brian adored having a near-constant audience of people in the neighborhood coming in to ask what all of that commotion had been about, and he loved talking about his time behind bars. He was only in jail for a day but still made his stint sound like an episode of *Oz*.

Turned out the chief was an old friend of his father's.

William had helped him with some sort of spooky business — and got Brian and the gang released with a phone call.

The cops never made it all the way into the lab. And their fog of confusion spread throughout the neighborhood. No one seemed to know what was true and what was a trip, not that any of the officers would admit to ever having tripped before or come anywhere near doing something illegal.

Clarence ordered Kip to clean up the mushrooms and handed him a hazmat suit with *Property of the United States Government* stenciled on the back.

"Can I help?" I asked.

"Just the one suit," Clarence replied. "But I do need your help preparing some slides. I need to study those spores a bit more."

Gnomey got moved to a lead-lined box that Clarence seemed especially proud of. "Superman himself couldn't see through this shit!" He looked down at the sturdy latches and hinges with pride like he had made the box himself. Maybe so, but even a crappy lead box would keep Superman from seeing inside.

"Why don't you just, you know, get rid of Gnomey?" I'd been dumb enough to ask him.

Clarence chastised me for a half hour, going on and on about how I didn't understand how exhaustive his studies had been and that he couldn't just get rid of a wildly energetic garden gnome because a few mushrooms had gotten out of hand.

"I *am* having fewer headaches," Ariel said, on my side about getting rid of Gnomey for good but allegiant to Clarence as she should be.

"I bet you'll feel better all around if you get rid of Snuggles," I tried again.

But Ariel never wanted to talk about the truth that she would be better off without her abusive teddy bear.

I even kept my promise to Justin and spent a few afternoons playing Mansions of Madness with him. It wasn't as bad as I thought it was going to be, although I couldn't help but shudder when the Dark Druid card came up. I had finally convinced him to reach out to his fan, SmileyTime44, and it turned out she only lived about an hour away. He was set to meet her soon, although he kept putting it off.

He was doing live streams on his blog now and responding to every one of his commenters. He was obviously happy, and it filled me up to see him smiling, knowing that I'd saved his life twice in a way.

Everything was going great, except when it came to our total lack of proof that either Monique or Rudolph was behind the bomb at the shop. It felt like Darrow & Grimes had a pair of enemies, united in the dark and waiting to pounce on us.

Until I had an idea. One that everyone at D&G wanted to hear.

"I like it!" Brian declared.

"It's ballsy but not out of line," Jackie agreed.

"The odds of that working are high." Clarence nodded at Beatrice, and she returned the gesture while glowing slightly brighter.

Ariel pumped her fist and smiled at me. "Fuck yeah!"

That would be gas in my tank for weeks.

My plan worked. We had sneaked into Monique's in the middle of the night and requisitioned her entire collection of dolls. All the ones I hadn't destroyed, anyway. Now, they lived as an extended family of hostages at our lab, with one doll returning to Monique each week, so long as she cooperated, working *with* instead of against us.

Monique was all apologies, trying to act like we were all the best of friends, her and me specifically, even though we had known each other for less than a month and she had tried to personally haunt me and kill my new family shortly after we met.

They wouldn't be giving Lulu back, now or ever. It turned out that Lulu was actually Dollie from the Carnivale Arcane. Monique did admit Lulu was the price for her planting bombs in our shop. But we weren't about to tell Monique that. The D&G gang would pretend to be friendly, but we would never trust her again.

Still, her connections to the arcane underworld were better than Brian's or anyone at Darrow & Grimes, so we all agreed to see Monique as an asset until she no longer was one.

But she still hadn't given up on Rudolph. There was a reason he suddenly wanted us out of the way, and the shop was exposed until we figured out what that was. But Monique either genuinely didn't know or was playing a stoic game I didn't really think she was capable of playing.

Rudolph, on the other hand, turned out to be the one who had set the cops on us. Why? It reeked of the *Saloon* painting. Him trying to eliminate people in a sideways manner.

"I'm telling you, I don't know!" Monique insisted, around the eighth or ninth time we questioned her. "We were only working together to get Lulu!"

But we were pretty sure that Rudolph only gave her the doll in an effort to ply her aid for a larger prize.

We just needed to figure out what that prize was.

Kip was full-time at D&G now that his cover was blown. He had only been willing to work at Nemicon because that's what Brian needed him to do.

"They're all such dickbags over there." Kip had plenty

of stories, but there was one thing that got him more than anything else. "Rudolph listens to Limp Bizkit," he reported with disdain, "and he expected us all to sing along."

I was still a bit worried that the boy wonder would keep making me feel like I barely knew anything and could accomplish even less, but that was just my own insecurities, so I told them to shut up.

The struggle was good. Healthy competition would only improve me.

I looked around the lab, feeling more secure than I had since before Dad passed away. I had found a home and the family to go with it. Of course, I loved Mom and Rashida and Malik, but everyone at D&G really saw me, and as it turned out, I really needed to be seen.

I finally had a place in this world where I could be myself, and that version of me that I loved and wanted to know better got nurtured and encouraged.

A staccato series of honks from outside announced Ariel's return from the latest auction. We were having a hard time keeping the shop's shelves fully stocked, and for all the right reasons. Those Agatha Raisin fans had spread the word about the best new shop in town, never mind that it had been there for decades.

It was a nice problem to have, and I was getting better at helping. I was always there for Jackie with whatever she needed up front, including becoming an expert on fudge. And I was there to help Clarence with whatever he needed in the lab — always with my gloves on, of course. But I looked forward to going on the storage runs most or helping out with inventory management whenever a load came back.

"Maybe we should get a storage unit while we rebuild the rest of the front. It seems like we're on a roll of getting some seriously awesome shit in this place," Ariel said. "Check out some of the crap I just brought back!"

Everyone filed out the back door behind Ariel. I lingered behind Beatrice's glowing form, trailing after Clarence, and found myself alone in the lab for what would have been a split second if I hadn't stopped to stare at the ghost phone.

I needed to know I could be better than I was.

So I stared the phone down, stretching a wanting hand toward the receiver and feeling my craving diminish as I neared the phone.

It wouldn't really be Dad on the phone. He was a wonderful memory and a special, necessary part of me. I wanted to feel haunted by my father forever. Even if he wasn't right there.

I dropped my hand from the receiver and felt something ice-cold ripple through the room. I turned to see the *Saloon at the End of the World*, the painting now safely inside the lab, with Montague in a similar pose to the one I was in now, facing the painting with my hand outstretched.

Only now, his posture was fully formed, his face open in terror, hand now pointing directly out from the painting,

I couldn't stop myself from looking over my shoulder behind me at the lab, wondering what terrifying thing Montague was aiming his finger at.

Then the ghost phone started to ring.

About The Authors

Paige Andrews is a forty something single mom, navigating the wild urban jungle of Detroit with her two kids and loyal sidekick, Shep—an adorable black mutt with a penchant for mischief. Once upon a bedtime, Paige spun whimsical tales to lull her little ones to sleep. As they grew, so did her stories, morphing from preschool fantasy into urban escapades.

One day, her oldest said, "Mom, you should publish these." So Paige set out to conquer the literary world. She's determined to be more successful as an author than she was in her ill-fated attempt at martial arts—a journey that ended with a wayward kick and an embarrassing encounter with a cardboard cutout of Bruce Lee. Join Paige as she juggles motherhood, magic, and the occasional dragon!

~

John Peragine - *Play or Perish* was born in a dark, dusty back room of a crowded antique shop in New Orleans. Surrounded by dolls' heads and reliquary, an idea began to form…

What if the game is cursed?

Award-winning author, musician, and journalist John Peragine writes while surrounded by his family and a menagerie of animals overlooking his hillside vineyard.

Travel and adventure are his passions. He's probably zip-lining through a jungle or hunting wild boar right now.

When he's not traveling or writing books for other people, he's creating even more fantastical worlds for readers of all ages.

Also By Paige Andrews

A Forty Something Fury

A Forty Something Fury

A Forty Something Frenzy

Arcane Auction Wars

Play or Perish